ANOTHER Chance

A WILDCATTERS HOCKEY BOOK

BOOK 7

ALEXA PADGETT

ISBN: 978-1-945090-50-9

Edited by Jessica Royer-Ocken
Cover by Chris Philpot

For Jessica, who has been my thoughtful, detail-oriented editor for years. These books, my work, is better because of you. Thank you.

CHAPTER 1
Zaila

Houston's Wildcatters Arena on a game night brimmed with excitement—even for a charity game. This evening, hockey teams made up of celebrities would be vying for a large donation their preferred nonprofit. Throbbing bass from the pre-game playlist, stomping feet, and the scents of popcorn, cold beer, and melted cheese enveloped me in that unique hockey experience as I stopped at the top of the stairs to assess the Wildcatters' home ice. Lights flashed from the Jumbotron, bathing the crowd in blues and golds as people searched for their seats.

I loved every second of the chaos as I navigated down the concrete steps, my plastic cup of soda sweating against my palm as the ice sloshed inside. Twenty-plus years of dreaming from my daddy's knee, and I was finally here—but not as a fan in those nosebleed seats where we used to sit. Nope. As a Wildcatters employee.

My chest ached with a weird combination of excitement, pleasure, and grief that I hadn't yet gotten used to. I wanted to tell my daddy in person. I wanted him standing next to me. But that would never happen again. At twenty-five, I understood grief and loss all too well; I longed for one more big bear hug from the best man to ever grace my life.

The row numbers blurred past me…26…25…24…as I

juggled my phone in my other hand. Seat 14B was just a few more steps down. My thumb hovered over Dad's old number, and I typed quickly before I could talk myself out of it. Mom hadn't gotten around to canceling it, though she'd put the phone away.

"*One day*," she'd said. But one day hadn't come yet, and I still sent him little updates, as if he was just out of town.

Zaila: I did it, Daddy! I got our dream job! I'm here, ready for the first of what I hope are many games.

I hit send and tucked my phone in my pocket as I trotted down the steps, a rolling tide overtaking the crowd. The whispers turned to cheers mixed with jeers, camera flashes strobing like a storm. I glanced up in time to see him.

Gunnar Evaldson, the Wildcatters' owner and former junior hockey phenom in his own right, continued to be a man everyone talked and wrote about in the industry. He was an enigma billionaire who'd built a franchise in less than ten years that most other organizations only dreamed of becoming.

His jaw was a hard line, his mouth unsmiling, and his pale blue eyes scanned the crowd more quickly and efficiently than a goalie reading a breakaway. Gunnar had played goalie in these charity games before, but regardless of the endeavor, the man was versatile, athletic, intelligent, and ruthless.

He was also taller in person, with broad shoulders and thick arms visible even under the team-issued sweater. His walk—even in skates—was all contained power as he marched down my aisle, where I still stood, gawking. He should've been on the ice, not up in the stands. I guessed as the team owner, he had more leeway, especially when one of the people he'd been talking to was the state's senator.

"That's the Wildcatters owner," someone in the stands said. "The commissioner guy called him up here, Stef."

Ah. That explained why he was in the stands.

"Yeah… I've never seen someone in skates come into the stands," Stef replied. "Oh my gosh! I didn't think I'd get a picture with so many famous people together. Ooh, there are some of the Wildcatter players. Man, this place is lit!"

Behind him, a cluster of fans surged forward, phones out, calling his name. One of them shouted something about "last year's record" that sounded less than complimentary. Another man reached for his arm, but Gunnar didn't stop. He didn't even slow his pace.

I tried to enter the row of chairs behind me, but the guy in the aisle seat stood up to high-five his buddy, blocking my escape. I sidestepped straight into the path of a teenage boy in a Cormac Bouchard jersey. He barreled into me, laughing, his shoulder slamming mine hard enough to send my soda sloshing.

The lid popped off as I stumbled. "Oh—no—no—no—"

A firm hand caught my elbow before I could face plant into a cement step. My gaze snapped up and found those eyes.

Icy blue. The kind of eyes you fell into.

"Easy," Gunnar said, steadying me. His voice was deep enough to cut through the roar of the crowd, and the timbre sent a shiver down my spine.

"Thank you," I said, heaving a sigh. "Oof. That was scary."

Another fan jostled past, shoving my arm. My soda lurched

in a sticky arc…straight across Gunnar's chest. It hit his sweater with a soft glug, darkening the Wildcatters logo.

"Oh my gosh! I am so sorry," I squeaked, my face rivaling the Texas summer sun that still shone outside. I scrubbed his shirt with my sleeve, a Wildcatters long-sleeve T-shirt my new boss had given me earlier today. Though I tried not to notice the impressive pec underneath, I did, and I liked the suppleness of Gunnar's physique.

Don't notice anything *about your boss's boss's boss, Zaila!*

Gunnar glanced down at himself, then back at me. "No harm. I'm just a little wet. And sticky."

Oh Lordy, did he have to say that? It's getting hot in here…

"Again, I'm so sorry," I stuttered. My mind seemed incapable of another thought as I fell further into his beautiful, frosty gaze.

His lips twitched like he was suppressing something… annoyance, amusement—Oh, God, maybe both. "You always greet people like this?" he asked.

"Only the famous ones," I said before my brain could stop me. "Makes me memorable." Then, because my brain was an asshole that wanted to embarrass me more, I added, "You're Gunnar Evaldson."

His eyes came back to mine, cool and assessing. "Last I checked."

"My dad used to tell me what an incredible leader you are. He was a big fan."

"Used to?"

"He passed away. Last year." The grief welled up, choking me.

Something shifted in his face. He was still guarded, but the edges softened. "Sorry."

"Thanks." I rallied a smile. "Anyway, you're kind of a big deal to me."

That earned me a dry huff as his eyes softened further. "Because of your father. So, I'm basically vintage now."

"Vintage is sexy," I mumbled.

I almost missed the faintest of flickers in his eyes, like I'd surprised him.

"Gunnar!" a woman's voice snapped from a few rows down.

I glanced past him to see a woman with sleek black hair overlaid with a headset, glaring like she could cut steel with her eyes. That woman, Lydia Breitbart, was my actual boss. I'd met her earlier today when she'd given me the tour of the floor, my official Wildcatters badge, and the T-shirt I now wore. Instead of the friendly smile she'd offered earlier, Lydia glared at me from under lowered, pinched brows.

I was so, so screwed, and I would not enjoy whatever she said next. As I contemplated disappearing into the concrete floor, two women slid through the crowd and appeared at Gunnar's shoulder. One exuded Texas charm, and the other oozed chic. They blocked Lydia's evil eye, but I was sure she was still planning my painful demise.

"Well, what happened here?" the Texan asked, her big blue eyes darting between me and Gunnar.

"Oh, nothing much, Ida Jane. Just making friends the old-fashioned way." Gunnar gestured to his damp jersey.

I bit back a groan at the growing audience for my humiliation.

"Gunnar," Chic drawled, "There's no need for dramatic pre-game rituals, especially not with the league commissioner.

Now get going. I want to see you score goals like you rack up dollars." She waved him off, though Gunnar gave me a last, lingering look before he clomped down the steps to the ice.

The elegant beauty turned to me. "I'm Naomi, and that bubbly bit of perky is Ida Jane."

"Nice to meet you." Ida Jane grinned. "Don't worry about Gunnar. He's survived worse in the boardroom. Probably will tonight as well, seeing as my husband and the rest of the team have been ribbing him about his…er, performance." Her eyes went wide and her cheeks pinked, as she realized what she'd said.

Naomi threw her head back and laughed. "Oh, that was too good."

"I'm Zaila," I mumbled, mostly to be polite, and to stop any more innuendos. My body couldn't take additional embarrassment, even second-hand. "And I'm supposed to start as the team's social media intern tomorrow, but my boss is staring at me like she wants to skin me alive."

"Oh, honey," Naomi purred, "*what* an entrance. Planning on dousing all your superiors?" She offered a warm smile to ease the sting. "Some could use the wake-up call, including Lydia, the witch. Though, good for you—going straight to the top."

I shuffled my feet, desperate to get away and sink into my seat. Maybe I should go home.

"Oh, she is glaring." Naomi's lip curled as she looked toward Lydia for a moment. "If you want me to finish your soda in her lap, I'm game."

Ida Jane linked arms with me. "Stop, Naomi. Lydia's…

something else, bless her heart, but she doesn't deserve a lap full of Coke."

"You sure?" Naomi asked with a toss of her head.

"Nope," Ida Jane said. "But tonight won't be when we find out, because then we'd lose Zaila, and I have a strong suspicion our new social media hire is going to shake things up in the best possible way." Ida Jane turned her soft blue eyes toward me, her smile ratcheting into Cheshire-grin territory. "Let's find your seat, Zaila, and make plans for a lunch sometime soon."

As we walked, the women's curiosity was palpable. I didn't understand why they were being so kind to me.

Naomi cracked first. "So, darling, spill the tea...or cola, rather."

I gulped. "I got bumped. A fan hit my elbow and blam! Soda everywhere."

Ida Jane clucked. "That's not even your fault. Though it certainly made an impression."

"Indeed." Naomi's eyebrow rose and fell like a gymnast. "And Gunnar's reaction? He's usually...wintry."

"He was nice," I admitted. "Like, really nice."

"We noticed," Ida Jane said.

"That's why we came over," Naomi added. "Gunnar finding a woman intriguing is...well, intriguing."

We reached my seat, and I collapsed into the cushioned comfort with a grateful sigh. Ida Jane patted my shoulder. "We've all had our moments. I once called a ref something unmentionable into a hot mic." She shrugged, her eyes narrowing. "He deserved it, but I didn't like the way my behavior reflected on Maxim. That's my husband." She pointed toward the big

Wildcatters D-man, who sat two rows in front of my seat, along with the rest of the team and their partners. I glanced at Lydia, but she was engrossed in a conversation with a celebrity player at the rink level. I sighed in relief.

"Enjoy the show—just don't be the show," Naomi said with a little finger wave.

I nodded. That woman's confidence was something to aspire to.

"We'll stop by this week. Break you out of the work prison," she added. "Don't worry, we have enough clout to make your jailer set you free for an afternoon."

I couldn't help laughing. Maybe my faux pas wouldn't be a total disaster. It might not even destroy my evening—or my job.

CHAPTER 2

Gunnar

I stepped through the gate to the ice that one of the security guards opened for me and glided onto the rink with the ease of decades of practice. While I didn't enjoy schmoozing, it was good press for my organization and the charities involved tonight when I was seen with the league's commissioner. Plus, the locker room was likely a nightmare right now. The celebrities my marketing department had brought in for this event were weenies who had little respect for the game and probably too high an opinion of themselves. I pressed my lips together to keep from smirking—I knew what was coming. This game might not have the professional hits and physicality of a typical one, but we were all going to work hard. Excitement fizzed in my belly.

The roar of the crowd was a familiar symphony I loved more than just about anything else in the world. I might not have played at a professional level, but I'd taken part in enough games during my youth and college years to appreciate all aspects of the sport.

Getting out on the ice where my brother and I used to spend hours a day reminded me of better times, and of what I missed most in my life: my older brother, Karl. I still couldn't believe he was gone. His loss tried to slam into my chest like a sledgehammer, but thoughts of the cola tsunami with Zaila—I'd caught her name as I tromped down the stairs—replayed in my mind, overriding the pain Karl's passing always brought.

The pretty young woman, who hadn't paid enough attention, had mentioned something about the Wildcatters to Naomi and Ida Jane. Hopefully she was involved with my team. We'd hired a new physiotherapist, and I wondered if it was Zaila, even if she handled cold beverages with the precision of a rookie goalie. I suppressed a chuckle.

Get it together, Gunnar. You're the team owner, not a lovelorn teenager.

Thankfully, the puck dropped, pushing thoughts of the soda spiller and my absent brother from my consciousness. I was off like a shot—with something to prove to the guys I paid millions, who tonight were sitting in the stands. I felt spry, though I spent more time in a boardroom than on the rink. I'd spent the last fifteen years juggling my business so I could focus on what I wanted most: a hockey team Karl would have been proud to play for.

And I'd achieved that goal faster and with more success than I could have hoped for. In the process, I'd made community involvement and giving back to those in need a central part of the Wildcatters' mission, which was why I was playing in this celebrity charity game tonight. The money from the event went to the cause closest to my heart: hate-crime prevention.

I snatched a pass meant for an agile celebrity chef and began my offensive maneuver.

"Evaldson's got the puck! Can he still bring the heat?" the announcer boomed, his voice laced with manufactured excitement. I rolled my eyes. "Twenty-five years ago, our owner was a force on the ice."

I grinned, dodging a clumsy attempt at a check from reality star Tiffany Caraway, who skated with the grace of a newborn giraffe. I threaded the needle through the other team's defense, spotting my opportunity. A quick feint, a subtle shift, and wham—the net vibrated, followed by the eruption of cheers from the crowd.

Oh yeah, baby. Just like that! This middle-aged man still could score.

High fives and backslaps came from my teammates, but my eyes drifted toward the stands. Was Zaila impressed by my display of athletic prowess? I hoped she'd noticed my skating technique... *Focus on the game. You're supposed to be a role model, not a man looking to score with a woman half your age.*

Okay, so she probably wasn't half my age, but she had to be at least fifteen years younger, and that stung. I prided myself on delivering hard truths and taking the time not to react, but to process and decide. There shouldn't be any confusion here. Zaila was young. She was beautiful and fresh and not for me.

Thankfully, the rest of the first period was a chaotic mix of flying pucks and near-misses. Then the Zamboni driver had to brake hard to keep from running over the celebrity chef when he headed back onto the ice too soon.

During a brief respite on the bench, I scanned the crowd yet again, pretending to adjust my helmet as I sought Zaila. The young woman had burrowed into my consciousness after a simple look into her sherry-colored eyes. Panic set in as I couldn't find her. I wanted to talk to her again...more...

Stop it, Gunnar.

Back on the ice for the second period, I vowed to channel my inner hockey star and ignore all thoughts of the beautiful woman who'd spilled her drink on me. But try as I might, Zaila kept popping into my head. I wondered if she thought I was too forward. Or maybe too friendly. I wasn't known for my easy, chatty manner. Perhaps the soda-stained jersey turned her off...

The whistle shrieked, jolting me back to the present. Before I could react, a linebacker on skates—or, more accurately, Bradley Dunbar, who'd starred in a few subpar action movies back in the '90s—bore down on me with the force of a runaway freight train. I sidestepped just in time, avoiding a collision that would probably have sent me straight to the physical therapist's office. Oh wait, maybe Zaila was the team's new physiotherapist. *Maybe I should let Brad hit me.*

"Close call for Evaldson," the announcer boomed through the speakers. "Looks like he's dodging more than just pucks tonight, folks."

Embarrassment rose to my cheeks. The announcer had noted my lack of focus, which wasn't like me. I always stayed ahead of the game. But Zaila had gotten to me, and I didn't like that. At all.

That was the lie I continued to tell myself for the rest of the game.

As the clock ticked toward the end of the third period, the score was a nail-biting 3-3. Every pass, every shot, every bodycheck was magnified by the pressure. The air in the arena crackled with anticipation when I intercepted a desperate pass from Tiffany, who then cowered against the boards at the far end of the ice. My lungs screamed as I propelled myself toward the net. Ten seconds left.

I ignored the burn in my legs and focused on the chance to redeem myself.

I wound up for a slap shot that would make Bobby Orr proud. I forgot about sodas, sexy young women, and hockey wives. This shot was all that mattered. As the puck rocketed off my stick, it turned into a blur of black against the bright white ice. The goalie—some tech billionaire with questionable skills but an ego too big to see his lack of talent—made a lackluster attempt. That guy was terrible at hockey and in life, and I hoped never to see the douche again.

Oh, that felt good. The buzzer blared as the puck nestled into the back of the net, Tech Bro threw off his helmet as he melted down on the ice. The crowd went ballistic. My team had snatched victory from the jaws of defeat, just as we should have.

For you, big brother.

I brought my fingertips to my lips and lifted them upward. Karl was the reason I'd strapped on skates, the reason I'd worked my ass off to make enough money to buy a team, and the reason I'd created a team he would have loved playing for.

My teammates swarmed me, their celebratory yells echoing in my ears. I ignored their back pats and scanned the stands.

Zaila stood near her seat, clapping and cheering, a grin on her beautiful face. When she caught my eye, her joy smoothed down into a small, shy smile that was just for me. And in that moment, despite the cheering crowd and the adrenaline pumping through my veins, all I could think was: *I'd let her spill soda on me again. Anytime she wants.*

CHAPTER 3
Zaila

I strode into Wildcatters Hockey headquarters the next morning, ten minutes earlier than my designated time, with my head high, just as my parents had taught me. *Being early shows respect for the other person's time. Project the confidence you want others to perceive in you.* Those two statements had served my daddy well throughout his forty years in the military.

I missed him; I'd come to realize I'd always miss my father.

I smiled at the receptionist as I stopped at the front desk. Casually, I placed my hand on the gleaming surface, but that was so I didn't face plant into the polished hardwood floor as my knees shook like a skyscraper during a Houston thunderstorm. If Gunnar Evaldson saw me today, would he throw me out?

I desperately hoped he'd forgotten the whole Soda Incident.

"Zaila Monroe. I'm the social media intern," I said without my voice cracking. Minor victories.

"Of course, Ms. Monroe. You're a few minutes early, which will win you brownie points with Lydia. She's a stickler for time. I'm Flora."

Nothing was going to win me points with Lydia, but I kept my mouth shut as I shook Flora's hand, noting how well put-together she was. The Wildcatters organization must've been flush with cash because everything gleamed and sparkled, including the workers. I glanced down at my outfit, suddenly feeling like I'd shown up to a black-tie gala in pajamas.

"Can I tell you a secret?" I leaned in, lowering my voice. "I'm so excited to be here. My father was a huge hockey fan."

Flora smiled. "Totally understand. I knew nothing about the sport, but I learned once I got the job because this organization is fire, not just in the league but as a place of employment." She winked. "You're going to love being a Wildcatter."

My smile grew as excitement hummed under my skin. "I sure hope so. Though Lydia's not impressed with me because I spilled my soda on Mr. Evaldson last night at the charity game."

Flora laughed. "No, Lydia doesn't like you because you're young and attractive. And she has a thing for Mr. Evaldson. Fair warning, most of the people who work here do because, OMG, that man is…" She waved her hand in front of her face, and I giggled. "If you do a good job, others will notice, and that means Lydia will have no choice but to acknowledge you as well. Mr. Evaldson runs a meritocracy."

"Good to know." I nodded and returned to my game face, ready to start the day and my career. This internship had been highly coveted among those in my graduate program. Getting the spot had taken an insane number of dedicated hours and lots of letters of recommendation. My hope was to turn this position into a permanent one at the end of the season or use the social media skills I learned here to move into marketing at a large firm. Thankfully, Houston had many to choose from, but the Wildcatters had been top of my list thanks to their consistent high marks from current employees and the generous pay package.

Still, as Flora led me to Lydia's office, it felt like I was walking into the lion's den—if lions wore designer suits and discussed social media strategies.

Lydia might be a stickler for time, and she clearly hadn't forgiven me for the Great Soda Incident, but she seemed to have determined that encounter would mean Gunnar didn't like me. That allowed her to be much nicer than I'd expected. She walked me through my job description, showed me the main pages I'd help manage, and ensured that I met the other three people on the socials team, which included two guys named Jay and Tim, as well as Veronica, who handled copyediting.

Jay Welks—I remembered his last name but not the rest of the teams'—smiled warmly at me, flashing a deep dimple that paired well with his straight, white teeth. He seemed to be the resident expert. The rest of the team was polite, if guarded. Tim offered a small, awkward wave.

"We're lean, but we're awesome," Lydia said with a chuckle. "We take care of our players and organization because they're the best in the league."

A recurring theme of the day for sure. Everyone who worked for the organization gushed about the quality of the players and personnel.

"Mr. Evaldson hand-picked every senior staffer," Lydia said. She leaned in closer, her eyes wide. "And everyone stayed." She gave a slight nod to emphasize her point about no turnover.

But I already understood. My father spent decades working his way up to the military brass; I recognized the need for loyalty and charisma, and Gunnar Evaldson had enough rizz to inspire the loyalty. That probably meant good things. I hoped.

Anyway, none of this was new information. Like my dad had taught me, I'd done my research, treating this job post as a potential operation for which I needed to gather intelligence.

Lydia went on. "We're under the marketing and promotions department, and Noelle Fischer is a truly excellent boss. She works really, really hard to showcase the best of the organization and its employees, not just the players. In fact, next week, we're starting a new series that highlights the equipment team. Those guys know their stuff."

"That sounds interesting," I said.

"It is. Oh, don't worry, you'll settle in quickly."

She offered a smile, though I noted it didn't reach her eyes. Maybe she still wasn't sure about me. But she seemed to be thoughtful, so I needed to give her the benefit of the doubt.

"We have a lot of images and ideas, and the reason we chose you over the other candidates was your eye for aesthetics," she explained, "and your ability to condense difficult concepts into hashtags."

I nodded. I'd gone through a rigorous interview process to get here, to my dream position.

"In fact, we'll start now with the images we want to sprinkle in throughout this next week. I'll walk you through our current process, and then we have a meeting with Noelle and Gunnar to discuss how we can clarify and improve our messaging."

I licked my lips, throat suddenly dry. "I'm meeting with Mr. Evaldson today?"

Lydia frowned as she nodded. "Yes." She drew out the word.

"We all meet regularly with department heads and top management, and you met him last night, anyway. While that was super awkward, dumping soda on him, we can't let that stop us." She smiled, one full of calculation and teeth. "This will be better."

No, it wouldn't, which was precisely why Lydia was putting me in this position. I rested my hands on my fluttering stomach. "Oh-kay."

Lydia's confused frown morphed into understanding. "There's no need to be nervous. We'll have checkpoints in place to make sure we catch any potential errors. And that's not because you're new," she added. "It's because this is the public face of the team, and we want the brand to reflect our values."

"No pressure," I murmured.

Patting the back of my desk chair, she said, "Oh, there's pressure, but you brought that on yourself by acting the fool last evening. Now, I'll let you finish getting settled. The meeting's at three."

My stomach plummeted to the bottom of my stylish pumps. I'd been right to be nervous, as it seemed Lydia was determined to keep me off balance. Everyone in the city, possibly the world, knew of the billionaire oilman turned NHL owner. Gunnar Evaldson's philanthropic achievements rivaled those of the Rockefellers, and his team's rise through the ranks of the NHL were storied, but equally as well-known was the fact that Gunnar Evaldson suffered no nonsense and even fewer fools. He created a plan, stuck to it, and saw it to completion. Rinse and repeat.

That was why, even with his generous seven- and even eight-figure donations, he remained one of the world's wealthiest.

My mother used to say white stuck to rice because it knew a good thing. I'd never completely understood that saying, but it seemed to apply to Gunnar Evaldson.

And now I knew he was even more charismatic in person. I might have spent all of one minute in his company, but I suspected the man's icy blue eyes—more crystalline and more precise than any I'd ever encountered—had catalogued everything about me. What he'd done with that information after the fact, though, remained to be seen.

While I enjoyed the morning of meeting my coworkers and getting to sign in to my laptop for the first time, I dreaded three o'clock. But that didn't stop it from arriving. When it was time, I followed Lydia to the meeting with a pounding heart and sweaty palms.

"Ms. Monroe. I've been looking forward to meeting you," Gunnar said as Lydia introduced us—thankfully not bringing up the Great Soda Incident.

I blinked up at him, noting the nearly imperceptible gray at his temples that fanned lightly into his thick blond hair. It looked as effortless as the cut of his bespoke suit. Now that I could study him, Gunnar Evaldson was like Chris Hemsworth with more money and the ability to buy a hockey team. My ovaries did the cha-cha.

"I'm glad to see you without your soda today," he added, his voice like warm honey over gravel.

I smoothed my hair. "Well, I'm pretty sure I'll never order another one. I don't really like the stuff, and last night was enough to end any positive vibe it might have had." I shrugged.

"It's just something my father used to get when we went to hockey games together, mainly because my mother refused to let us have sugary drinks at home. It was our thing." I pressed my lips together to stop my rambling.

"I make you nervous." His mouth compressed, though his eyes sparked, causing an answering fizz in my chest.

I'd never been this aware of a man before.

And I was not just aware; I was attracted. I swallowed, trying to force down the blush of awareness and need that had crept up my neck. "Nervous? No, not at all." My inner snark kicked in. "Just contemplating whether I should feign a sudden illness to escape this meeting. Totally normal first-day jitters."

"Unnecessary. I get the best ideas from engaged professionals who understand that they have more expertise in their area than I do. I'm here to learn. From you."

Was there anything sexier than a successful man looking me dead in the eye and telling me I could teach him? Nope. Nothing.

While I'd teetered on the brink before, I now fell into complete infatuation, right then and there.

I lowered my lashes, not wanting Gunnar to see the desire that had to be broadcasting from my face. He was everything I wanted and more that I hadn't yet fantasized about. Gunnar Evaldson had become my unattainable sex god, better than any book boyfriend, and all in the last sixty seconds. I was so fucked…because I wouldn't ever get to fuck him.

Sigh.

"Let's get started," he said. "You can share your knowledge with me."

His eyes warmed, so I forced a smile. "Sure, Mr. Evaldson. I'd be thrilled to share my limited knowledge with you, so long as you understand that I'm still learning."

I locked my knees as I raised my head, meeting his gaze, just as my father had taught me. "*Make the connection, even when it's hard—especially when it's hard, Zaila. That's how you get ahead in this world, by making that connection.*" My father hadn't meant to connect with a future of twisted sheets and sweaty bliss, but that's where my mind went. *Sorry, Daddy.*

Gunnar's lips parted as his pupils dilated, making me wonder if he felt the connection between us as well. To me, it was as clear as the Great Wall of China. But who knew what Gunnar perceived. It was possible he was humoring me, or just wondering whether he'd left the stove on at home.

CHAPTER 4
Gunnar

For the second time in twenty-four hours, Zaila Monroe had stunned me. That never happened. And yet…she'd done so effortlessly, just by being herself.

If Lydia, Jay, Tim, and Veronica hadn't been in the room, I could have had a massive sexual harassment suit on my hands. Because said hands would be on Zaila's sweet ass, tucking her in close to my chest, to the heart I worried she could easily burrow her way into.

Time to face facts: my attraction to this woman was not simple appreciation. My infatuation was something stronger—something I would have scoffed at if I weren't reeling from my new Zaila-infused reality.

I shoved my fists into my suit pants so hard, I heard a stitch pop. Then another. At this rate, I'd be pants-less by the end of the meeting, and that would be another way to a sexual harassment lawsuit. I forced my shoulders down, relaxed my jaw, and bent my arms at the elbows. Control was my specialty. Ice cold and rigid, that's how I held myself. That approach had won me ever-larger oil contracts and allowed me to bring hockey to Houston. It kept me making informed business decisions instead of acting on impulse.

Control. I had it in spades, and I'd executed it on a daily, if not hourly basis—until now.

In this moment, as my control threatened to shred, I longed to thread my fingers through Zaila's thick, dark mass of waves, tugging her head back to expose the smooth expanse of her neck and plunder those pink lips until we were both drunk on pheromones and lust.

"Didn't I tell you this intern knew her stuff?" Lydia's peppy comment snapped me out of my fantasy.

Intern. My jaw clamped tight. Zaila was my company's intern. I spent a long moment examining her features. Christ, she was young. Too young for me.

"You did," I said, managing a nod.

I made my first million while she was learning to tie her shoes. *Great, now I feel like a creepy older man and a robber baron.*

"I'm so glad you think so, Gunnar." Lydia smiled brightly at me, inching closer, a calculating gleam in her eye.

Lydia steered Zaila toward a chair at the opposite end of the table, all the while talking about the Wildcatters' social media presence. The babble was excellent cover for me to get myself under control.

Unlike a lot of men, the idea of spending time with a younger woman had never appealed. I enjoyed being able to talk to my companions. Intellectual discourse was a form of foreplay. Zaila and I wouldn't have anything in common, so this ridiculous need would fizzle as soon as she spoke again. It had to.

Lydia came to my rescue. "Zaila, why don't you give us an overview of what you'd like to do with the Wildcatters' social media presence, emphasizing our corporate wellness?"

Zaila fumbled with her notepad, her hands shaking.

"N-now?" she squeaked.

I sighed as tension eased from my shoulders. Zaila was not a poised, successful businesswoman. I'd have to give Lydia a raise for showcasing her youth and inexperience. Saving me from myself.

"Yes," I agreed. "That's why we're meeting."

Zaila bit her lip, which trembled slightly, before pulling in a deep breath. "I thought I was here to observe the process," she said with quiet dignity.

"Oh, come on, Zaila. I know you have ideas," Lydia needled. "This is your big chance to impress the owner."

I sat forward, my forearms on the table, ready to step in. Ultimately, managing my desire for the young woman was on me. I didn't want Zaila to be uncomfortable or thrown to the wolves because I couldn't control my feelings.

But before I could postpone the meeting, Zaila flipped a page in her notebook—without looking at Lydia, which I had to admire. She refused to let the woman intimidate her.

"All right. Well, you wanted to showcase some of the staff who work with the players, which makes sense, seeing as the team wouldn't function optimally without support," Zaila began. "I haven't had a chance to get to know any of the key players in those roles because I've only been in the building for approximately five hours, but from what I know about the team's structure, I'd suggest we start with the nutrition and PT teams. These two groups are the ones who ensure the athletes are in top condition, which makes them nearly as valuable as the players themselves. I'd like to ask each of them a series of questions and request detailed, fact-based answers we can use to show regular people they don't need to spend six-plus hours a day training to achieve healthful results. In fact, I think it might be useful to explain how the staff use these strategies in their own lives, which would connect to Joe Everyman more quickly than a specialized D-man diet-and-workout regimen."

As she spoke, Zaila looked me square in the eye most of the time, sometimes including Jay, Tim, Veronica, and Lydia. And once she got going, she rarely looked at her notes. I was impressed.

Also, I wasn't giving Lydia a raise. I was going to fire her for throwing this smart, beautiful woman under the bus. I leaned back in my chair as I studied my social media manager with impassive eyes. Slowly, the vindictive glee faded from Lydia's face. I suspected she'd done this to Zaila because she sensed my attraction to her, and she wanted to quash it. I'd certainly sensed Lydia's attraction to me, and I'd done my best to quash that.

I shifted my gaze to the new intern. "Well, Zaila, that was an impressive presentation, especially since you'd been told you were here to observe. In fact, it's more interesting than anything I've heard from the social media team in months. Thank you for bringing the idea to my attention."

Before I could say or do something I'd regret regarding Lydia, I rose from my chair, gave them a nod, and strode back to my office. Once inside, I shut the door and leaned against it, eyes closed.

Zaila Monroe was smarter and even sexier in full profes-sional mode. She was a badass. And she had a perky little ass. I rubbed my hands down my face. I worked closely with the social media team on the organization's brand and messaging, so I'd see Zaila often, especially once I fired Lydia. And if the dose of sexy professionalism amped up any higher…

I'm totally fucked. And not in the fun way.

CHAPTER 5
Zaila

After Gunnar Evaldson departed, Lydia asked for details to hash out the plans he had agreed to, and Jay, Tim, and Veronica backed all my suggestions. That portion of the meeting ran until nearly five, so once we were finished, I just needed to shut down my computer and collect my bag from my office before I could leave for the day. At least the lengthy conversation had given my legs time to stop shaking.

Before I managed to leave, though, Lydia appeared in the doorway, her glasses atop her head, nearly buried in light brown curls.

She offered a smile that I struggled to believe was genuine. "You did really well today."

I offered a stiff nod. "Thank you."

Lydia sighed, her lips compressed. "Look, Zaila, you're young. You're lovely. You have a lot to learn about corporate America… and I want to help you."

I bit my cheek, refusing to respond to her condescension.

"He's interested in you," she blurted. Taking a step back, no doubt to make sure the hall was clear, Lydia walked into my office. She flung herself into the chair as if she were auditioning for a furniture commercial.

This was my first office. My first professional job, despite the title of *intern*. What I'd thought was my dream company. Spoiler alert: this dream apparently involved a passive-aggressive boss and potential HR violations.

Be careful what you wish for… Those words had never rung truer than today.

My father had been such a hockey fan, not just of the Wildcatters but of the corporation's leadership, and I'd wanted to be part of that, for him. Now I wasn't sure. I kept wondering what my mother would say about my mixed feelings. She was the best at teasing out the critical pieces, letting the rest fade so it no longer bothered her.

"I'm looking out for you," Lydia said, her voice and expression plaintive. "I need to remind you that romantic relationships between coworkers are frowned upon. And starting something on your first day, particularly with the owner, won't be a good look for you."

I centered myself. She was looking out for me the way a cheetah looks out for a gazelle. And I'd read the handbook and my contract twice. Time to showcase the skills Daddy taught me. I lifted my chin and met Lydia's gaze.

"Actually, I understand that relationships may cause potential loyalty issues or conflicts of interest and are to be brought to HR immediately," I told her. "That's typically used for if and when players get involved with staffers. I haven't been romantically involved with anyone here. Now, I don't control the owner's thoughts or feelings, and I don't control yours, either. But you told me one thing and did the exact opposite today, and I didn't appreciate being unprepared. I'll always do my best to rise to the occasion, but as my boss, I assume you'll want to make sure I'm not put in that position again since my performance reflects on you."

I gripped my tote so hard the straps dug into my palms. But I didn't back down.

Lydia exhaled sharply, and a dull flush crept up her neck. "You're right."

"Thank you." Short. Simple. *No need to rub it in, Zaila.*

Lydia pursed her lips, tilting her head. "You're not what I thought you'd be."

I snorted. "A pushover? I'm here because I want to be, and I worked hard to be. That said, I have no problem walking out that door and continuing to walk, especially if you try to use fake concern or lies against me again."

"That's unnecessary."

Lydia and I startled, turning toward where Gunnar now stood in the doorway.

"Gunnar," Lydia said, rising to smooth her suit jacket over her hips.

Ah. Flora had called it. Lydia lusted after Gunnar, and she saw me as competition. I'd walked into a professional and emotional minefield.

"I came to the same conclusion Ms. Monroe seems to have reached," Gunnar said, inclining his head toward me. "Which is why I'm going to say this plainly: This is a professional organization. We work here. I have never and do not plan to be romantically involved with my staff. Ever. Not because it's against corporate policy, but because I believe each member of this team deserves to earn their achievements." He gave Lydia a long and pointed look, and she wilted.

"Not just that, but I won't have talent bullied or wasted because of competition. You may have hired Ms. Monroe, Ms. Breitbart, but she's my employee, and she'll be working with me on the upcoming season's social media campaign, as you and I have already discussed." He shifted his attention to me. "Therefore, I want it to be clear that you, Ms. Monroe, will report directly to me. I'll follow up with Gladys, the head of HR, whom I think you met during the interview process." Gunnar's icy gaze swung to Lydia and then back to me. "If you have any issues with a team member, Gladys will assist."

Great. Just freaking great. Not only was I irrationally attracted to the man who was now my actual boss, I'd gotten my previous boss in trouble with HR.

"You didn't do a single thing wrong today, Ms. Monroe," Gunnar continued, seeming to read my mind. "And HR issues are confidential, but I can tell you that the reason we had this opening was because our last social media expert no longer felt she could offer us her best work." Gunnar's cold eyes returned to Lydia's stiff form. "I plan to call Chantal to see if there's anything she'd like to add to her exit interview now that she's no longer working here—"

"I quit," Lydia snapped. Her chin wobbled, and she appeared close to tears. She fled the room, skirting Gunnar as she moved down the hall.

I stared after her, eyes wide, mouth gaping. Looking at Gunnar, I waited for the punchline. I was starring in a workplace rom-com, a drama, and a horror film all rolled into one. I should probably option my life story now. "Holy sh—*cow*. I did not expect that type of drama on my first day."

His lips quirked. "That about sums it up." He rocked back on his heels, hands in the pockets of those well-tailored slacks. "Seems I need to go see Gladys about this unexpected turn of events." His glacial gaze held mine. "I'll say it again, you did well today. Much better than some of my executives have in… similar situations. And I appreciate the opportunity to root out the problem before it became an even bigger one." He paused, seeming to argue with himself, perhaps wanting to say more. "Good evening, Ms. Monroe."

I inclined my head. "Mr. Evaldson."

He spun away, and the doorway was empty for half a second before Jay Welks—probably three years older than me and more sports-oriented than an ESPN anchor—popped his head around the corner. He had black curls that begged for fingers to muss, and I'd bet he had women falling over themselves for the chance.

"Damn, Z. You did what the rest of us have only wished to achieve. And on Day One. You overachiever, you."

"Oh?" My entire body shook, and while I told myself it was adrenaline, it wasn't. Standing up to Lydia had taken a lot out of me, and I was close to falling apart.

"Lydia's been a menace since she started here," he said. "But she delivers her threats so sweetly, everyone got a toothache—and a kick to the…er…" His face reddened.

"Pants?" I offered.

He smiled. "Yeah. Let's go with that. The worst part, though, was how she took all the glory and left us with the blame when things didn't go well."

"She was definitely not a leader," I mused. "Why didn't anyone say anything?"

"Because she gave us the impression that she and Gunnar had a special relationship." He waggled his eyebrows and dropped his voice.

I had to laugh at that, charmed out of the worst of my emotional hangover. "Well, I guess we know that wasn't true."

Gunnar had laid it all out, and while it had been a hit to my vanity and even my self-esteem, I understood his reasoning. Moving up the ladder on merit was essential. I didn't need anything to overshadow this opportunity to showcase my intelligence, ideas, and work ethic.

"We do now." Jay's smirk broadened into a full-blown and very relieved smile. "I'd say I owe you a drink or three for your maneuver. Whatcha say?"

I kept a smile on my face. "Thank you, but not tonight. I'm going to visit my mother." *You don't need to say more*, I reminded myself. No one had a right to my information.

Yet he was still looking at me, now quizzically, as if I was blowing him off.

"She's not doing well," I added, wanting to kick myself. I didn't want to be the girl with the elderly parents, but it was true. My mom wasn't well. She'd been heartbroken since my father passed away, and I wasn't giving up time with her—even to make friends with a coworker. No matter how cute his hair or how mesmerizing his smile.

He's no Gunnar Evaldson.

I nearly rolled my eyes at myself. There wasn't any point in making that comparison.

"But thanks for the invite," I added into the growing silence, slightly unnerved by the way Jay was studying me.

"You got a partner?" he asked.

I nodded before I had even decided to lie. But this would save his ego and let me maintain our work relationship.

"Ah, well." He shrugged. "You're smart, a badass, and pretty. Can't blame a guy for trying."

I laughed again, this time with more ease. "Thanks for trying to make me feel better about the Lydia thing," I said as I collected my belongings.

He shook his head. "Are you kidding? I still owe you drinks for that. You don't know how difficult she made everyone's lives."

Gunnar

I shouldn't have stopped to listen outside Zaila's door when Jay waltzed in. I knew such behavior was beneath me. But if Jay followed in Lydia's footsteps, I'd need to remedy that situation, too. I couldn't have incompetent people working for the Wildcatters. That impacted morale and created disharmony, which went against my ethos. Plus, it was important, since I was the boss, to make sure Zaila felt comfortable in her new role. That was my only focus regarding her.

That's what I told myself, and that was a lie.

Now that I'd heard Zaila's laugh, I knew I'd do everything in my power to make sure I listened to that crystalline sound again.

And again.

I sure as hell didn't want baby-face Jay taking Zaila out. My breath had passed my lips on a whoosh as she turned him down.

But a partner? Of course she had someone, and I wouldn't pursue her. I'd meant what I said about not involving myself with my staff. And I respected her choice, even if I didn't like the idea of another man touching her, kissing her, loving her…

With a faint grunt, I pushed myself off the wall and stalked toward the elevator. I'd get over this. The response was hormonal, and I was an adult. Finding her attractive wasn't that big of a deal. I'd ignore her as much as I could, seeing her only in meetings. Better, I'd ask Noelle Fischer from marketing and promotions to take over the department meetings and only get involved when necessary. Zaila didn't work on my floor, and hopefully my interest would wane. I just had to hold to control myself until then. I could do that. I'd been doing so for decades.

CHAPTER 6
Zaila

I settled onto the couch next to my father's favorite chair, a leather recliner that had seen better decades. The soft, worn upholstery cradled my mother, who huddled in its depths, draped in her housecoat. She told me she'd changed into it after her shower, but I'd bet she'd worn the horrid thing all day.

The housecoat itself wasn't horrible; what it represented, however, upset me.

My mother was getting worse. She'd slowed down physically, and now she didn't even want to get dressed. Instead, she hid in her nightclothes, growing paler and thinner—such a change from the vivacious, smiling woman who'd raised me.

"Mom," I said, taking her hand in mine. Her skin was cool to the touch, and I could feel the bones beneath. "Do you want dinner?"

She opened her eyes and smiled. "Zaila, my sweet girl," she said, her voice barely a whisper. "I…forgot what we were talking about."

"I asked what you wanted for dinner." Emotion rose in my throat as it tried to push up and make my eyes tear, but I shoved it down.

"Oh, I can just get something later."

Her vague answer told me what I'd feared: my mother wasn't eating. "I'm moving back in," I told her.

She frowned. "Whyever would you do that? You should be out living your life."

The tears I'd tried to force away now welled up. "I am living my life. I just told you about my job, remember?" I could tell she didn't. "But you…" I blinked back tears. "You're not."

She reached over, fumbling until she could squeeze my hand weakly. "You have to, Zaila. You have to live your life, free and unfettered. Don't let me hold you back. Your father would be appalled."

He would, but not for the reason she'd cited. My mother had always been the backbone of our family, so seeing her reduced to this wisp of her former self destroyed me, just as it would have him.

"I'm going to make stroganoff."

My mother loved the creamy pasta dish. I rose and headed to the kitchen, unsurprised that she didn't follow me. Just two years before, my mother would have been bustling around the room, a smile on her face as she ensured that Dad and I had our favorite drinks as we waited for a meal. I took out some of the day's frustration on the onion, then the mushrooms.

Once it was ready, I went back to the living room, where my mother was once again zoned out in Dad's chair. The sight of her firmed my resolve. I'd moved out the year before Dad died—the year I'd finished my bachelor's degree and started my master's. I might have stayed longer, but both my parents wanted me to "*experience a full life*," they'd said. While I loved my loft near the Galleria, it had become impractical. My lease was up in three months, and I'd let the place go. Mom needed me.

"Time to eat," I said.

"Zaila." She placed her hand to her chest. "Oh, darling. I forgot you were here."

And I'd start moving my stuff back sooner than that. No way was I leaving Mom alone, even if it meant a longer commute.

We settled at the round oak table, and I dished up a plate for her, already knowing she wouldn't finish most of the meal. Dread settled in my belly, chasing away my appetite.

"I'll start moving my stuff back this weekend," I said.

She shook her head. "No, Zaila. You have your whole life ahead of you—"

"Stop it," I argued. "You and Dad…you're everything. Without you, I'd have spent my whole life in that orphanage. I'm here, happy and healthy, because of you. Don't you dare diminish what you did for me."

She smiled, her eyes filled with love and understanding. "Ah, my sweet girl. From the moment your father and I saw you, we knew you were ours."

My parents had been over fifty when they'd adopted me at age five; Dad's fifty-fifth birthday was a couple of months after they brought me home, and I'd enjoyed his big birthday bash more than anything in my brief life. I'd known from early on that my parents were older than most of my friends' parents, but they were so loving and so much fun, and I'd found so much joy in our bond, that I hadn't cared. Now, finally I did, because I'd lost my father before my twenty-fifth birthday, and my mother probably wouldn't make it to my twenty-sixth.

"I am yours." I nodded. "That's why you understand that I'm

going to love you the best way I can, with everything I have, just as you showed me."

"You have to live," she said. "Even better, find someone to love you. Your father was such a good man, so much integrity that came through in everything he did. Love a man like him, sweetheart."

My mind turned to Gunnar Evaldson, but I slammed the lid on that thought before I could yearn.

"Promise me you'll do that," Mom said.

I picked up her hand and brought it to my cheek. "I'll try."

She smiled, her gaze tracking the curves of my face. "That's all I ask, my darling Zaila. Just for you to try." She pulled her hand back and picked up her fork. "Now, tell me about your day."

When I walked into the Wildcatters' office building for my second day on the job, my heart thudded against my ribs. I half expected people in the office to glare, believing I was the reason Lydia had quit. Yet everyone seemed more relaxed and happier than they'd been the day before, just as Jay had said they'd be. It seemed the guy had appointed himself my office friend, and throughout the day, he kept me informed on the rest of the marketing team's reactions to Lydia's resignation. But I was determined to prove myself worthy of my position, so I settled at my desk and got to work sketching out my portion of tasks we'd put together based on my pitch to Gunnar the day before.

Later that afternoon, Jay, Tim, and I met with the Wildcatters' marketing director, Noelle Fischer, a kind but no-nonsense woman who reminded me of my mother. I left the meeting feeling more confident about my position with the team. I also met Natalie Patel, who handled most of the Wildcatters' PR, and she seemed polite and competent, but was much cooler in her response to me.

Regardless, I was finding my footing—especially now that Jay and I dealt mainly with Noelle—and I knew my stuff. Though Gunnar had said I'd report to him, he'd clearly changed his mind, as Noelle, Tim, and Jay had each taken over some of Lydia's duties, at least for now. That made for a more streamlined department with an obvious hierarchy—Jay acting as my boss and Tim managing the art department. Fortunately, I liked working with both of them, as well as Veronica and the designers. The days unfolded, and the week went smoothly as I began interviewing the team nutritionists and physical therapists to implement my plan for social media. And I spent every evening with my mother, brushing off Jay's continued coaxing to get me out for a drink, dinner, something, anything social outside of work.

Ida Jane and Naomi had invited me out to lunch, just as they'd promised they would, but I'd begged off from that, too. Not because I wasn't interested, but because I wasn't sure, exactly, of the line was I wasn't supposed to cross. My internship was for a full calendar year, giving me time to get a better feel for the industry and the sports team. At the end, I hoped the Wildcatters would offer me a position, so I didn't want to blur any boundaries that might complicate that.

Over the weekend, I moved more of my clothes and all of my toiletries into Mom's house, returning to my old bedroom. While some might see this as a step backward, I didn't. My mother needed me, and after just a couple of days, I was more than happy to see the color return to her wan complexion and interest brighten her eyes.

"Why didn't you tell me you were lonely?" I asked her on Sunday afternoon.

We'd gone out for mani-pedis, and Mom had even agreed to get her hair cut and colored. She looked beautiful in her silk blouse and wraparound skirt, so much more like the mother I was used to. My heart warmed. This is what I wanted—to see my mother again.

"I was worried." At my questioning look, she sighed. "That I was being selfish, wanting you here with me. I never want to be a burden."

I leaned over so I could rest my head on her shoulder. Peace filled me. "You could never be a burden, Mom. Please don't say that."

She wrapped her arm around my shoulders and hugged me. "You got it, Zaila. Thank you for being such a sweet girl."

"I'm who I am because of how you raised me."

Monday morning, I got up extra early and put on the outfit I'd chosen the night before: dark blue, flowing pants and a tailored, white linen blouse that made me feel feminine and pretty. I pulled my hair back into a high ponytail and applied my makeup. Today, the social media team would meet with Gunnar about the new campaign we'd developed.

The memory of our first meeting still made my cheeks flush, but I was determined to demonstrate that I was prepared and capable, that I deserved the trust he had shown me.

I drove to work, and as I approached my desk, I noticed something odd. Sticky notes in various colors covered my entire workspace. I couldn't help laughing. "Jay!" I called out, knowing exactly who was behind this.

He appeared, leaning against the wall with a smug grin. "Yes, Ms. Social Media Guru?"

"How long did this take you?" I asked, gesturing to the sticky note disaster zone.

"Oh, you know, just a few hours after the game last night," he said. "But it was worth it to see the look on your face."

As I began the tedious process of removing the sticky notes, an idea struck me. "Wait a minute," I muttered. "This could be perfect for our Day in the Life series!" I glanced up, my voice as bright as the ideas now bouncing through my mind.

Jay raised an eyebrow. "How so?"

"Okay. Picture this," I said. "We film the players pranking each other in the locker room, but we also show them helping clean up afterward. It's a great way to showcase their personalities and team camaraderie, as well as responsibility."

I was so enthusiastic, I hadn't noticed Gunnar walking up beside Jay. But I sure noticed his nod and the glint of approval in his eyes. "I like it," he said. "It humanizes the players and gives fans a glimpse into their relationships off the ice. Let's bring the group together to discuss options."

We settled in the conference room, but as the social media team discussed the logistics of implementing this idea, Gunnar's phone soon buzzed with a notification.

He glanced at it, eyes widening. "I have to go. Consider this our meeting for the day. I looked over the posts you've readied, and I approve. I'll have my assistant send out an email to that effect so it's official."

A moment later, he was gone, taking the air with him. Jay continued to study me as I busied myself with jotting down additional notes from our brief meeting.

"Gunnar's the guy, isn't he?"

"What?" I asked, my gaze rising quickly to Jay's. I willed my cheeks not to flush, but I must have failed because Jay sighed.

"Are you two dating?" he asked.

I shook my head, deciding my best bet was to say as little as possible.

"But you want to be," Jay pressed.

I bit my lip, but I hated lying, so I gave him a brief nod.

Jay's shoulders folded in as he accepted defeat. "Dammit, Z. I really like you."

"And I like you," I assured him. "But I'm not interested in a relationship right now, especially one that has no chance of ever happening. That's what my stupid crush is. Can we never mention this again?"

Jay's face softened. "Yeah. I can do that."

"Thanks. Because my mother is my full focus, like I said before."

He gave me puppy-dog eyes. "If that changes, you'll tell me?"

I smiled, but it was sad because I knew there was no hope for Jay and me. My mother would continue to come first in my life, and Jay, while nice, wasn't the man who caused my heart to pound or my mind to create fantasies I both relished and abhorred.

Nonetheless, I decided it cost me nothing to be kind. "You'll be the first to know," I assured him.

Gunnar

On Wednesday, when I should have been focused on the financial reports that my assistant, Leon, had brought me, I jogged down the steps to the third floor, where the social media team worked. I'd done my best to steer clear of Zaila Monroe, but thoughts of her had assailed me as I slept, causing sexier dreams than I'd had since puberty. While shocking for a man of forty, and a little humiliating, they'd also left me more stimulated than I'd been in years.

I also had to admit that what I felt for her hadn't waned; it wasn't going to dissipate as I'd hoped. Zaila intrigued me, and I wanted more of that heady feeling. Craved it.

I stopped before I reached the open pen of long worktables and computers set up in the middle of the floor, where the various teams met to discuss and work through creative issues. While each of my employees had an office, the open setup in the center allowed for easy communication and had increased both productivity and creativity by double digits. The layout had proved to be a game changer for the Wildcatters, as well as the oil and gas business I still ran, though I did that mainly from Wildcatters headquarters these days.

I stood to the side in the hallway, out of sight as Zaila spoke with Tim, head of social media graphic design, who had two high school boys and a wife he adored.

My jaw clenched as Tim scooted closer to Zaila, speaking animatedly about a filter they both liked. I relaxed as I noted Tim's focus was on the conversation, not Zaila. I struggled with the part of myself that wanted to beat my chest and claim her as mine, as the urge to at least check in on Zaila had overpowered my good sense already. Her enthusiasm was infectious, and I smiled as she gesticulated, Tim hanging on her every word.

An unfamiliar warmth spread through my chest—I'd experienced this more than once recently. I tried to push the emotion aside, reminding myself yet again that I was her boss and more than fifteen years her senior, but I couldn't help myself. I basked in her glow.

As a result, I nearly jumped out of my skin when Jay Wilks, newly promoted to social media manager as of yesterday, tapped me on the shoulder. He held up a stack of paperwork.

"Here are the engagement numbers you asked for," he said as he glanced past me, a sly grin tugging at his lips. "Zaila's really settled in well, hasn't she?"

I nodded, trying to keep my expression neutral. "She's an asset to the organization."

Jay raised an eyebrow. "An asset?"

I felt my jaw clench. "Yes. She's smart and capable."

Jay's smirk widened, and I saw calculation in his eyes. "You two work well together. She seems quite…taken with your management style."

Jay was fishing, probably because he was also attracted to Zaila. I didn't have time for these games. They weren't professional.

"She seems to fit right in here," I said carefully. "Just as you

are an asset to the Wildcatters office culture. I enjoyed your…
interesting way of getting Zaila's attention with the prank earlier
this week."

His smile turned smug. "That was a good one."

The truth hit me like a puck to the mouth: Jay was young,
attractive, and a much better match for Zaila, at least on paper.
My long-clipped rebellious side roared to life—the one that
had often left Karl rolling his eyes at my ridiculous attempts to
garner his attention.

I cleared my throat. "It was. And it brought about some
exciting new ideas."

Jay looked thoughtful. "So…you're saying I could do
something like that again?" His eyebrows rose.

Was I? That would be spontaneous, possibly chaotic, and
potential repercussions ricocheted through my mind. But it
would show Zaila that I wasn't a stuffy suit who didn't know how
to enjoy life…

I forced a nonchalant shrug. "In good fun and nothing that
could embarrass or endanger a colleague, then sure." What the
actual hell had I just said?

"Really?" Jay asked, disbelief twitching across his features.

"I have to tell you, I didn't make my fortune by coloring
inside the lines, Jay." I patted his shoulder a bit too forcefully,
slightly mollified when he winced. "I appreciate creativity."

*And you're not the only one who can play, asshole. I learned and
perfected this game before you were in high school.*

Jay studied me for a long moment. "So you'd be okay with me
setting up a week or two of office pranks, just to see where the

creativity flows, of course?"

I shrugged. "It's the off season. The players aren't practicing, and this is the least busy time of year. Seems like a good time to try it."

"Which is why we do that team-building retreat in September," Jay concluded. "I really thought that was as interesting as you'd allow us to be." He blinked, as if seeing me for the first time.

I chuckled, glad for the diversion from Zaila. Karl and I had always enjoyed pranks. Maybe bringing that here would inject some much-needed lightness into the organization, and into me. I'd been in a rut for so long I no longer even realized it was a rut.

By all measures, I was in my prime, but I'd spent over two decades mourning my older brother, my hero, even as I'd tried to continue his legacy by playing hockey through college. It was time to let loose.

To be fun. To see if I had anything in common with Zaila Monroe. As much as I still struggled with whatever this was happening to me, I liked her, I respected her, and I desired her. I wasn't ready to ask her out, but I did want to see if I'd overblown my interest. If I hadn't, perhaps I'd come up with a new plan.

As Jay left, I turned] toward Tim and Zaila in time to see her throw back her head and laugh. Her smile was radiant, even from this distance. I sighed, running a hand through my hair.

~

When I got back upstairs to my office, I was surprised to find the Wildcatters' team captain waiting for me.

"Did we have an appointment?" I asked.

Cormac Bouchard shook his head. "No, but can I have a few minutes?"

Since Cormac rarely came to see me and typically handled player issues with the coaching staff, I was intrigued—and worried. "Of course." I ushered him into my office and waited for him to take a seat at the table I used for informal meetings. I grabbed us each a water and sat down across from him. "What's bothering you?"

He began with a deep sigh. "Some of the new guys," Cormac said, shaking his head. "They think this place is just one big party with excellent perks and sweet money. I've never met a group less interested in hard work and toeing the line." He leaned closer, his expression tense. "I think Jeff Cross is close to going off the rails—much worse than his college coach let on."

I settled back in my chair, absorbing this additional detail. On paper, Jeff Cross had been a solid offensive addition with strong statistics and athleticism, but his personal choices hadn't been well-documented. I could see now that it was likely intentional. If they had been, neither Silas nor and I would have picked him. As it was, perhaps I should have seen that red flag more clearly and not been so focused on one-upping Leon Johanson, Karl's former coach who was now the offensive coordinator for Boston and had been very interested in Cross. Such pettiness had a way of biting the vindictive person in the ass. "What does Coach Whittaker say?"

Silas Whittaker was the team's head coach. Cormac raised an eyebrow. "He's talking to Jeff right now, for the fourth time in the last two weeks."

That revelation weighed heavy on my chest. "He's not a team player," I surmised. "And he's not settling in because he's used to being the star."

Cormac nodded. "With an even bigger ego. He's a rookie in the NHL. You and I both know he'll have his ass handed to him in the first period of the first game. I'm worried, Gunnar. This guy's already changed my locker room. If nobody shuts him down and puts him in his place, he'll mess up the team. I planned to go out on top, and Jeff's already caused enough adversity to make me question that possibility."

"That serious?"

"Well, Maxim wants to pound his face in, and Stolly's had it out with him because he made comments about Stolly's wife."

I sucked a breath through my teeth. "He said something about Millie?"

Cormac's face soured. "How hot she was from the back, but how the glasses detracted from her overall appeal. Took me and Maxim to peel Stol off the snotty little shit. And Jeff laughed."

"Is that why Silas is talking to him today?" I asked.

Cormac shook his head. "Today he overslept by three hours. Missed practice and weight training. But he said it's fine because he can skate around all of us old men any day of the week."

Yeah, those comments and that cocksure attitude were only going to cause more problems. I didn't have patience for the Jeffs of the world, so either the rookie would fall in line or he'd be slap shotted into a better fit for him, which would mean a less-successful team. That was the deal when you came to Houston: Silas's word was law. Everyone believed in and followed the values of inclusion and hard work, my mainstays.

If they didn't, they didn't last.

"I'll talk to Silas, and we'll keep you in the loop," I told him.

If the locker room was splintering before preseason, I needed to get ahead of the fracture fast.

"Thanks." Cormac stood and stretched, tension still etched into his face. "By the way, you need to tell your new social media intern to take the CATS up on lunch. Keelie's gotten her feelings hurt by the rejection, and that pisses me off, too."

"Zaila's been mean to your wife?" I couldn't fathom such behavior.

"Nah, man. It's just that Keelie's pregnant again, and everything makes her cry," he clarified. "Currently, it's Zaila trying to keep a professional distance. I thought about talking to her myself, but Keelie would get angry, and I hate that shit. So, I'm telling you." He turned toward the door. "If you want me in a good-enough mood to deal with that rookie's assholery, make your intern play nice with the CATS."

I shook my head and raised my hand in a wave as he departed. Now I was in the middle of a friendship dispute? I just wanted this day to be normal. I reached for my phone to check the schedule and got hit with a flood of alerts—mentions, tags, and texts from players and even a few board members.

One stopped me cold: #GunnarTheGoalie is trending! 🖤

I clicked the link and blinked. There I was, in a photo from the end of the charity game when I'd scored the winning goal. Except in this version, someone had Photoshopped me into goalie pads that looked more like a bad Superman suit.

The caption read: "When your billionaire boss can score goals, stop pucks, AND fund the team."

A breath hitched in my chest before I realized it was a laugh.

Soft, surprised. *Hell.* It was stupid…and really funny.

I scrolled farther, finding meme after meme. Fans were already adding their own. This gag was blowing up, and I'd bet quite a bit of my bank account that Zaila Monroe had come up with it. That woman kept me on my toes, and damn if I didn't love every second of it.

CHAPTER 7
Zaila

On Wednesday, after I met with Phoebe Goldstein, the head nutritionist for the team, I returned to my office, excited about the next round of posts she'd helped me develop. Settling into my chair, I pulled out my phone, and my jaw dropped. The top trending hashtag in our city was #GunnarTheGoalie, accompanied by a photoshopped image of Gunnar in full goalie gear, looking comically out of place. Tim and I had created said image earlier this morning, not long after Jay, glee clear in his expression, had told us we had authorization for a week of pranks and free-flowing creativity.

I shook my head, incredulous as I scrolled through the tweets. Fans were having a field day, creating memes and sharing the image with increasingly ridiculous captions.

I bit my lip as I struggled not to laugh. "Tim," I called, pushing away so quickly that my chair rolled into the credenza behind my desk. I rushed to my office door just as Tim sped through it. We collided with a grunt and a squeak as I toppled backward and Tim fell on top.

"What the hell is going on?" Gunnar demanded from down the hall.

I heard his footsteps approaching, but with Tim's elbow still pressed into my diaphragm, I couldn't breathe, let alone speak.

He'd smacked his head on the door frame as we fell, and he groaned, his warm breath in my armpit.

"That hurt..." He moaned.

"It'll hurt more if I have to pull you off of her," Gunnar growled. He came into view over Tim's bony shoulder as I gaped like a fish. "You're squishing her, Tim."

Gunnar took Tim's elbow and hauled him off me. I curled into the fetal position and struggled to breathe, my breath between a pant and a gag.

"Zaila?" Gunnar knelt at my shoulders, cradling my head against his thigh...his very firm thigh. The man was so strong and sexy, and I wheezed like a goose dying of emphysema. "Are you okay? Should I call an ambulance? Did Tim break you?" My vision cleared in time to see Gunnar give Tim a death glare.

I reached for Gunnar's hand and gripped his fingers as I struggled to push out the words. "Wind. Knocked. Out."

His icy gaze softened as concern replaced rage. "You had the wind knocked out of you?"

I nodded.

"I'm bleeding." Tim moaned again, touching his forehead with his fingertips. "I don't do blood."

"You work for a hockey team, my man," Jay said, squatting beside him. "And you cheer loudest when there's a fight."

"Not my blood..." Tim gagged.

"What happened here?" Gunnar asked as those pale blue eyes darted back and forth, like he was scanning me for injury.

I held out my phone, because my diaphragm was too busy seizing. Thankfully, it was still open to the team's social media page. "This? I saw it a few minutes ago."

Gunnar met my gaze briefly before he swiped through the comments. His scowl lightened, and then his eyebrows shot upward. A smile lifted his lips.

"You're fine," Jay said as he handed Tim a bandage. "It's barely a scrape, but it might bruise."

Gunnar had looked up to confirm this diagnosis, but he now brought his attention back to my phone. "I have to hand it to you," he said. "This is pretty clever. But how did you pull it off?" His icy eyes settled on me, but they didn't seem cold. They were warm, like the hottest of flames.

I shivered. "I may have had some help from Tim," I admitted, finally able to breathe again. Reluctantly, I sat up. "He was more than happy to assist."

I leaned over so I, too, could view the screen. Even some of the players had joined the fun. We had stumbled upon social media gold.

"You know," Gunnar said, "we could use this to our advantage. What if we actually put me in as goalie for a practice session? We could livestream it and have the players take shots. It could be a fun twist on next year's charity event."

"It might get more interest than this year's game," Jay grumbled. "Those celebrities were awful."

Gunnar raised his eyebrows. "I thought I played well."

Jay's face suffused with color. "You did. I meant the others. They were…"

"Tiffany was a hot mess," Tim said, looking a little better now that his Band-Aid was in place. "And it was great publicity for her because she's grown her audience with the videos she posted. Who knew falling on your ass would garner so many millions of views?"

I rolled my eyes, not interested in Tiffany or Jay's embarrassment. I smiled at Gunnar. "I like your idea. And we could have fans vote on which player gets to take the last shot. It's interactive, it's entertaining, and it shows that the Wildcatters don't take themselves so seriously that they've forgotten hockey is a game."

"Let's talk more after we get you two casualties off the floor," Gunnar said. He gripped my hands and tugged me up. Once I was on my feet, he continued to hold my hands, his thumbs brushing back and forth over my wrists. "You okay? Steady?" he asked, concern in his eyes.

I nodded as I blushed, then glanced at Jay, whose eyes had zeroed in on where Gunnar caressed my skin. "Y-yes. I'm good. Thank you."

"Be more careful," Gunnar murmured, his words low, just for me. "I was worried."

I lifted my eyes, and my breath caught. "Okay." Then, because he didn't appear satisfied, I added, "I promise."

Offering a lopsided smile, he let go of my hands after one more caress. He placed his hand at the small of my back and ushered me out into the large workspace in the center of the floor. We followed Tim and Jay to a table, and Gunnar pulled out a chair for me—right next to his. I swallowed my giddiness and tried to keep my professional demeanor intact, though I knew Jay was burning with questions he wouldn't let me sidestep.

Not that I had answers for him. I didn't know what was going on with Gunnar, and I didn't know what I wanted. Well, that wasn't quite true. I wanted Gunnar. He was witty, urbane, and effortlessly sexy, confident without being overt. My lady bits had taken notice, and those glacial eyes, when they warmed for me, made me swoon.

But I didn't want to be the woman dating her boss. I hated the idea that people would believe I'd landed here because of my bedroom skills.

I took a breath, my lungs functioning normally now, and tried to get my libido and common sense back on the same page. It took some time as we fleshed out the details of what we'd now dubbed the "Gunnar in Goal Challenge," but eventually I reined myself in. Gunnar owned the company. He was my boss. He never crossed the line, so I wouldn't either.

"While we can nudge the direction, the excitement will more likely grow and interest increase if it's organic," I said as Jay created posts for the next few weeks.

"I disagree," he said. "This is our campaign, and we direct the content."

Gunnar looked back and forth between us for a moment. "Jay, you do the posts you'd like to do on your schedule. You'll need between fifteen and twenty to get us to the time when players are back for practice, so we'll need close to triple that before we can set up a time where I can act as goalie at an exhibition game. Those start six weeks after training camp begins." He turned to me. "Zaila, you create your posts based on users' responses. Then we'll have months of data to measure and aggregate. That will allow us to quantify which posts get more engagement."

Jay's expression turned haughty. "Fine. But when my measured approach wins, I want a victory lap."

"What's that?" Gunnar asked.

Until now, I hadn't realized Jay was taking this so personally, but his next comment proved it.

"We don't have anyone hired to be the new mascot yet, right? Zaila will do it."

"What?" Tim gawked. "No! She'd never get to see a game, take pictures, build the brand."

"That's my job." Jay sniffed. "Zaila's supposed to take my direction. Because she's the intern."

"I don't mistreat my employees because I disagree with them," Gunnar said, his tone teetering on the edge of annoyed.

Jay narrowed his eyes, perhaps readying himself for a verbal assault.

I might not have liked Lydia, but I did like Jay. Well, I had. Now, I wasn't so sure. But I knew I wasn't ready to take on his position, and I didn't want him to hate me.

"I'll agree to that," I said, "as long as you do, too. Should I be right and you wrong, you take on mascot duties."

Gunnar looked ready to argue, but I caught his eye and shook my head. This was my battle, not his. I needed to earn Jay's respect. More than that, I wanted our department to be harmonious, so I'd take the knock on the chin for the team.

"I reserve the right to end this ridiculousness at my discretion," Gunnar said. "But as long as you both understand the terms and agree to them, I'll abide by them as well. For now." He turned the full force of his glower on Jay, who shrank back. "And for the record, this is not how I want any department run. I've found that working *with* my colleagues improves situations and morale. Pranks are one thing, but I think this might be another."

But Jay couldn't opt out now. He'd forced the issue, perhaps without thinking it through. I could see the concern in his eyes. He'd gotten himself on the wrong side of Gunnar Evaldson, and there was no easy way to repair that damage.

With that, Gunnar rose from the table and took his leave. Tim and I shared a long look that spoke volumes—and put us firmly on the same page. We both seemed to understand what was at stake here, Jay's ego. Tim's quirked eyebrow reinforced what my gut was saying: this wasn't going to end well for me.

CHAPTER 8
Gunnar

Friday evening, after I left the office late, I got a front-and-center schooling on Jeff Cross, the rookie player Cormac had come to talk to me about. I'd wondered if Cormac's frustration was magnified, based on his need to secure his legacy.

But that wasn't the case.

Even after the offensive coach's interviews with Jeff's college coach and Jeff himself, he continued to sidestep our typical protocols and showcase himself as a toxic element set to bring down everything I'd worked so hard to build. This evening, the dimwit had posted videos of himself and two teammates at a college party full of underage students. If their red plastic cups didn't scream alcohol, the keg and bottles directly behind him, centered in the shot, did.

So, instead of having a quiet night at home, I'd rushed back to the office to join Noelle, Jay, Zaila, and the rest of the PR team working to mitigate the fallout. Two members of my public relations team scrambled with the head of marketing to get to the phones, offering the pat answer the group had worked out: Our organization was aware of Jeff's posts, and the team and staff would never endorse underage drinking.

I watched as Zaila scooted to the corner of the chaos, her head bend over her phone. "What are you doing?" I asked as

I approached.

I should have been working with the team, but as usual, I was drawn toward Zaila. Her dark hair was pulled up in a haphazard bun, with five or six pens or pencils stuffed into the mass.

"I'm messaging Jeff and telling him to post a photo of himself getting into a rideshare and talking about what a bad idea it is to drink and drive." She glanced up as she hit send. "I'm trying to find a silver lining in this shitshow." She rubbed the back of her hand across her brow.

"Not what you expected from the job, eh?" I asked.

A faint smile tipped her lips before she shook her head. "I know young people are impulsive, sometimes foolish, but this is a disappointment from a guy who's been handed everything…" She shook her head again, her lips pressed together in disapproval.

According to my calculations, Zaila was three years older than our newest addition to the team, yet she had more sense in her pinky finger than Jeff had in his entire body. The feelings Zaila evoked in me grew stronger the more time I spent with her.

"Ah!" She brightened. "He actually answered. Good."

A few minutes later, a post popped up featuring a video Jeff had posted of himself walking unsteadily down a sidewalk, away from the noise spilling from the house behind him. "Just learned some people here are underage." He hiccupped. "That's not cool, man. Not cool. I mean, I prolly shouldn't be drinking like I did tonight, but those kids back there…" He waved behind him, where the party continued. "That's not right. I'm calling a ride to get home safely. Got training camp next week. No reason to be reckless when I've got so much on the line. For the record, those kids do, too—their whole lives are in front of 'em."

I'd seen enough of Zaila's text to know Jeff was reading her words for the camera. "Gotta sober up and play smart. That's the best option for me..." He pointed at the screen, blinking owlishly. "And for you. Party smart, everyone! Jeff out."

The video ended with the collective release of groaned-out breaths from the team.

Jay rubbed his palms down his face, tugging the skin so hard that his eyelids pulled downward, too. "That was a total clusterfu—*hi* there, Mr. Evaldson."

"At least he smartened up," Natalie, the PR director, muttered. "Damn fool could have made everything much, much worse."

I waited for Zaila to tell them she'd gotten through to Jeff, but she didn't. In fact, she stayed tucked against the wall, head bent over her phone. Twenty minutes later, after we determined Jeff was home, the team packed up and filtered toward the exits. I kept out of the way but continued to observe, fascinated by their conversations and their insights into the players and what Jeff's hard-partying attitude would do to the team.

"I hope he doesn't screw up the chemistry," Jay said to the PR guys as they walked past. "The Wildcatters are known for being hardworking, focused, and goal-oriented. This one yahoo might undo all that, and then we'll have to fight tooth and nail for our brand."

Silas would have Jeff on a short leash after this, and I expected the kid to either rebel harder or get with the program. Only time would tell. I'd have to talk to Silas again tomorrow about how he wanted to handle the rookie. Personally, I was leaning toward Cormac's method: slap shot the little shit as far from my organization as possible.

Soon, the room had emptied. Though I noted that Zaila was still hunched in the corner with her phone. As I watched, she dropped her head into her hands and heaved a deep, shuddering breath. This hadn't been a fun night, but it seemed unlikely that she was this distraught because she worried for Jeff's reputation.

Something else was bothering her.

"You okay?" I asked, sliding into the seat across from her.

Zaila's head snapped up, surprise and embarrassment flashing across her face. "I didn't see you there." She glanced around. "I thought everyone had left."

"They did, congratulating themselves for getting Jeff to see reason." I waited a beat. "Why didn't you tell them you'd managed to get through to him?"

She sighed as she rolled her head, trying to loosen the tension in her neck. "Because who talked him out of the dumb situation doesn't matter."

"It matters to me. You deserve recognition," I said. "You did well tonight."

A ghost of a smile flickered across her face, but it quickly faded. "Thanks, but I don't care about recognition as much as I wanted to make sure he didn't drive." She blew out a long breath. "He really doesn't get it, does he?"

"No, he doesn't," I said. "But I think for you, this was personal."

She looked away. "My father was badly injured in a car

accident. He died two years later because of complications. Technically, it was renal failure, but that started with lacerations sustained in the wreck."

I covered her hand with mine. "I'm so sorry."

"Thanks. Mom and I handle some days better than others. The idea of Jeff getting in a car, doing that to another family…"

"I understand," I murmured. I knew what it was to lose someone you loved because of others' negligence. My frustration with Jeff roared back to life.

For a moment, I considered telling Zaila about my brother, about that night twenty-five years ago when ignorance and hatred had taken him from me. But the words caught in my throat. Speaking about Karl was too personal, too raw, even after all this time—even to share with someone who'd understand.

Instead, I said, "I've seen what that kind of ignorance can do. It has no place on this team or anywhere else."

Zaila nodded. I had an uncomfortable feeling she could see right through me. "I agree," she murmured. "I just wish everyone else did, too."

We sat in silence for a moment, unspoken words weighing down the space between us.

"Thank you for your efforts this evening, Zaila," I said finally. "The team's lucky to have you."

She gave me a small smile. "Thank you. That means a lot."

I stood to leave. "Need a ride?"

She shook her head. "I have my car. I'll head out soon. Just… need to regain my composure."

I hesitated, shifting from one foot to another. "If you ever need to talk...or stress-eat ice cream—my brother used to do that—my door's always open."

Her eyes widened, and her mouth dropped open just enough for me to catch the soft pink of her tongue. My abdomen tightened again, but for a different reason.

Then she straightened, her professional mask sliding back into place. "I appreciate that," she said, her tone polite but distant. She rose, smoothing her slacks over her nicely rounded hips. She gave me a polite, businesslike smile that I detested. "Have a good evening, Mr. Evaldson."

"Gunnar," I said. "Please call me Gunnar like everyone else."

She paused and glanced over her shoulder. It could have been the light, or it could have been wishful thinking, but I could swear yearning flitted across Zaila's expression, and desire darkened her eyes. She licked her lips. "'Night, Gunnar."

Her voice stroked my skin like a physical caress.

"Dream of me," I murmured once I knew she couldn't hear my quiet words. Still, I shouldn't have said it. But I knew I'd dream of her, just like I did every night.

CHAPTER 9
Zaila

The Monday morning air thickened with tension, the kind that smothers thought and makes clothes stick, as the players slid into their seats in the large conference room on the top floor of the Wildcatters' office building. I clutched my coffee mug as if it could protect me from the angry words and anxiety I worried were coming.

Typically, I would have enjoyed the view out the window of Houston's sprawling city center. Instead, my focus remained on Cormac Bouchard, who sat ramrod straight at the far end of the table, his arms crossed over his chest like the last barrier to a castle's courtyard. Gunnar stood by the whiteboard, his expression flat. Jay fidgeted beside me, clearly wishing he could be anywhere else, and then Jeff came in with Coach Whittaker and goalie coach Adam Kramer. He was basically a prisoner in chains.

This meeting was going to be brutal.

Finally, Cormac leaned forward. His voice was low, controlled, and infinitely more dangerous than if he'd shouted. "What Jeff did on Friday wasn't just stupid, it was a slap in the face to every guy in our locker room who's earned his place."

Nearly every player nodded and voiced agreement. Jeff and his other rookie buddy, Brayden Blackwell, turned pale and dropped their gazes.

Then, Brayden lifted his head, jaw clenched, and gave both Gunnar and Silas Whittaker a sharp nod. He turned his focus to Cormac next. "I get what you're saying. I'll do better."

"Good," Gunnar said.

"I'm glad to hear that, Brayden, because you have talent, and you'll be a hella good scorer soon." He refocused on Gunnar. "You brought us here to build a culture. Family. Legacy. And Jeff? Unlike Brayden, who says right now that he wants to be part of the team, Jeff has pissed all over it."

Jeff looked up, his expression mutinous, but when he caught the fury not just in Cormac's expression, but also on the faces of Wildcatter legends Maxim, Stol, Naese, and Cruz, the core guys who'd been here for the championship and held the Stanley Cup, his fire flickered out.

My breath caught in my throat at the raw power in the room.

"Ms. Monroe, I know you're here because you talked Jeff into going home," Maxim Dolov said, and I startled. "Thank you. That didn't just save his PR image; it saved lives."

Jeff opened his mouth, perhaps to defend himself, but the growing volume of the rumbling in the room caused him to clench his jaw, and fists, instead.

"I've seen your work," Luka Stol added, looking my way. "You've been smart, fair. You get the brand."

Jeff shot me a glare that I studiously ignored.

"But you also understand that this is our city, these are our people, and we care about them."

"She shouldn't have been in that position in the first place," Cormac Bouchard said, enunciating each word with care.

"That's why we're here. Jeff's actions are causing problems not just for the team, but for the social media, PR, and marketing departments, not to mention the potential for injured people Jeff almost put in harm's way."

"We didn't need this PR shit-mire to start our season," Paxton Naese chimed in. "Everyone in the league was gunning for us because of our record, but now? They think we're divided. Though ironically, this brought most of us closer."

What he didn't say reverberated through the room: *You aren't one of us, Jeff.*

"Discipline starts at the top," Gunnar said. "Jeff's benched for the first two preseason games. He'll issue a public apology and attend the youth outreach sessions with Cormac and me. Voluntarily."

This was also supposed to show Jeff that his actions impacted others, according to Natalie's memorandum outlining how the public relations staff wanted to handle the incident. I wasn't sure that would work, especially now that the rookie's shoulder chip had grown to the size of the city of Houston.

Jeff jumped to his feet, face florid. "What? I'm your best—"

"You're nothing if you don't play." Gunnar's icy voice cut through Jeff's potential rant. "No professional stats, nothing to offer another team except what Silas has to say about your lack of work ethic and your lack of team spirit. And while I'm giving you another chance—one the rest of the team doesn't believe you deserve—if needed I will cut you and take the loss so you don't further damage my team and our season."

His words were soft, but the ruthless truth caused me to

shiver. Jay let out a low whistle.

"Protecting the shield means holding the line. Every time," Cormac said. "You didn't just fuck up for yourself, rookie. You tried to bring down my team." He rose, towering over the table as he leaned forward. "You either fall in line with what we're doing here or you're done."

The ultimatum settled. Coach Whittaker remained stoic, arms crossed, even with Jeff's beseeching gaze. "Don't look at me," he said. "I've already given you more chances than Mac and the other guys said you deserved. This is your fuck up. Own it. Make it right, and maybe the team will learn to respect you." He shrugged, seeming to say, "*I don't think that's possible.*"

Jeff's need to fight, to speak his piece, finally left him with a ragged sigh, echoed by Jay beside me. I'd noted the two of them together more than once the past week or so, and I wondered if Jay held more sympathy for Jeff than he should.

"Now we strategize about how to fix this," Gunnar said.

Jeff's lips twisted, and a dull red climbed up his neck and into his cheeks, cresting at his ears as Natalie began speaking about the plan her team had put together to head off further incidents and right the damage.

Cormac dipped his head when she finished. "We'll do that. What about socials?" He turned to look at me, and so, of course, did everyone else. Jay scrambled from his chair and stuttered through some of the talking points he, Gunnar, the PR team, and I had worked out.

"From her," Maxim said after a moment, cutting Jay off.

I straightened in my seat, throat dry. I didn't need to look at Gunnar, and I didn't dare look at Jay, because I already knew what I had to say.

"This isn't simply a PR issue, where a press conference and a few photos at youth camps will solve the issue. Though I think those are a great start," I added quickly. "What you're actually asking, I think, is what the organization is and what it isn't." I looked around, waiting for the players to nod or shake their heads. They all nodded.

"Got it," I confirmed. "So, while Natalie and Noelle are working on damage control, the social media department needs to provide the narrative that we are *not* an organization that drinks heavily and plans to drive themselves home. Jay, Noelle, and I have created a list of talking points for each of the players to communicate on your socials. Natalie has opportunities for you all if you'd like to do outreach, and they look really cool, so that's a great idea as well. This problem took one night to create, but it could take months to clean up, so we need to be diligent and patient."

Cormac exhaled, with a slight nod. "I'll do my part, but if the rookie's late to even one of those youth events, I'm pushing for him to be cut."

Cormac waited for Coach Whittaker's nod, then he rose and strode from the room. When he was gone, I finally let out the breath I'd held and the other players buzzed with conversation as they began to disperse.

Gunnar turned to me, quiet but intense.

"You okay?"

I nodded, hoping my dizziness would pass. "Yeah. I mean, I will be."

Gunnar smiled. "You handled yourself well." He looked over at the exiting players and Jay's sweaty chaos as he spoke to Jeff and two other young players huddled in the corner.

"I've never had a situation quite like this," Gunnar said. "What's your take? Honest, no filter, please."

I looked around, taking in the dynamic between Jeff and the rest of the team, including the staff. "He's isolated and feels put upon—treated unfairly. This will probably blow up even bigger."

Gunnar sighed. "That's my feeling, too." He shook his head. "Still, it's worth a try to get him to see the light."

I shrugged. *Maybe.* My father had talked about soldiers who refused to follow protocol. They always caused problems, big ones, and I had a strong suspicion Jeff would, too.

CHAPTER 10
Gunnar

I stared at the analytics dashboard on my computer screen, a grin spreading across my face. The results were in from the social media team's six-week posts contest, and the results were even stronger than I'd expected. I reviewed every post and then the aggregates for each of the contestants, pride blooming in my chest as I noted the engagement Zaila had created.

As I took the stairs down to the marketing floor, I greeted employees along the way with a nod and a smile. Today was a good day—not just for our online engagement but for the future of the organization.

I didn't need to gather the team in the open meeting space in the center of their floor. They were assembled there already. One constraint I'd imposed on the competition was that after the first two weeks, I was the only person allowed to review the numbers. This had allowed Zaila and Jay to make tweaks based on quantitative analysis for the first half of the month, but then both were blind after that, so they couldn't do anything to sway the eventual results. I wasn't exactly sure what they could have done to skew the outcome, but then again, no one liked to lose, especially when ego was on the line.

"The numbers for our latest campaign are in," I noted, keeping my expression neutral even as most of the staff leaned forward, clearly interested in the result. The entire organization, even the players who'd recently come back for training camp, was aware of the competition and the bet. The wagers had remained friendly, but they were fierce. That's what happened with a group of such highly competitive people, after all.

Zaila stood on one side of Tim, Jay on the other. He'd been so confident about his posts that he'd talked them up with the team. I'd learned over my decades in boardrooms and corporations that true confidence was often much quieter than insecurity.

"It was a good run, Zaila," Jay said, with a gallant smile that didn't quite seem genuine. "I'm sure my posts crushed it."

I chuckled as I shook my head. "Jay, I've got some news for you. Your posts didn't exactly crush it."

His face fell. "What do you mean?"

"I mean," I said, pausing for dramatic effect, "your last five posts came in last."

The office erupted in a mixture of gasps and congratulations to Zaila.

Jay's jaw dropped. "No way," he scoffed. "How is that possible?"

I pulled up the stats on the big screen for everyone to see. "The numbers don't lie, Jay. Your posts about the team's pre-game rituals didn't resonate as much as you thought they would. Unfortunately, the players are going to be upset, which means they're going to need reassurance that they're still admired." I looked over at the PR staff. "Can you put together something that showcases how much our fans love the players?"

Natalie nodded. "Of course. I'd love to plan an event."

As the group gathered to look at the results, I did feel a twinge of sympathy for Jay. He'd been with the Wildcatters just over three years and was eager to prove himself as the new division head. Even more, he'd navigated his role successfully under Lydia, who'd made that hard for everyone. This loss had to be a tough blow. But a bet was a bet, and he'd been the one to push it in the first place.

As I'd suspected, Zaila had a better knack for creating engagement. She was more in touch with the online world, perhaps. I'd have to keep an eye on the social media group to ensure Jay was nurturing Zaila's gifts, rather than stifling them.

"So," I said, turning to Jay. "I believe you set a little wager about this."

He groaned, covering his face with his hands. "Oh, no. Don't remind me."

But the rest of the team was already buzzing with excitement. "The mascot!" someone shouted. "Jay's going to be the mascot!"

I nodded, trying to keep a straight face. "That's right, Jay. You'll be donning the Wildcatters mascot costume for home games for the first half of the season."

The color drained from Jay's face. "You can't be serious. I…I was just joking around."

I shrugged, turning to Zaila. I wouldn't punish my staff, but I wasn't going to make this easy for him either. But even before I could ask Zaila how she felt, Tim said, "You shook on it, Jay."

"So? It was just a silly joke." Color appeared in his cheeks, and he clenched his fists.

"But you told me yesterday how much you were looking

forward to Zaila sweating it out in the costume. You laughed," Noelle said, narrowing her eyes.

"Me? In that...that thing?" Jay sputtered.

I pulled up a picture of Gusher, the Texas Wildcatters' mascot, and sent it to the screen. The oversized, cartoonish oil derrick with a hockey stick and a mischievous grin stared back at us.

"I'm holding you to your word," Tim said. Noelle gave a firm nod, and more people crowded closer, offering their support.

"Starting next month, you'll be bringing Gusher to life for thousands of fans," Noelle said. "What a gift you'll give them."

Tim grinned. "You can post about it, complain good-naturedly, too. I bet those posts will get a ton of engagement."

Jay groaned as he sat and buried his head in his hands, muttering something about regretting his life choices. But I couldn't stop smiling. This unexpected turn of events might actually be good for our in-house team and the Wildcatters on the ice.

As everyone separated and went to their offices, Jay lingered, so I did, too— though I stayed behind him. "They love you now, Zaila Monroe," Jay muttered at her doorway. "Hope you can keep it up when the spotlight shifts."

Zaila

That evening, after my big win in the social media challenge, my coworkers dragged me to the Frozen Puck, a karaoke bar across the street from the arena. I'd never been before, and Noelle insisted I needed to unwind after the stressful month. She wasn't wrong, but my worry wasn't for the reason she assumed. I wasn't overly stressed about Jay or work; I was concerned about my mother and my inability to stop thinking about Gunnar Evaldson.

He was my boss—actually my boss's boss's boss, and my little crush embarrassed me almost as much as it annoyed me. Gunnar was good-looking. He was suave and confident, and those eyes seemed to laser into my soul and pull out yearnings for cuddles and kisses I hadn't known I had inside me. But nothing was going to happen between us.

Because he was the team owner. And the wielder of immense power…that I found so sexy.

The moment we walked through the door of the bar, some of the younger Wildcatters players—including Jeff Cross, that troubled one who'd caused the social media storm a couple of weeks ago—raised their voices and glasses toward us.

"The winner is here," Jeff shouted.

I rolled my eyes. So much for him toeing the line. Though I guessed as long as he met the criteria laid out by the rest of the team—namely, not posting about his partying and attending the PR events—his current beers with teammates weren't a problem. It just felt like one, and I sighed as I noted his glassy eyes and too-wide smile.

"Hey, it's your PR savior!" one of the other players called out, waving us over.

I hadn't learned his name yet, mainly because he wasn't on the first line and had done nothing noteworthy. I had a strong suspicion I would remember his name—ah, he just said it was Brady—after tonight, especially when he spoke up again.

"Let us buy you ladies a drink!"

"I'm okay," I said, hands up, trying to back away. I wasn't much of a drinker. My father always said alcohol rotted the mind, and the one time I'd had a few hard seltzers in college, I'd learned I did not like being hungover.

"C'mon, have a drink with us," Jeff wheedled. "We've gotta say thanks." A waitress dropped off twelve shots, and Jeff shoved one into my hand. "On three!" he called.

Brady counted down, and they slammed their shots back, Noelle following suit. She widened her eyes and darted them to the glass before she grimaced.

I looked down at my shot. Gunnar would probably sound like my father, telling me shots were a terrible idea. And I needed Gunnar Evaldson out of my head. I was so tired of batting away thoughts of him.

So I picked up the glass and slammed it back.

The burn of the liquor seized my lungs, making breathing impossible. Noelle shoved a second glass in my hand, saying it would chase the drink. I took a long sip before realizing it was some other form of alcohol.

My lunch-less afternoon caught up with me immediately. Before I knew it, Noelle, Brady, Jeff, and I were several rounds in, and the room had started to spin. As the opening notes of "Love Shack" by The B-52s filled the bar, the karaoke machine and screen beckoned, and in my alcohol-infused state, belting out my favorite party song seemed like a brilliant idea.

"I'm going to sing!" I announced, stumbling towards the stage.

Nadine hooted and cat-called while the guys howled. I grinned as I picked up the mic. I strutted across the stage, mimicking exaggerated model poses as I warbled out the lyrics. I'd just hit the last stanza when I glimpsed a familiar face at the bar entrance. Gunnar had arrived, his expression a mix of amusement and concern.

Fucking Gunnar Evaldson. I'd spent a good bit of time this evening not thinking about him, and now he was here, ruining my fun. I stumbled off the stage, giggling as I for some reason made my way directly toward him. "Gunnar! You came to hear me sing!"

He frowned, his eyes darting to the group of players at our table. "Not exactly. Coach Whittaker is on his way," he informed Brady and Jeff, his pale eyes now glacial with…something my muddled brain wanted desperately to understand, especially after the two players swallowed hard. "He heard you were here. Since I was still at the office, I told him I'd suggest strongly that you head home in a rideshare. I'm also here with a warning: You, Jeff, are past your two strikes. I've never had a player hit three, but I'll remind that you signed a contract that includes a cut clause should you be unwilling to abide by team rules."

"Hey! That's not fair," Jeff began.

But Gunnar's expression turned dark, and Jeff fell silent, his lips compressing. After sharing a look, Jeff and Brady made a beeline for the exit, and Nadine slunk away during the exchange, making it impossible for me to suggest she share a ride home with me.

"Oh," I sighed. "I was having fun."

Gunnar turned back to me, a thick eyebrow shooting up. "I think it's time to call it a night. Let me take you home."

"But the night's just getting started!" I protested. *Do my words sound slurred?*

Gunnar's jaw clenched with apparent irritation that even my drunken self recognized. "You've had enough fun for one evening," he said. "Come on."

"Fine, but only because you chased off my friends." I hiccupped softly. "And because everything is spinning. And because I'm really going to hate myself tomorrow."

"Then why drink?" Gunnar asked.

I had enough self-preservation intact not to give him the main reason. "I thought... Jeff likes to party, so connecting with him might be a good idea."

"Yes, but now the rest of the team thinks you've gone to the Jeff-side." Gunnar shook his head, disappointment tightening his mouth. "I thought you were smarter than this, Zaila."

As we stepped outside, the cool night air hit me, and I swayed. Gunnar steadied me with a hand on my elbow, guiding me back toward the Wildcatters' building and his car.

"I...wasn't at my best," I conceded.

Gunnar chuckled as he shook his head. "Not much of a drinker, are you?"

"Nope. I never drink. My dad said it rots the mind."

Gunnar looked over at the two players, now huddled on the corner, as we passed. At least they were smart enough not to get behind the wheel of a car. I wasn't too drunk to notice that.

"He's right, and I'm more worried about you than those two knuckleheads."

I giggled, enjoying his attention. Then I remembered my mom, and I gasped.

"What is it?" he asked, instantly on alert.

"Oh, I just, uh, should have gone straight home. My mom... She's not doing well."

"You live at home?" Gunnar asked.

"I moved back this month," I said with a sigh. "My mom's having a hard time. Since my dad died..." I trailed off, blinking away tears. "She needed me. I make sure she eats, goes to the doctor, takes her pills..."

"On top of a more-than-full-time job where you're paid an intern's salary?" Gunnar's eyes held a strange light, almost as if I mystified him.

But that couldn't be right.

"Well...yeah. This is the first time in my life I've been able to do something for her. She was always the one to take care of us. She doesn't like me living there, though," I confided.

Gunnar stopped in front of a sleek silver vehicle. I didn't know what it was, just that it was clearly new and clearly not American. "Why doesn't she like you there?"

"Because I'm supposed to be living my life, she says, not taking care of her. But she's my mom. She and Daddy took me out of that awful orphanage, gave me a home. As if I wouldn't be there for her now." I scoffed at the very notion.

Gunnar studied me for an intense moment.

I dropped my gaze and tucked my hair behind my ear. "What?"

"You are so young one moment—getting drunk and making a spectacle of yourself—then the next, you're explaining how you've put your life on hold for your mother." He stared at me, and I had to drop my gaze before he peered into my soul. His eyes were so pale and yet so deep. Both secrets and hurts swam in those icy depths, and I wanted to know them all. "You, Zaila Monroe, continue to surprise me."

I cleared my throat. "Well, you continue to confound me." I slapped my hand over my mouth. "I need to stop talking."

Gunnar opened the car door, but I noted the upward twist of his lips. My cheeks burned even brighter because I'd amused him. "You know," I said as he helped me into the passenger seat, "you're really handsome when you're all protective and stuff."

Gunnar paused, his face inches from mine as he leaned in to fasten my seatbelt. For a moment, I thought he might kiss me. But then he stepped back, clearing his throat. "Let's get you home, Zaila."

As we drove, I couldn't stop giggling. "Did you see me singing? I was so good."

Gunnar chuckled. "You certainly were something up there."

"You should've joined me," I said. "We could've done a duet."

"I don't think the world is ready for that," he said, shooting me a grin. An actual grin!

Oooh, he was so attractive when he smiled, and that made me want him. The next moment, sadness overwhelmed me because I couldn't have him. I looked out the window.

As we pulled up to my parents' house, Gunnar helped me out of the car. I leaned against him, suddenly feeling very sleepy. "You're a good man, Gunnar," I mumbled. "A really nice, handsome guy."

He sighed, his arm around my waist to keep me steady. "And you're drunk, Zaila. Let's get you inside."

As we reached the door, I fumbled with my purse, searching

for my keys. Once I had them, Gunnar took them from me, unlocking the door. For a moment, we faced each other, the air between us charged.

"Goodnight," Gunnar said as he handed me back my keys. My breath caught as he skated his knuckles down my cheek. "Drink some water and get some rest."

As he headed back down the sidewalk, I called, "Hey, Gunnar? Thanks for being my brave, shining knight tonight."

He smiled. "Anytime, Zaila. Anytime."

Though even now, I knew there'd better not be another time.

He chuckled. "See you Monday, rookie."

I snorted at the nickname, mostly so I didn't melt at the sweetness. "I'm nothing like Jeff."

"Don't I know it. And aren't I glad," Gunnar said, waving over his shoulder.

I melted. Total goo right there in the foyer.

"Zaila? Is that you?" Mom called.

Gunnar tipped his head, silently commanding me into the house.

I shut the door with a sigh. "Here, Mom."

Gunnar Evaldson might not be for me, but that didn't stop me from yearning.

CHAPTER 11
Gunnar

The staff retreat had arrived, and because I'd had two meetings early this Thursday morning about one of my other business ventures, I flew my private jet to the small airport near the retreat location. This year it was Horseshoe Bay, which sits on the Colorado River about an hour north of Austin and nearly two hours north of San Antonio. Typically I considered this annual team-building event a necessary evil at best and a complete waste of time and money at worst. This year, however, I was looking forward to these three days away from the office and the lull before the hockey season started.

And though I'd steered clear of her the past couple of weeks, I was really looking forward to seeing Zaila. I'd spent more of my meeting this morning mooning over how cute she'd looked with those big, luminous eyes focused on me when I found her up on that karaoke stage than I had on the financials for the newest alternative-energy options my team had brought to the table.

That sort of lack of attention wouldn't do. Still, I wasn't sure how to reframe my ever-growing interest in Zaila so I could compartmentalize her as I did most everything else in my life. If I kept everything in a place of my choosing, it couldn't affect me, unless and until I allowed it to. Spoiler alert: I refused to be affected. Icy control had made me billions and kept me at the top of my field.

And yet…Zaila Monroe affected me. Deeply. Often. I'd stayed away, expecting my interest to wane, but it hadn't. In fact, I was more interested in Zaila now than I had been before I decided to steer clear of her. I'd finally admitted that whatever this was with Zaila, it was different. I hated that I loved her stubborn presence in my thoughts.

I continued scowling as I settled into the air-conditioned vehicle waiting for me—a sporty and nimble all-wheel-drive powered as much by solar as possible. I'd also requested a standard transmission, which improved fuel efficiency. While I'd made my money in gasoline and oil, we had one world, and I was partial to the pretty parts, wanting to keep them that way for many generations to come. I also preferred manual shifting to the mind-numbing boredom of letting the car's computer manage the engine for me.

I navigated away from the small airport, and within a few minutes, the lakeside resort sprawled before me, a picturesque setting that did little to ease my irritation. As I exited the car, I smoothed down my tailored suit, a habit I'd developed over years of board meetings and press conferences.

"Mr. Evaldson!" A shrill voice pierced the air. I turned to see Brenda Hernandez, the overly enthusiastic retreat organizer, practically skipping towards me. "Welcome to our Trust Trek scavenger hunt!"

I offered a tight smile. I couldn't think of any bigger waste of my time than a scavenger hunt. "Brenda. Nice to see you."

"I've paired you with Zaila Monroe for today's activities," she chirped as she gave an exaggerated wink. All she needed to do was elbow me to make it more obvious I'd insisted on this arrangement. I tipped my chin in acknowledgment.

"Understood. Thank you. Is everyone here?"

"They are. The lunch hour is nearly complete, and folks should meet in the lobby for their pairings." Brenda trotted at my side, so I held open the door to the building when I arrived, and she ducked past me. "I think your complementary skill sets will shine today," she added over her shoulder. "It was a good idea to pair mentors with the younger team members. This set of clues is a doozy."

When we entered the lobby, it seemed most everyone had gathered. Brenda clapped her hands and waited for the noise to die down enough to run through the same spiel she'd just given me. Then she continued into the rules of the game, the timeline, and the grand prize: a two-night stay on one of the luxury properties along the River Walk in San Antonio.

"So, find your partner and grab your envelope, but don't open it yet! " Brenda said. "Cheating gets you immediately disqualified. All righty, we move out in fifteen minutes." She pulled on a headset that looked like something NASA might have designed and bustled off toward her team, no doubt to ensure a smooth and fair competition.

Zaila worked her way through the crowd. "We meet again, Mr. Evaldson."

"Gunnar," I corrected, though I knew she was trying to put a barrier between us. Intelligent woman, though I couldn't tolerate the distance. "You've been in my car," I reminded her. *In my mind.* "I think we're past formality, especially since I know you find me handsome."

She raised an eyebrow, a hint of embarrassment blushing her cheeks. She was striking with those soft curves, brown eyes, thick hair, and quick wit. "We'll never bring that up again," she declared. "I've decided befriending Jeff is outside my skill set."

"On that we agree."

She stood next to me as I greeted more of my staff. Jay Wilks, I noted, remained off to the side, glowering at us. Rather than having fun with his coming time in the mascot costume, he'd been sulky since he lost the social media competition. I made a mental note to monitor him.

I turned just in time to find Brenda at the top of the staircase in the large entry area. She clapped her hands. "The scavenger hunt has officially begun! Good luck, Wildcatters!"

Pairs of people hurried to the exits, though Zaila and I hung back. And it wasn't because we lacked a competitive streak. She'd just chosen to open the envelope here and look over the clues before busting through the doors and bottlenecking with the rest of the teams.

She was strategic like that. I loved how forward-thinking and imaginative she'd proven herself to be.

"Don't worry," Zaila said as we studied a Polaroid of a golf cart and a riddle. "I'll try not to let my skill set outshine yours."

I chuckled. "I welcome the challenge."

She hesitated, taking a breath before meeting my eyes. "Thank you for that night. For taking me home from the bar. I…" She shook her head. "I'm glad you were there to make sure I didn't do something I'd regret more than bad karaoke."

Warmth radiated from my chest, heating my belly, too. The

energy was so comforting, so sweet, I almost didn't recognize it—affection. "I want to be someone you can lean on, Zaila." My fingers itched to brush her hair away from her smooth cheek, to run my thumb along the curve of that lip. But that would be selfish and stupid, especially since I'd put the barrier between us.

"Gunnar," she breathed, her pupils expanding as those lush lips parted, inviting...

Brenda bustled over. "Y'all need to hustle. Your first clue awaits! Remember, teamwork makes the dream work!"

I cleared my throat, seeking a level of neutrality I didn't feel. "Shall we get started?"

"We better," Zaila agreed. "I don't like to lose."

"Noted," I said, fighting a smile. "The golf carts are behind this building. Let's go grab one as we think about what the image means."

Zaila dipped her head, her brow furrowing as she contemplated the clue. "See these lines on it? I think to get the rest of the clue, we have to find this golf cart," she said.

"Good eye. Right. So it may be on the course, because there's a tournament that starts tomorrow."

"Why would Brenda do that?" Zaila asked as we went outside. "Seems unsportsmanlike."

"Probably because they goofed on the scheduling," I said. "We got a discount on our typical rate, but my guess is that Brenda's ability to control the damage is much smaller than she thinks." I pointed. "The course is there, and our cart isn't one of the ones out front. We're going rogue."

"What does that mean?" Zaila asked with a laugh.

I turned to face my…intern. "You said you wanted to win. Well, I only win. So, we're going to take the necessary measures to ensure a W."

She narrowed her eyes, though I wasn't sure if it was against the sun or for me, specifically. "Ethically."

I scoffed. "I don't cheat to win. Normally I just glare, and people cave."

"Oooh, so intense," Zaila snarked.

"That's awfully sassy for someone who hasn't proven her abilities."

"I beat Jay," Zaila said, raising her chin. "And our golf cart is at that tee—there." She pointed.

We jogged up to the cart and were searching it for the clue when a red-faced woman in a visor stormed over, her driver lifted over her head. She waggled it at us.

"Hey! What do you think you're doing?" she demanded.

"Ma'am, we're just—"

"This is my lucky cart." She poked the driver closer to my chest. Zaila pulled in a breath. "I'm about to break eighty for the first time."

Zaila stepped in, her voice smooth as silk. "We apologize for the confusion. We're part of a scavenger hunt and thought this was our assigned cart."

The woman's face softened, but she still eyed us with suspicion as she got behind the wheel. "I see. Well, good luck."

As she sped away, Zaila turned to me with a smirk. "So much for your billionaire charm, huh?"

I rubbed my hand down the back of my neck. "I'm more effective with the hockey crowd. She was scary."

"Lucky for you, I got the clue." Zaila held up another picture, her face beaming with a dazzling smile.

"Where was it?"

"Taped under the passenger seat. Says we need to take a picture of this cake before it's cut, which will happen for the afternoon tea…" She glanced around. "I don't know what time it is, so I guess we should trot back over there now to get it done."

I glanced at my watch, shaking my head. Zaila wasn't the first of her generation I'd noted who seemed averse to clocks. I knew they used their phones, but a quality watch was so much better. But we didn't have time for my lecture on the matter because we had a competition to win. "It's two."

"And the cake's cut at two thirty." She peered more closely at the photo. "I think that's the main hall."

She showed me the picture, and I squinted at the surroundings before nodding. "Looks like."

Zaila trotted back up the hill toward the main hall in the distance. "I guess I'll get my steps in today."

I was pretty sure she got them every day, as did I, but I appreciated her positive outlook on this rather silly game.

Our clue led us to a massive birthday cake, now on display in the center of the dining room. Zaila snapped her shot moments before chaos erupted as a toddler, moving with surprising speed, darted past us and face planted directly into the cake. Frosting flew everywhere, including onto my suit, face, and hair.

Zaila snapped a photo of the disaster, then one of me. "Got one before he body slammed it, so it wasn't just uncut, it was untouched."

The child's mortified mother rushed over, apologizing profusely. "I'm so sorry! I didn't know. We're only here for the golf tournament. Oh, Zack, look at you…"

Zaila's eyes met mine, sparkling with mirth, and as I laughed I felt my initial irritation slide into a warmth that had nothing to do with the Texas heat.

"No problem," I assured the mother. "Honestly, that's something my brother and I would have done." I swiped at my face with a napkin.

Only after I said it did I realize I'd mentioned Karl. I never talked about Karl. His memory was mine—the only piece of him I still had, really.

I excused myself to the restroom and removed as much of the icing as possible. Then I splashed cold water on my face, as much to calm my nerves as to get rid of the sticky residue. "Don't make a big deal out of it," I murmured to the mirror. "Karl would have found that kid's stunt hilarious. Mentioning him is understandable."

Once I'd calmed myself, I returned to meet Zaila in the entry. She didn't mention my brother, and I didn't bring him up again. She was now all business. "The cake had big roses on it, so I'm assuming we head out into the garden," Zaila said.

"Good thing we got there before the message was smooshed," I said, holding open the door to the resort's lush gardens. As we searched for our next clue, I overheard a snippet of conversation from a nearby gazebo.

"We're almost finished here," a man's voice cut through the thickening afternoon air. "We need to move fast before someone else swoops in."

I grabbed Zaila's arm, my eyes wide. "Did you hear that? It must be about our next clue."

Zaila looked skeptical, but I was already marching towards the gazebo. As I rounded the corner, I found myself face to face with a young couple, the man down on one knee with a ring box in his hand.

"Uh...congratulations?" I stammered. The woman looked mortified, and the man glared at me as if I'd just checked him into the boards.

"I'll just..." The woman darted away, leaving Zaila, the would-be fiancé, and me staring at each other.

"Erm...gotta go," I said, my face flushing as I grabbed Zaila's arm and we retreated. "I swear, I'm usually much better at reading situations," I muttered.

"Sure you are, Mr. Billionaire," she teased. "Though, I think the lady was happy to have you gate-crash."

"Seemed like it," I agreed. "She dodged a bullet, seeing as there was nothing romantic about that proposal."

Zaila glanced up at me, the corners of her mouth lifted. "Ah. Then I'll know what to expect should you ever propose—promises of undying love and lots of flowers and balloons and candles."

"Who said anything about that rubbish?" I asked as I buttoned my suit jacket. With a sigh, I swiped some additional icing onto the handkerchief I kept in my pocket.

"You did," Zalia said.

"No, I didn't. Quit wasting time; let's find the actual clue."

We eventually found the next envelope, which contained a paper that read: *Capture the spirit of Texas in one shot.*

"Easy enough," I said, pulling out my phone. I scanned the area and spotted a cactus near a decorative wagon wheel. "Perfect! Nothing says Texas like a cactus, right?"

I lined up the shot, ensuring that both the cactus and the wagon wheel were in frame. As I was about to take the picture, a resort employee dressed as a cowboy walked by.

"Even better!" I exclaimed, snapping the photo.

Zaila peered over my shoulder and burst out laughing. "Gunnar, I don't think that's quite what they meant."

I looked at the photo and realized I'd captured the cowboy-costumed employee mid-sneeze, his face contorted and hat askew, with the cactus appearing to sprout from his head thanks to the angle.

"You know, for someone who owns a hockey team, you're surprisingly bad at following instructions."

I chuckled. "Maybe I should stick to what I know best."

"I don't think people want another lecture on quarterly profits," Zaila said. "So maybe you just need the right partner to keep you on track."

Our eyes met, and for a moment, I forgot all about the scavenger hunt. "Maybe you're right," I murmured as awareness sparked along all my nerve endings.

"Th-the answer," Zaila said, pointing to an envelope taped to a saddle atop the chuck wagon.

"Hmm... That's a way to do it," I said. "My photo was a better idea."

"Sure it was. Except it didn't take us to the next clue."

"Final one," I said, reaching for the envelope. "Most teams won't finish this hunt, but thanks to your excellent sleuthing skills, we've got a solid shot at winning."

I read our last clue, which had us searching for a piece of ice, of all things. I spotted a cooler and charged for it, determined to beat Zaila to the punch. However, in my haste, I slipped on a patch of wet grass. I grabbed for something to steady myself, but instead of finding support, I found Zaila's hand. We went down in a tangle of limbs, sliding toward the lake and sending ice cubes flying everywhere.

Thankfully we stopped before reaching the water, and for a moment, we lay there, stunned. Then Zaila started laughing, and I did, too. After a moment, I realized how close we were, her body warm against mine.

"You know," she said, her voice low, "you're not very graceful on your feet."

I grinned, making no move to get up. "I'm usually more coordinated, both on and off the ice."

"I'd like to see you play again," she replied, her eyes meeting mine.

When we finally stood and brushed ourselves off, I decided this corporate retreat had turned out far more entertaining than I could have imagined. As we walked towards the resort entrance, I glanced at Zaila. Maybe, these team-building exercises weren't so bad after all.

CHAPTER 12
Zaila

When we began the scavenger hunt, the Texas sky had burned a brilliant, cloudless blue. But now at the end of it, a churning mess of dark gray clouds had boiled up from the horizon, and the wind began to howl like a banshee. The downpour hit as we hurried back to the resort's main building.

I squealed as the rain pounded my skin with its stinging needles. Gunnar grabbed my hand and towed me toward a building I couldn't make out through the sheets of rain, but once we entered, the musty smell and grass-covered tools informed me that we were in a garden shed. I heaved a sigh as I shoved my wet hair from my forehead. Looking out onto the resort grounds through the torrent of water, I felt a pang in my chest.

"It's so pretty," I breathed. "Like a blurry watercolor."

"You mean a painting?" Gunnar asked. He ran his hand through his hair, ruffling the ends to get the strands dry.

"Yeah. Kind of dreamy. Like a…a…Susan Weintraub."

"Who is Susan Weintraub?" Gunnar asked. "Should I know her?"

I shrugged. "Probably not. My daddy liked art, especially watercolors. Said it soothed him. I used to go with him when he toured galleries."

"You, Zaila Monroe, continue to surprise me," Gunnar murmured as he stared out at the downpour.

"Your suit's clean, thanks to the rain."

He barked a short laugh. "So it is. A bit of good to come out of what's been an eventful day." He paused. "You know, I never talk about my brother. Ever. But I mentioned him to you earlier today. It seemed so natural."

I shoved my chilly hands into my pockets. The ambient temperature still had to be over eighty degrees, but this conversation had turned heavy, and I wasn't prepared after the lightness of our day together. "You don't have to say anything," I murmured.

Gunnar turned to look at me, blinking as if to bring me back into focus. "That's the thing; I want to, which has never happened before." He shook his head, rubbing his large palm across the back of his neck. "I'm old enough to be your father."

"Uh…not my dad. He was fifty when he adopted me. You're not even fifty now."

Gunnar offered that tiny lip flip I craved. "Getting close, though."

"Whatever. You can claim age or maturity or…whatever, but you know what really matters? Connection. Respect. Intimacy."

A clap of thunder shook the shed, and I yelped and shrank back, away from the opening.

Gunnar never flinched. "You don't like thunder," he said.

I shook my head. "Bad things happen during thunderstorms," I whispered.

"Like what?"

I had only hazy memories of my time in the orphanage, but I

had a clear memory of one of the older boys taking things from the little kids during storms. He often hit or pinched them, timing their cries with the claps of thunder, which allowed him to get away with his cruelty.

That wasn't something I would share, though. "My dad was injured during a thunderstorm," I said instead.

"You mentioned the car accident. I'm sorry, Zaila."

I shrank from another crack of thunder, my eyes fixed on the sky. Gunnar moved closer, shielding me from the spits of rain that splashed up from the growing puddle in the doorway.

As another bolt of lightning seared across the thick, roiling mass of clouds, Gunnar asked, "What do clouds have on?"

I stared at him, my mind blank. "I do not know, and frankly, I don't want to know."

"Thunder wear."

I stared at him. "That's…terrible."

"I know!" he said, his grin widening.

Gunnar's brain operated on a different frequency than mine. "You actually like those jokes?"

"Love them," he confessed, his eyes twinkling. "The cheesier, the better."

"Why?"

His smile slipped a little. "Karl." He turned wistful. "My brother used to tell them when I was scared—and I was scared of a lot when I was young."

I tried and failed to picture Gunnar cowering. A moment later, another thunderclap boomed overhead, even closer this time. I wrapped my arms around myself. "Tell me another joke."

"Why are piggy banks so wise?"

I sighed even as my mood lightened a little. "Why?"

"They're full of common cents."

My lips tipped upward. "Okay, that one was marginally better."

"What do you call a hot dog on wheels?"

Thunder rumbled, but I ignored it. "What?"

"Fast food!"

I couldn't hold back the giggles. "You are ridiculous."

"Guilty," he said. "One more? I promise this is a good one."

"Fine," I said. "But if it's a knock-knock joke, I'm walking out into the storm to let the lightning end my misery."

"What did the ocean say to the beach?"

"No clue."

He leaned closer, his voice dropping to a conspiratorial whisper. "Nothing. It just waved."

I groaned even as I chuckled. Was a groan-chuckle even a thing? "These comments—I won't call them jokes—are so awful that they're hilarious."

"Exactly." Gunnar clapped, his blue eyes warm with humor. He was gorgeous—completely open and engaged. I knew instinctively that few people saw him like this. "I knew you'd come around."

The rain showed no signs of stopping, but I wasn't as miserable as I'd thought I'd be. In fact, I was having fun.

"Okay, your turn," Gunnar said. "Tell me your best joke."

I hesitated. I wasn't known for my comedic timing or my karaoke. "I don't really do jokes."

"Everyone has a joke inside them," he insisted. "You just have to find it. Come on, I shared some of my best material with you."

"Oh, wow," I retorted, but my smile grew. "All right, all right. I'll try. But don't say I didn't warn you."

I took a deep breath as I remembered something my daddy used to tell his buddies. "Why did the scarecrow get an award?" I asked.

Gunnar raised an eyebrow, intrigued. "I don't know, why?"

"Because he was outstanding in his field!" I said even as I cringed.

Gunnar stared at me for a moment, and that grin—that gorgeous, carefree smile—broke out across his face once more. I caught my breath, shocked by how beautiful he looked in this moment. I'd never tire of seeing him like this. Never.

"That's surprisingly good," he said. "I'm impressed."

While the storm continued to rage outside, we became two people sharing a moment of unexpected connection, bonded by the unending number of dad jokes in Gunnar's arsenal. Somewhere in there I realized that when this retreat ended, I would miss this version of the Wildcatters owner, the unguarded, real Gunnar Evaldson, the most.

CHAPTER 13
Gunnar

The storm broke in about a half hour, and I regretted it hadn't had the staying power of some tempests that hit the state. This afternoon spent with Zaila had been the most carefree I'd had in years, definitely since losing Karl.

"Thanks for the fun," I said.

"This was fun. And you're welcome," Zaila replied with a pep in her step that faded as we walked out onto the steaming grounds and found many Wildcatters staff looking our way, eyes heavy with disapproval. Even worse, some seemed downright hostile.

"Ahhhh…" Zaila said, reaching up to smooth her hair, which likely made the whole situation seem more sordid.

"Janice and Laurie were sure they'd seen you two flee into the shed. Were they *right?*" Jay asked her.

"What are you implying?" I asked, my tone so cold, I gave myself goose bumps.

Jay took a step back, as if he'd felt the danger wafting from me. While I aimed for a contented workforce, I wasn't one to suffer fools—or people who got in my way.

Most people understood not to push me, and based on Jay's bobbing Adam's apple, he'd figured that out as well.

Zaila stepped away, likely wanting no part of this confrontation.

Jay shrugged, shoved his hands into the pockets of his wet chinos, and whistled as he walked away. He seemed to feel he didn't have to say anything further; his point had been proven just by me being here, next to Zaila.

Dammit. My fury rose, sizzling through the good mood that had been so fleeting. I met the eyes of those still lingering close, letting them feel the weight of my displeasure. We all headed back toward the main building, and when we entered, I kept to the back of the room, as far from Zaila as possible. I wouldn't create more drama. Instead, I watched, impassive, even as my mind whirred.

I had to admit something I would have preferred to deny: each time I interacted with Zaila was better than the last. She relaxed the hard shell I'd coiled around myself and left me wanting to go loose. The feeling was freeing, like coming home. More and more, I'd come to miss the kid I'd been when Karl was alive. That Gunnar was affectionate and playful. Zaila brought those memories out of me, made those qualities seem possible again, and I could love her for it.

No, no, that was a big step too far. I appreciated her for bringing joy back into my life, just as I found her fascinating. If only I weren't so much older than she was. Being that wealthy man who dated women too young for him gave me a severe case of ick. I hated that cliché.

As people milled around, laughing as they dried off with towels provided by the staff, I made a point of going over to Jay. "If you're willing to use rumor and innuendo to destroy another person's promising career, I don't want you on my team."

He held up his hands, palms out, but his mouth stretched into a grin that made the hairs on the back of my neck rise. "I didn't do anything. Nor do I intend to."

Brenda clapped her hands, trying to get people's attention.

"I won't have to," he muttered.

"What was that?" I asked.

Jay blinked up at me, all innocence. I didn't trust him, and I fought the urge to fist his shirt and threaten him. Instead, I inhaled slowly and exhaled even more slowly, a trick Karl had taught me that allowed me to stay calm even in dreadful moments like this one.

Brenda's chipper voice came through her microphone as she called for attention, but I'd had enough. I spun on my heel and walked out of the building, out into the dusk, and away from Zaila Monroe.

CHAPTER 14
Zaila

That night at the awards banquet, Gunnar and I won the scavenger hunt and, awkwardly enough, a two-night stay at a five-star luxury resort in San Antonio. But when our names were announced, he'd already disappeared.

I learned later that he'd flown back to Houston on his private jet, much like a little boy would race home, but, well, richer and more ostentatiously, leaving me to look even worse in front of my colleagues. For the remainder of the two-day retreat, Jay vacillated between glee and attempted commiseration that people were gossiping about me trying—and failing—to seduce Gunnar.

And just like he'd disappeared from the retreat, Gunnar withdrew quickly and completely from my work life when we returned to the office. I never even had a chance to ask him what he'd said to Jay. Perhaps that was for the best, and at least the overt gossip died down after the retreat was over, though everyone still seemed a bit distant and distrustful. But my hurt at Gunnar's abrupt dismissal of me festered. So I threw myself into my job. Despite the moment I'd thought we had during the storm, the man had made it clear he didn't enjoy my company or respect me enough to explain why he no longer wanted to be seen with me—though I was pretty sure he knew about the gossip and part of me wondered if he was trying to protect me.

Still, I'd have preferred an honest and thoughtful conversation. Heck, just a text explaining his position would have been welcome. Such authenticity was essential to me; I'd watched my parents discuss most decisions, and my father was always attentive and listened to my mother's reasons. He treated her as an equal, and I would settle for nothing less than a true partnership in my own life.

While I spent two weeks worrying over Gunnar's withdrawal and my coworkers' tittered conversations and long stares while they kept their distance—all except Tim, who'd become my friend and champion—I also had the long-put-off lunch with the CATS. One afternoon Naomi Kramer, Ida Jane Dolov, Keelie Bouchard, Vivian almost-Cruz, and Paloma Whittaker walked into my office and surrounded me, herding me out of the building and into a waiting SUV, driven by another hockey wife, Millie Stol. They took me downtown to a well-known Italian bistro and plopped me into a chair. The best part was them all cupping their chins around the table and staring at me like I was a butterfly pinned to a display board.

"Spill," Naomi said. She was married to Coach Adam Kramer and one of the original CATS. I'd noted that the others looked to her as a leader.

"What? That you abducted me?"

"Pssh. That wasn't even close to an abduction," Ida Jane cut in. "But now that I think about it, we should try that sometime. Keelie's so good with her golf clubs—"

"Hush, Ida Jane. You're scaring her," Paloma said.

She was older than the other women by a few years and had a Zen quality that reminded me of my mother. She was also married to the head coach, Silas Whittaker, so she held a lot of sway—Ida Jane hushed.

I blinked as I considered Mom's recent return to declining. She'd perked up for a while after I moved in with her, but that wasn't holding as a long-term trend. I'd come into the kitchen last Saturday and found her at the round oak table that had been scrubbed nearly white. Her eyes were dull, her hair lifeless, and her back bent. This had to be more than continued grief. But when I asked, she hadn't been willing to tell me anything, just said she was seeing her doctor. Her current state nibbled constantly at the edges of my consciousness, making concentrating difficult.

"I'm curious," Vivian said with a shy smile, smoothing her red hair back from her face. She had freckles across her nose that made her look soft and friendly, and her eyes smiled even before her lips quirked. I knew, deep in my bones, that I liked this woman. She seemed like someone I could get close to. I didn't know much about her story, or even her last name, just that she was engaged to Lennon Cruz, the big, gruff D-man who seemed to be a second team captain to Cormac Bouchard. I suspected it was his emotional intelligence that earned him players' respect, but I didn't fully understand him yet. I just knew I'd liked him the few times we'd spoken.

"We're all curious," Naomi said, leaning forward.

My palms began to sweat. "I can't imagine why you're interested in me."

"Well," Keelie said. She set her chin on her palms, and her big engagement ring flashed. Cormac had made quite a statement with her jewelry, and from what I'd read and seen, those two were madly in love. "Gunnar likes you. Like, a lot."

I scoffed, an instinctive reaction that caused Ida Jane to wag her finger. "Honey, I saw it with my own eyes. That man is enamored."

"He sure is, and I heard about the canoodling at the retreat." Naomi's eyes sparkled. "And I have to know how good that was."

I swallowed, my throat dry and my eyes and nose stinging. "There's nothing between Mr. Evaldson and me. I earned my position. In fact, Lydia hired me, and I'd never met Mr. Evaldson until the day I dumped soda all over him—"

Vivian rubbed my forearm while Paloma reached across the table and patted my hand. "Forgive Naomi. She has a tendency to think everyone's as forward as she is," Paloma said.

"For what it's worth, we were all *hoping* for canoodling," Millie explained. She was quiet, one of those who watched interactions before jumping in. That seemed to balance out Luka Stol's impetuousness. The league sportscasters had commented on how levelheaded he'd been on the ice since marrying and the birth of his daughter. "Gunnar is way kinder and much lonelier than the world realizes."

Vivian pulled back her hand and resettled in her chair.

"It's because we care about him so much that we want to get to know you," Paloma said. "He's a good man who has developed an influential organization, and we want to see him happy."

"And you do that," Ida Jane said, clapping her hands and looking every inch the cheerleader she must have been in high school.

"Don't pressure her, Idge," Millie murmured.

"No pressure," Keelie said. "Just…affection and interest."

"Also, once we adopt you as a CAT, you're one of us for life," Paloma added.

I forced a smile as I ran my finger down the menu and swallowed. These women were kind, open, and interested—so unlike the current office dynamic where everyone avoided me… so they could talk about me. What did I have to lose? "I'm attracted to him," I said softly.

Hoots followed.

"I sense a *but*," Ida Jane said.

"But he told me he'd never get involved with an employee, and I respect that."

"Oh, pish. He's just being rigid," Paloma said.

"And it's clear he wants more," Vivian whispered. She offered a smile. "I may be one of the newer CATS, but I've seen how Gunnar lights up when he talks about you. His eyes go…"

"Warm," Millie finished.

The waiter walked over, dropping off waters and taking orders. I was so overwhelmed that I requested what Vivian had chosen, without understanding what it was.

"We're here to support you and your relationship with Gunnar," Paloma said. "Whatever you need, you can come to us."

"Not only will we make your dreams come true—like sexy, smart fairy godmothers—we'll offer a shoulder or an ear when Gunnar undoubtedly does something stupid," Naomi added.

"Because he's a man." Paloma sighed.

"And these men, especially hyper-competitive men, are

ridiculous when it comes to feelings," Ida Jane added.

"I…" Dropping my gaze to my lap, I decided to take the leap of faith. I missed having someone to talk to. For a long time I'd been so close to my parents that I hadn't needed many friends my own age, but that wasn't the same anymore. These women were all interested in me. Their care was genuine, and they wanted Gunnar and me to succeed. Though I wasn't sure what I wanted. Everything had been so tense and weird since the team-building retreat that I was desperate for advice.

So I spilled every detail of my time with Gunnar, from Lydia's resignation to my karaoke evening, to waiting out the storm in the planting shed and Jay's strange and snarky behavior. I even told them about my mother's illness and my need to help her.

Vivian turned out to be an oncology nurse who cared for Lennon Cruz's mother. She made me a list of questions to ask my mom, and Ida Jane probed a bit—no doubt psycho-analyzing me, as she was a therapist—while the rest of the women offered encouragement and insights into Gunnar's life. They said he was a workaholic who always managed to make time for his players and their families but seemed to hold himself apart from the exuberant get-togethers Cormac and Keelie liked to host.

By the time I finished my salad topped with the most delicious salmon, I was full and flush with that good feeling of friendship. "I need to get back to the office—"

"You'll do no such thing," Paloma said, all business as she signed for lunch. I offered to pay, but she waved me off. "It's something we do whenever we can get the Glam Team together. Too bad Hana's presenting her rocket design this week."

"That's Paxton Naese's wife. She's an actual rocket scientist," Vivian said. "These women are all amazing. And so kind. I can't believe I get to be part of this group. Much as I love Lennon—and I do with every fiber of my being—being part of the CATS is the best thing that's ever happened to me."

I returned her smile. I could already see what she meant.

"Now that that's settled, we're going to get our nails done for tomorrow's game," Naomi said. "You must join us. Oooh! You could use it as part of the social media campaign to show off how the hockey partners support and cheer on our players. That is, if you want to. We'd have so much fun. Even though Adam's now a coach, I wouldn't miss these days for anything."

Not only did I have lovely Wildcatters-themed nails and some very fun photos for the team's pages at the end of it, but spending the afternoon with the CATS gave me the courage that evening to ask my mother the question that had been simmering between us all week. I sat in the ladderback chair next to hers at the kitchen table, taking a page from Vivian's book and squeezing her hand as I asked, "What's wrong, Mom? Can you please talk to me."

She looked up and held my eyes a moment. "I...don't feel great," she said with a pained expression.

"Let's go to urgent care," I said, rising from my seat.

She shook her head. "Thank you, darling, for looking out for me, but I already know what's wrong." She patted my hand and waved me back into the chair.

I hesitated, gripping the chair's back, terrified of what I was about to hear.

"Sit, Zaila. Please. I know you're worried about me, but it's all right."

I returned to sitting and sucked my lower lip into my mouth, a bad habit I'd never been able to break. Much as I wanted to ask another question, I couldn't. My vocal cords froze, while my legs jittered with too much tension.

"My darling girl. Please believe me when I say you will be fine, and I'm okay right now." She patted my hand again. I noted that her skin was dry and cool—like a piece of paper left in a freezer.

"Mom…" Tears welled.

"The moment I looked into your sweet little face, when I saw those big, dark eyes, everything clicked into place. You were mine, Zaila. You were always meant to be mine." She smiled with a soft, loving sweetness that made me both warm and deeply sad. My tears spilled over, blurring Mom's image. "I'm so scared."

"I know, Zaila." She swallowed. "I am, too. That's why…" She shook her head. "The prognosis isn't good." She took a breath. "I have coronary microvascular disease. Basically, plaque has built up in the small spaces, the linings of my arteries."

"So you have surgery," I said. "A—a bypass or something."

Mom shook her head. "The inner areas of the blood vessels are at risk. It took time to figure out why I was so fatigued, unable to sleep. You saw me; I was unaware of the world."

She paused, and I remembered those days, the heaviness of not doing enough for her. I should have known. I should have—

"I thought it was grief, too, darling," she continued. "And I'm sure that was part of it, but this is something much more serious and less fixable."

My lower lip wobbled as tears spilled down my cheeks. "There's nothing the doctors can do?"

Mom shook her head. "Nothing that can reverse or remedy it. And there's no way to improve my day-to-day life." She handed me a cloth napkin. "I'm seventy-four, and this is one of those times when the treatment would be worse than the disease." She swallowed, her gray eyes soft and warm as they remained firm on my face. "I wouldn't be able to get out of bed, and there's no way I'd let you wait on me, nurse me. Give up your career, your life."

"Of course I will," I exclaimed, pushing back so quickly that the chair flopped over. "I'll quit right now—"

"You'll do no such thing, Zaila Alice Monroe. You'll continue to work at that job you love." Mom offered a mischievous glance. "And maybe bring home the man who's caught your attention."

I shuddered, not liking that my mom had used my full name. But that issue was about a million steps from the fundamental problem. "You're going to d-die," I breathed.

"Oh, my darling girl. We all die. I'll just have to do it sooner than I wanted to." She squeezed my hand. "Sooner than either of us is ready for."

I shook my head. I didn't want her gone, too. Then I'd be an orphan once more. My palms turned sweaty with the realization that without my mama, I'd again feel alone in this big, scary, painful world.

CHAPTER 15
Zaila

The roar from Wildcatters Arena during that Tuesday evening's preseason game echoed even through the glass of the press box, but I could tell this wasn't celebration. Tension rippled through the space like its own entity.

I leaned forward, fingers flying over my laptop, even as my gaze stayed locked on the ice. Jeff had the puck again, streaking down the left side like he was the only man on the team. He refused to pass to Stolly, who was open. Instead, he took the shot, and...missed.

Again.

Groans rumbled through the stands. The Jumbotron cut to Cormac on the bench. The team captain's jaw clenched, his eyes burning a hole into Jeff's helmet.

I felt that same frustration. This wasn't the junior championship or even the college-level Frozen Four. This was the national professional hockey league. The season hadn't even started yet, and Jeff was failing.

I clicked open my dashboard. Fan sentiment continued to trend negative, with the #TradeJeffNow climbing. My stomach sank.

Tim nudged my elbow, his face a mask of resigned disappointment. "He's going to blow it. God, and to think we could have had Brokowski."

That was the other rookie the Wildcatters had looked at instead of Jeff. He'd been picked up by the team just before Houston's turn in the draft, so that wasn't an accurate statement. But nonetheless, everyone was talking about Brokowski's fantastic preseason and how seamlessly the young player had clicked with his teammates. That had to be part of why Jeff kept pushing—he and Brokowski had competed for everything for the last fifteen years. Jeff Cross had something to prove, but each time he got on the ice and tried, he failed.

Returning my eyes to the ice, I watched Jeff ignore another wide-open teammate, go for a wraparound, and get flattened by the other team's defenseman.

Turnover.

I sighed, my shoulders tucking as if I'd been the one to sign him.

Two minutes later, the puck hit the back of the Wildcatters' net, and we chalked up an overtime loss. Cormac snapped his stick against the boards. Tonight and tomorrow would be long, as no one was happy with this loss, even if it was preseason. There was no way around it: Jeff was throwing off the whole team.

I typed in *Tough loss. Tougher lessons.*

Then I deleted it, because something told me Jeff had learned nothing. And based on Cormac Bouchard's fury, the Wildcatters' locker room was about to light up. I hoped no one filmed the confrontation and posted it online. I really needed a good night's sleep.

"The rookie is all yours," Jay informed me as he walked by. "I'm done babysitting egos."

"What? No…" I began, but Jay was gone. That butthole wanted me to clean up the mess when he was the one in charge of the department? *Talk about ego.*

"He can't do that," Tim said.

"He's my boss, so he can." I shrugged.

"He shouldn't," Tim said.

"That's something entirely different," I muttered as I settled back in my seat, eyes still on the ice. Jeff skated toward the locker room without looking at the crowd. "I hope they make the call to trade him soon," I said, my voice low. "He's throwing off the team's chemistry."

"Jay can't handle Jeff," Tim mused. "So he expects you to work your magic on the clown, I guess. Or maybe this is a punishment for the mascot thing." He shrugged. "You can always go to Gunnar—"

I shook my head. "No. I'll manage."

Tim turned to face me. "I don't like the way Jay's been acting. He and Jeff chat way too often, and I can't see anything good coming of it, especially if he's putting you on the account when he's been so involved until now."

I bit my lip as I nodded. "I have to do my job, Tim."

He narrowed his eyes. "Just…be careful. With both of them."

After a long week, on Friday evening, after my colleagues had left, I was still in the office because I couldn't face going home. I'd put together two different extensive social media plans for Jeff and was working on a third, mostly because I didn't want to see my mother slowly fading in front of me.

Cowardice remained as unbecoming now as it had been in second grade when Nora Kramer had called me a slimy gypsy orphan. I'd been terrified to stand up to her, and I'd suffered stomachaches and headaches for two weeks until my father took me out for ice cream and pried the details of her taunting from me.

During that hour together, he'd said something I'd stuck to every day of my life: "*When someone is mean or tries to bully you, remember that their behavior is a mirror of their struggles and insecurities, not yours. You don't have to drop to their level.*"

He'd gone on to tell me he knew me, knew that I was a kind, confident person, and all I had to do was stay true to myself. "*Keep on doing you by standing up for what's right,*" he'd said. He'd told me I was stronger than I thought and so special to him and my mother. "*Never—and I mean never—let anyone make you feel otherwise,*" he'd concluded. "*Or like you should be anyone other than yourself.*"

I was letting my mother's prognosis steal precious time with her. I wasn't being brave or myself and the fear, the spiraling thoughts, had won this week. I was angry about that, but unable to stop myself from falling prey to my worries.

"Zaila. Hey. What are you still doing here?" Gunnar asked from the doorway, startling me from my thoughts. He leaned against it as if he had no cares weighting him to his desk. Maybe he didn't. He was wealthy and, according to the internet, one of the most sought-after bachelors in the country, not just the city.

I held up a stack of papers. "I put together some more social media plans after I went through this past week's analytics."

Gunnar nodded. "I appreciate the effort, but it's late. You should go home."

"I will soon. I wanted a head start on next week's presentation, which is about fixing Jeff's image."

Gunnar frowned as he stepped into my office. "Wait. Why are you working on Jeff's image? That's Jay's job. He and I discussed it at length a few weeks ago—right after that meeting with the players."

My jaw clenched as I stared at him. How dare he meddle in my job and how I did it? Now suddenly I had value to him? If he had questions, he should talk to Jay. I lifted my chin. "Well, my boss gave me the account."

Gunnar narrowed his eyes. "What's going on with you?"

"I'm working," I said, stressing the second word.

"But I don't pay you to work this late on a Friday night. You're young. You should be out with friends, partying, making bad choices—"

"Regardless of what you saw at the karaoke place," I broke in, too annoyed to be appropriately respectful. "I'm not interested in that. Never have been. I…" I shook my head. "You know what? My personal life is none of your business, Mr. Evaldson. Now, if you'll excuse me, I'd like to finish this." I looked down at the stack of papers, my gaze sliding across the words and numbers without a bit of comprehension.

"I do mind." Gunnar strode forward with soft, steady footfalls until he was right in front of my desk. Then he had the audacity to round it and lean his lean hip against the edge, lifting one muscled thigh straight into my line of sight.

I hadn't needed the reminder of his attractiveness, nor did I want it. My eyes still worked just fine, even in the dimmed lighting the building shifted to after six p.m. With a mulishness I hadn't exhibited since childhood, I dropped the paper to my desk and swung my gaze up to Gunnar's. "What do you want?"

He studied me for a long moment. The silence turned oppressive as my mind once again chewed over my mother's illness. I wanted to be there to hold her hand when she went, but I couldn't bear to say goodbye, and it would be forever...

"Why are you working on Jeff's account?" Gunnar asked again.

"Because Jay told me to." Suddenly I wanted to say more, to tell him Tim was worried about Jay and Jeff and whatever they were concocting, but both men were already on Gunnar's bad side. Tattling wouldn't help anyone, least of all me.

"That's outside your scope—"

"Jay's my boss," I cut in. "So, if he hands me an account, I take it on." I squeezed my hands tightly, trying to keep myself together.

Gunnar had hurt my feelings, made me feel small and unworthy when he'd ditched me at the retreat. I drew a deep breath and released it slowly, trying to regain my composure and my ability to have a rational, calm discussion.

"We'll see about that," Gunnar said, his gaze narrowing.

"No, we won't. Just...leave it, Gunnar. Between the gossip about me from the retreat and Jay's piling on, I'm..." I dropped my head into my hands, unwilling to admit the depth of my hurt and embarrassed by my inability to hold my feelings closer. "I'm tired."

"Okay," he said, more softly than I expected.

I closed my eyes and soaked up the silence, enjoying being

near him even as I recklessly wished he'd make a damn move—
put us both out of our misery.

"Mary," he said.

I frowned, confusion growing as I looked up at him.

"Laura, Jennifer, Sarah, Helen, Elizabeth…ummmm…"

"Why are you saying women's names?" I asked.

"I'm guessing your middle name." He raised an eyebrow.
"Caroline, Sasha, Patricia, Ruth, Martha, Kristin, Ellen, Nora,
Isla—"

"Oh my God." I laughed. I couldn't help it; this man was
utterly ridiculous, and he didn't seem to care. "No, none of those
is my middle name."

"All right, let's see… Bertha, Martha, Madelyn, Carmen,
Cara, Carina, Courtney, Cassiopeia…"

I giggled until tears slid from the corners of my eyes and I
gasped for air. "N-no." *How did he do that?* I'd been so frustrated
and hurt, and now I was laughing so hard my sides ached.

"Damn." His lips quirked and those glacial eyes warmed
into the hottest flames. "Who knew there were so many
women's names?" He thought a moment. "Susan, Isolde, Esme,
Charlotte—"

"I don't have a middle name," I said between gasps for air.

"Really? That's unusual."

I shrugged as my gaze returned to the table. "Okay, I do, but
I'm not telling you."

"Fair enough. Now that you're not glaring like you want to
stab me with your pencil, please tell me what's bothering you,"
he coaxed.

I closed my eyes, blocking him out, wishing I could block out my overactive mind. "My personal life has no bearing on my work here—"

"I find it fascinating that people believe that," Gunnar said. His tone was conversational but his eyes, now much cooler, assessed me carefully as I opened my own. "Because I've found that personal issues have a great bearing on stress, and thus work performance." He leaned closer. I could feel his warm breath on my cheek. "That's true for the athletes and my employees."

My scowl deepened. "I may be employed by this organization, but I'm certainly not your anything." I plunged my teeth into my bottom lip, wishing those last words could be returned to my foolish mouth.

He straightened. "And that bothers you?"

I shrugged. "Why should it?"

"Why, indeed," he murmured.

Before he could interrogate me further, my phone beeped. I glanced at the screen, noting MOM as the incoming call, and answered immediately. "Hi. Are you okay? Do you need—"

"I'm fine, darling. I'm just fine," she assured me. "I know I gave you a scare, but I'm not dying tonight. Not even tomorrow." Her laugh was hollow.

That could never be a funny joke. I swiveled away from Gunnar, wishing he'd leave, but hoping he could hear my conversation almost as much as I hoped he couldn't.

"When will you be home?" Mom asked.

"Well, I..."

"You can't avoid me and my diagnosis forever," she said in that gentle voice that felt like sandpaper across my nerves. She'd never had to raise her voice to get her point across. I strove for that level of emotional mastery…and so far failed.

"I'm not."

"You are, and I get it. You're still grieving your father. But, Zaila, I'd like to spend time with you." She paused, likely gathering her thoughts and composure. "It's one more memory I'll get to add to my beautiful bank of them."

I swallowed the thorny lump of emotion that clogged my throat. "I was just packing up. I'll be home soon."

After saying goodbye, I pocketed my phone, turned off my computer, and picked up my purse, aware of Gunnar's remaining presence. "I'll see you next week," I told him with the briefest of glances as I moved past him toward the door.

Even that was enough to see his expression now held a deep sadness. Had he heard what my mother said? He nodded. "Until then," he murmured.

CHAPTER 16
Gunnar

As Zaila moved past me and strode down the hallway toward the exit, I marveled at her enthusiasm for her work, even if it didn't come from an entirely healthy place at the moment. Zaila had found so many new ways to showcase our organization. The posts she'd created about the CATS and their preparations for preseason games had been another tremendous boost for the team's social media presence. The fact that those women were both brilliant and down-to-earth made them relatable to our female fans, and I was proud to say we had a multitude.

I pursed my lips as I stared at Zaila's desk. She'd circled in red a lunch date with Paloma and Vivian next week. Clearly, she didn't want to miss it.

Paloma had told me at yesterday's preseason game that I'd hurt Zaila when I pulled back after our afternoon at the retreat. I'd tried to stay clear of her, hoping to avoid adding fodder to the gossip mill, but I hadn't fully considered how that would feel to her. That had been glaringly true tonight. I'd broken her confidence, and that made my chest ache. I hated to be the cause of the bleakness in her eyes, but after listening to the call from her mother, I knew I wasn't the main reason for her unhappiness. And Jay and Jeff were adding to her stress as well.

I knew better than most how important having a person to

lean on could be during difficult times. Karl had held me while I cried after our parents died. He'd taught me to acknowledge that grief, letting me sit in it and with it until I was ready to move forward and begin the more painful process of healing. Zaila seemed to be flailing against her grief and her changing reality, same as I had when I learned of my parents' boating accident.

I'd have to inquire about into Jay's decision to offload Jeff's account, because I had a feeling the situation was worse than Zaila had let on. I didn't trust Jeff Cross at all, which made my path forward clear. The season hadn't yet opened, but I'd made known my interest in trading him. I'd take a loss on his contract if it meant getting him out of my organization before he did permanent damage to my carefully crafted world.

I sighed. Who was I kidding? Jeff had already damaged it, which was why I was still in the office this late on a Friday, planning to talk to another owner before I headed home.

The appointed time had come, so I dialed the phone and endured a conversation that went nowhere—pretty much as I'd expected since Jeff was proving to be a liability and not worth his salary. At the end I clicked off, disappointed but unsurprised as I looked around Zaila's office. My thoughts had remained on her even during the call. She didn't seem to have anyone to help her through these bleak days ahead. I frowned as I stared down at her desk. Until now, I'd never considered how much Karl had helped me through my parents' deaths. Without him, I wouldn't be the man I was today.

Perhaps Zaila could find support in the CATS. Paloma and Keelie seemed to have taken her under their wings, and Vivian had chatted my ear off about how smart and fun she was. I knew that group took good care of one another. But Zaila didn't have a partner, didn't have someone to stand beside her, to catch her when she stumbled.

But perhaps she could have that. The fundamental question was whether I could be that man. Because if I was going to try, I had to be all in. There was no halfway with Zaila. She deserved commitment.

My eyes fell on the coffee mug at the edge of her desk, one of my favorites from the team's merchandise line. I touched the rim where she'd left lipstick. Then I shook my head, trying to clear it. Zaila was my employee, not to mention two decades my junior. But I couldn't deny the connection I felt, the one others seemed to see as well.

That awareness wasn't just physical attraction; it was a meeting of minds, a shared passion that went beyond the superficial. And it already went much deeper than what I'd found with any of the women I'd dated in my infrequent relationships over the years.

I finally went back to my office, slinging the coffee cup at my side. I smiled as I considered the fact that I'd done something for the very first time in my life: I'd stolen. Sure, it was a coffee mug. And one I'd most definitely replace, but I'd broken one of my cardinal rules, just because I wanted something of Zaila's.

She'd never have to know. She might never figure out that I'd swapped her mug for another. But I'd know. And I didn't regret my action, which told me more than my continued waffling ever could. I wanted the young woman any way I could have her. I wanted to be the shoulder she leaned on. I wanted to be the person she turned to in her grief but also in her joy.

So I needed to step up now and show her she could count on me. That would take some effort. "Luckily, I'm disciplined and good at following through," I said to the empty hallway.

Entering my office, I set Zaila's mug on my desk, right where many of my colleagues had pictures of their families. I had to tread carefully. Whatever this was between us, it was too precious to rush. For now, I was content to let it develop, and I wanted to savor each moment of our association.

As I switched off the lights and shut my office door, Zaila's laugh echoed in my mind. Tomorrow was another day, another chance to explore what could potentially be between us. I'd make sure she had the support she needed while proving she could trust me, eventually perhaps with all aspects of her life.

CHAPTER 17
Zaila

When I finally got home, my mother bustled around the kitchen that Friday evening, chattering as she dished up one of my favorite meals: chicken paprikash over homemade spaetzle. The dough for the small dumplings didn't take long to make, but cooking them in batches, standing over the boiling pot of water, was a process and had caused Mom's cheeks to turn rosy.

"I thought we could watch a movie tonight," she said. "Then, tomorrow, I booked us both a massage and some treatments at the spa you like."

I wrapped my arms around her and hugged her, resting my cheek against the curve of her neck. I breathed in the soothing scent of cold cream, shampoo, and lavender sachet I'd always associated with this woman. "Thanks, Mom, for pulling me out of my funk. I'm sorry I was in that place."

She cuddled me closer, though I knew she held a bowl in one of her hands. "Not a thing, my darling girl. You never worry over it. You, Zaila, are my moon and stars." She pulled back with a soft smile and love shining from her gray eyes. "I never believed I'd be so lucky to have a daughter as smart, capable, and beautiful—inside and out—as you."

"Flattery will get you everywhere." I laughed. "I'd love to watch a movie tonight and go to the spa tomorrow, but I'd really like you to let me buy."

"Nonsense." She waved that away. "It's not every day I get to spoil my professional daughter. You let me do this."

More words hung between us, needing to be said, but she didn't offer them, so I ignored them, too. The weekend lay before us, maybe one of the last ones we'd have together. If Mom insisted on splurging, I should let her—no, I would let her, so we'd both have the memory to cherish. I poured water while she finished setting the table, and we sat down to the home-cooked meal I loved so much.

We filled our plates, and the first bite sent me straight to my happy place. "It's always so good." I moaned. "I don't know how you do that."

She chuckled. "Years of experience. And patience. You can't overcook the chicken during the searing and the simmering."

I rolled my eyes because that's often what I did, and we both knew it. She smiled, but there was a hint of sadness mixed in. "I tripled the batch, so there are a few containers in the freezer."

I managed to swallow the bite in my mouth, but I couldn't take another. Those words, the reminder, roiled my stomach. Setting my fork down, I offered her a smile and asked about her day. She, too, pretended everything was fine as she filled me in on her trip to the grocery store and her talk with Mrs. Chao, our next-door neighbor, who'd been old when my parents brought me to the house twenty years ago.

"I've got the dishes," I said when Mom made a move to rise, reaching for my plate. I shooed her. "No, no, I insist. You made this delightful meal." We both ignored the fact that more than half of mine was still on the plate. "So I'll clean up. Why don't you pick out a movie?"

Mom agreed and headed to the living room. Once I heard the TV click on, I bowed my head and breathed, trying to gather my shredded composure. If I let grief grip me now, these last memories would be tainted, and I'd have to contend with that guilt. Blowing out a breath, I refocused on my desire for positive interaction.

I'd finished putting away the leftovers when the doorbell rang. I rinsed the suds from the pan in my hand and laid it on the drying rack before grabbing a dishtowel and heading toward the living room, where Mom had just closed the front door.

She turned to me, mild shock in her gaze. "You just received a gift card for the fancy spa we're going to tomorrow—the one with the wine bar. Apparently, we both have a full day of treatments booked. How did you manage that while you were in the kitchen?"

I shook my head, mystified. "I didn't."

"Zaila." Mom used her no-nonsense tone.

"I didn't…" I trailed off as I noted the elegant scrawl on the envelope. "Gunnar."

"What? Who?"

Mom's confusion was understandable. I tugged the card from her hand and read the note he'd written. How he'd had time to write a note and book full-service spa treatments in the last couple of hours was beyond me, leaving me as mystified as my mother.

I hope you and your mom can enjoy some relaxation together. Consider it my apology for being an ass. You deserve the very best in life.

-G

Mom raised on her tiptoes so she could read over my shoulder. I felt her puff of breath as she exhaled a soft *oohh*.

Lowering my arm, I tried to ignore the warm, fuzzy feeling in my chest, but I couldn't. Gunnar apologizing, Gunnar taking the time to do something so kind for me… I'd fantasized about such things, though I'd never expected them to happen.

"And who is Gunnar?" Mom asked, coming around to face me. Her eyebrows were up, her lips curled in the faintest smile, one I mirrored because… How could I not? Gunnar Evaldson had just given me the best gift, and he'd included my mother.

"Gunnar's the Wildcatters' owner."

Mom's eyebrows shot up so high and with such speed that I giggled, imagining them flying off her face altogether.

"I'm going to need more than that," she said. "And you know what? I think I need wine and popcorn—the chocolate kind—for this conversation."

I opened a bottle of Mom's favorite chardonnay as she poured popcorn into a bowl, all while I told her about meeting Gunnar at the hockey fundraiser just before I'd started my internship and our subsequent interactions. We went back to the couch as I explained how Gunnar had been my partner for the scavenger hunt at the retreat and his good humor throughout the day.

"Nothing fazed him, Mom—not the kid covering him with frosting or the rainstorm. It's not that he doesn't care or thinks he knows all the answers… It's more that he just doesn't let the problem overwhelm him. He knows he'll resolve the issue. He's dogged like that—not giving up."

Mom's eyes never left my face, not as she ate the treat or sipped her wine. When I finally stopped talking, she smiled at me, her big, bright one I'd always loved most. "You like him."

"I do. He's a great leader—"

"You *like* him, Zaila. You want something romantic with him, and based on his present, he wants that, too."

I scowled down into my wine glass. "Sometimes I think so, but then he pulls away. He keeps bringing up our age difference."

"Does it bother you?" Mom asked. She set aside her wine so that she could pull a pillow into her lap and hug it.

I shook my head. "I've thought about it a lot, and the age discrepancy doesn't bother me."

"But something does."

I nodded. "His wealth and power. I don't want people to think he gave me my position because we're together."

"And if they do think that?" Mom asked.

"I…"

She leaned forward, folding the pillow in half. "Zaila, that's your worst-case scenario: what other people might think. So, what happens to you—to your relationship with Gunnar—if people talk about how you slept your way to your job?"

I wrinkled my nose, though not because my mother had stated my concern so bluntly, but because she was making the point I should have foreseen.

"Let them," I said with a shrug.

She snagged a handful of popcorn, tossing a couple of pieces into her mouth. "Let them what?" she asked after she swallowed.

"Let them say what they will about me. They will no matter

how I met Gunnar or what field I'm in. They're going to talk because they're jealous or petty or because they like to gossip." I raised my glass to salute her. "Thanks, Mom. That helps put it in perspective."

She gave me her stern look. "I'll go tomorrow because this is prepaid and a kind gesture from a man who can afford to spoil you like you deserve to be. But I insist Gunnar join us for dinner next week so I can thank him in person."

Mom likely meant *so she could decide if he was really good enough for her daughter*. But I just nodded and sipped my wine so I wouldn't blurt out that I was much, much more concerned about her daughter being worthy of the man.

CHAPTER 18
Gunnar

After dinner on Saturday night with my executive team, in town for the weekend to review financial reports for my oil and gas company, I arrived home exhausted but pleased. Things were going well, and I needed to schedule my return to Sweden to check in with my staff there and tour our facilities, something I did at least twice a year. Those trips helped me understand the changes in the business and speak to my staff about the challenges they were navigating.

Our diversification into cleaner energy had progressed faster than expected, and the cost of inputs had dropped sufficiently enough to allow for a significant increase in production. That would eliminate a substantial volume of pollution over the next decade. I remained a man who'd made the bulk of his wealth from petroleum products, but I wanted to leave the world in as healthy a place as possible.

I flipped my phone over in my hands, debating whether I should text Zaila to ensure the spa experience for her and her mother had been satisfactory. Okay, I was going to message Zaila, but I needed to decide how to start the text.

Casual? Flirty?

The indecision irritated me, so I typed, Hey, how was the spa day? Did they pamper you enough? I hit send before I could change my mind.

Her reply took several nerve-wracking minutes to arrive. It was amazing! I feel like a new woman. ● Thank you. I can't tell you how much it meant to both Mom and me.

I grinned at the screen. A new woman, huh? Do I need to reintroduce myself to this upgraded version of Zaila? Will she still tolerate my hockey obsession?

Her response came more quickly this time. Hmm, she might. But she's definitely expecting you to step up your game now, goalie.

I chuckled, imagining her smirking as she typed that. Step up my game? I'm already in playoff form.

Her response was quick: We'll see about that. My mom would like you to come to dinner this week. We can make any night work.

Dinner with the parent. I chuckled as I dragged my palm across the nape of my neck. I hadn't ever met a woman's parent before. Though with Zaila, I wanted to. Thursday?

Zaila: That's great! I'll let Mom know. She'll ask about food allergies, your favorite dish, everything, so if you have any goodies to share, now's the time.

I eat anything, I wrote. While I detested shellfish, I wouldn't tell Zaila that, because there was no need to stress out her sick mother.

Zaila: Hmm...that's not true. You dislike shrimp.

Ah. Right. The team nutritionist, Phoebe, had mentioned that in one of the interviews she did for Zaila's social media campaign.

Gunnar: Caught me. But I would have eaten them for you and your mom.

Zaila: No need. I'll tell her you might be Scandinavian by birth, but you're a meat-and-potato guy like my dad. She knows what that means.

I shook my head and typed, I don't.

Zaila: Sure you do! And if you really don't, it'll be a surprise. A good one. Now, I'm signing off. Goodnight, Mr. Playoffs.

It's Lukas, I typed.

Zaila: What?

Gunnar: My middle name. One day you'll tell me yours, Ms. Fancy Spa.

As I set my phone down, I realized my cheeks hurt from smiling.

~

A pleasant surprise flickered through me when I received a text midway through the following morning.

Zaila: Good morning! Hope your day is as relaxing as mine was yesterday.

Relaxing? Not really how I operated. To prove the point, I snapped a picture of my desk, where the laptop was open with game footage and a coffee mug sat next to a stack of notes, even though it was Sunday.

Gunnar: This is what relaxation looks like in my world.

Zaila: Wow. Living the dream, huh?

Gunnar: Absolutely. Who needs beaches when you've got defensive zone breakdowns to analyze?

Zaila: You have an incredible group of coaches who are paid to do that for you, but you're such a nerd about hockey, I know you can't help yourself. It's rather adorable how into the stats you get.

Adorable?

Gunnar: Careful. Call me adorable again and I might start thinking you like me.

Her response made me laugh out loud.

Zaila: Don't get cocky, wannabe coach.

That interaction kept me peppy all day, and I even took an hour off to enjoy the latest thriller novel by my favorite author. For the first time in ages, I went to bed before I was dragging, and I slept well—better than I had in a long time.

The sight of Zalia walking into the office on Monday morning was enough to freeze my thoughts in place. Yes, I'd been waiting for her, but no, I would never admit it. She had this way of commanding attention without even trying—confident strides and a warm smile that could light up the room.

"Zaila," I greeted her as she approached my office door. "You look lovely." *As always.*

"Thanks. I had a great weekend, thanks to a very generous donation."

"Really? How lucky for you."

We'd moved closer to each other. Zaila must have realized that because she lurched back. *Ah.* She wanted to keep our time at work professional. I supposed we hadn't really discussed that anything was different. So I could do that for her. For now.

"I'd like you to have lunch in my office," I told her.

She licked her lips. "All right."

Her voice was a bit breathy, and her chest rose and fell, telling me I affected her, probably as much as she affected me—which was good to know.

"I need your help to splice some video for our socials over the

next couple of weeks. Gotta get the fans ready for the season."
No, I didn't. She did an excellent job of creating engagement with
no input from me. "I'd like you to make time for this hockey
nerd," I said anyway.

Her lips parted, and her pupils dilated. "Lead the way, coach."

I itched to touch her, but I managed to resist. "Twelve thirty?
I'll have lunch waiting." With that I scooted past her and moved
toward the elevator, fleeing so I didn't tug her into my arms and
kiss her...

Now that I wasn't trying to avoid my attraction, I wanted to
jump in with both feet. But I wasn't sure Zaila felt the same, and
she deserved to weigh her options with me.

Once I'd faked an errand and then returned to my office, I
told my assistant Zaila would be coming for a working lunch,
which was true if you counted watching hockey film as work.
Then I focused on reports from the Wildcatters as well as my
oil business for a solid two hours before I started counting the
minutes until I could see Zaila again.

I haven't been this into a girl since I was fifteen, I thought to
myself. Actually, I wasn't sure I'd ever been this interested in a
woman. Zaila made me fumble for my usual collectedness. And
somehow, I appreciated that I wasn't able to keep my cool with her.

I continued to contemplate this loss of control until my
fantasies took a not-suitable-for-work turn, and I forced myself
to rein them in. By the time twelve thirty rolled around, I'd
managed one additional hour of focus, for which I should have
received a gold star.

At precisely 12:30, Zaila knocked before sticking her head

through my double doors. "Is now a good time for our lunch meeting?"

Any time is the right time for you. I smiled. *I enjoy spending time with Zaila.* Even the little things were a revelation sometimes. "Perfect," I told her. "Leon's getting our lunch. Why don't we sit over here at the table, and that way we can go through the footage while we eat." I nodded toward the large, flat screen on the wall nearby.

She nodded. Once she'd taken her seat and pulled out a pad and pen, Leon knocked on the door. He brought in the food, setting a stuffed paper bag between us. Leon had worked for me for nearly five years, and I could see the interest in his gaze. I never had working lunches with Wildcatters staff. Coaches or players, sure, but not the employees. I'd tended to steer clear of them, until Zaila.

My gorgeous intern had changed everything, and she didn't even know it. I gave Leon a curt nod, and he exited the office, shutting the door behind him.

"Let's eat first, and then we can dig into the details," I suggested.

I'd ordered from a place I'd seen on her social media feed, betting she'd enjoy the dish she'd posted there.

She opened the container of chicken masala and raised an eyebrow. "Hmm... Cyberstalk much?"

I shrugged. "I consider this research."

Her eyes lit up. "Lucky for you, this is my favorite, so I'm not going to complain."

"Good, on both accounts."

We ate, and the conversation was easy—like we'd known each other for decades, not mere weeks. Zaila told me about her mother's illness, and I reciprocated with details about my parents' deaths and Karl raising me through high school. I didn't even hesitate to mention my brother, which was atypical for me. The words were out before I had time to consider them.

"We had to move twice because of his hockey commitments, but I didn't mind."

"Your brother plays?" she asked, clearly surprised.

I shook my head, setting aside my meal. This was why I never talked about Karl. I *hated* remembering how he'd been taken from me. "Not anymore," I murmured. Steeling myself, I met Zaila's concerned gaze. "He was murdered."

Zaila's fork clattered into her to-go packaging. She leaned forward, her eyes filled with so much compassion that my nose stung with answering grief. "I'm so sorry, Gunnar. I can't even imagine how much you must miss him."

I reached over and intertwined our fingers. "I do. I always will." I paused a moment. "I don't like to talk about it. I usually don't talk about him. But somehow…" I looked up at her and cleared my throat against the emotion crammed there. "He was beaten too badly to survive. His teammates found him outside a gay bar with his partner." *Because Leon had told them where Karl would be.*

I shoved down those thoughts, those memories, with the ruthless precision I'd mastered over the decades.

Zaila closed her eyes and took a deep breath. "That's such a tragedy. I can't believe people could be so cruel…" She opened her eyes and met mine. "That's why the Wildcatters have the CATS," she said. "Comrades, allies, teammates, spouses. Inclusive."

I nodded. "That's why."

"And that's why the organization is involved with domestic abuse shelters and does so much work to bring attention to hate crimes."

"Yes."

"That's inspiring—not losing your brother to violence," she hastened to add. "But the way you've chosen to channel your grief into improving others' lives. I'm sure he's very proud of you."

That squeezed my throat nearly closed. Noting my response, Zaila withdrew her fingers from mine and patted my hand. "I'm grateful you shared that with me. Thank you. I'll keep it close." She touched her chest.

I'd been ruthless for so many years now that these softer emotions startled me. Still, I soaked up the feelings Zaila evoked in me. It was as if she gave me better access my own emotions. She cleaned up her space, tucking the trash away in a paper bag. I took the cue and followed suit so we could get to work.

Once I'd disposed of the mess, I pulled up clips from our last few preseason games.

"So," she asked after watching an impressive goal replay, "what are our chances this year?"

"With or without Jeff?" I asked.

"You tell me," she replied.

I leaned back in my chair as I crossed my arms. "Without Jeff, if the rest of the players keep playing like they have in preseason?" Which they wouldn't because someone would get hurt. That was a fact of life in hockey. "The playoffs are ours to lose." I paused, glancing over to the door. "With Jeff? I don't think we'll make it to the playoffs."

"Ouch."

I sighed. "He's an albatross."

"And you don't think he'll see reason?"

"Youth and hubris are a fatal combination for a career," I said. "Maybe he'll settle down and get to better choices at some point, but the bad blood here already runs too deep. We need players who not only work with our vision, they believe in it. That's how games are won."

"You really love this sport," she noted.

"It's not just the sport," I said. "It's what it represents—the strategy, the teamwork, the commitment to peak physicality, everything."

As she studied me, the room felt smaller, as if it were just the two of us and nothing else mattered. With a soft laugh, she said, "You're such a nerd about hockey."

"Guilty as charged," I agreed. "But don't act like you're not impressed by my analysis skills."

"Oh, I'm impressed," she teased. "Just not sure if it's with your analysis or your ability to talk about hockey nonstop."

By the time Zaila left my office that afternoon, I felt lighter, as if her presence had lifted me out of the grind I'd allowed my life, and myself, to fall into. And with that realization came another: I was happiest when Zaila was nearby. I'd been in a holding pattern. She'd awakened me from a long sleep, and I was ready to live and love fully now, with her.

Clearing my calendar for dinner with Zaila and her mother proved more difficult than I'd expected, as it seemed there was always an issue that needed my immediate attention. However, stepping back and allowing Silas and the Wildcatters' general manager, Pete Riggs, to work on the trade deal for Jeff Cross was worth it.

As I parked outside Zaila's house on Thursday evening and walked up to the door, my nerves prickled. Meeting her mother, Susan, felt like crossing an invisible threshold in whatever this thing with Zaila might become.

The door to the red-brick bungalow with white shutters opened before I could knock, and Zaila stood in the entryway with a smile that put me at ease. She looked lovely in her capris and a flowy cotton blouse that made my heart skip a beat, not that I'd admit that out loud just yet.

"I'm so glad you could join us. Come on in," she said.

Susan greeted me in the living room. She was a petite woman with sharp gray eyes and a serene smile. "It's a pleasure to meet you," she said. "I wanted to thank you for the delightful spa trip." She leaned in closer and stage-whispered out of the side of her mouth, "And to meet the man who has Zaila mooning."

Zaila's mouth dropped open as her neck and cheeks flushed. "Oh my G—"

"She moons over me?" I asked Susan with a chuckle.

Susan nodded. "Mmmmm…yes. She talks about you often."

My gaze flashed over to Zaila, who now had her red face buried in her hands.

"That's good to know," I said. "No, this additional detail

is fabulous."

"I needed to see if you were serious about her as well," Susan added.

"So, what's the verdict?" I asked, my attention once again focused on Zaila.

Susan hummed. "Well, that's what tonight's for. So I can decide."

I chuckled, but nerves skittered through my belly. I wanted Susan to like me, to approve of me for her daughter.

"Can we eat, now that I'm so embarrassed I may never recover?" Zaila asked, but she smiled at her mother, genuine warmth in her eyes.

Over dinner, we talked about everything from hockey to travel to Susan's favorite books. She had this way of making you feel like you'd known her for years—a trait Zaila had clearly inherited—and the two women knew literature.

"So, Gunnar," Susan said, her eyes glinting with amusement. "What's your take on nonfiction? Big, boring lectures or roadmaps to a better you?"

I shrugged. "Depends, I guess. If it's about hockey, I'm game. If it's…I don't know, about whale migration or something, I'm out. I don't have time for subjects that far outside my business concerns."

"Well, if you want life changing and sports-related, there's a biography I'd recommend. But it's not hockey. It's about basketball."

"Oh?" I leaned back in my chair. "What's the title?"

"*The Last Shot* by Darcy Frey," Susan said. "Have you heard of it?"

I hadn't.

Before I could respond, Zaila leaned forward, resting her chin on her palm. "You'll like it. High school players fighting for college scholarships—it's gritty, raw, probably right up your alley."

I raised an eyebrow. "You've read it?"

"Of course," she said, her lips tipping into a smile. "I don't sit around painting sunsets."

Susan smirked. "Not a bad book for comparing dreams and reality. Or for discussing how sports reflect wider societal struggles."

"I knew you'd say that," Zaila teased. "And knowing Gunnar, he's probably more interested in the moments on the court. While it's not hockey, there's a lot of overlap I think you'd appreciate, Gunnar. Specifically about the necessary chemistry for team building."

I didn't know what was more disarming—the way they assumed I'd join in, or the way Zaila's laugh felt like a jump shot swishing through the net. Pure and clean, no pretenses.

"I guess that's going to the top of my reading list," I said.

"If it's in front of a nonfiction on business processes or World War II history, you'll be happy, because it's way more exciting," Zaila noted.

"Maybe I like my books super boring," I said. "To put me to sleep. I read a few extra textbooks for just that purpose."

"You're quite different from what I expected," Susan said, shaking her head.

"And what did you expect?" I asked.

She tilted her head. "Someone less...genuine."

The compliment caught me off guard, but filled me with quiet pride.

By the end of the evening, after a fabulous cherry pie, I was pretty sure Susan and I had charmed each other. As Zaila walked me to the door, I knew tonight had been more than just dinner. It had been a pivotal step forward.

"Thanks for making time for this," Zaila said. "I know you're busy."

"For you? Always," I replied.

Zaila reached out and hugged me, the first time she'd initiated that kind of contact. I was thrilled at the feel of her soft curves settling against my body. Unable to stop myself, I brushed my lips across her cheek, inhaling the faint aroma of her shampoo.

"This was really fun," Zaila said.

She stepped out of my arms, and I missed her. I wanted her back—close to me, at my side. Zaila wasn't just someone who fit into my life. She made it better in ways I hadn't realized I needed.

As I drove away that night, I couldn't wait to figure out what that meant. I began to plot how to keep her in my house, my life, and, hopefully, my bed.

CHAPTER 19
Zaila

Over the next few days, as the start of the hockey season approached, Jay's impending mascot performance became the talk of the office. Tim had created a countdown calendar, much to Jay's annoyance. Then, after a long lunch with Jeff one day, Jay's attitude had shifted. What had started as dread morphed into determination.

I wasn't sure what had caused the change, but it meant Jay was nicer to me, so I rolled with it.

The night of Jay's debut as Gusher the oil derrick arrived with much fanfare on social media and local news coverage. After some tense back-and-forth, Jay had agreed to be the one to update our social media pages with the story of his bet, loss, and resulting turn as Gusher. Those posts generated a lot of engagement, and all signs pointed to a fun night of fan support for Jay. The marketing department, including Noelle, had made sure to be at the arena early. Tim and I scurried around until we found Jay in the locker room, already half-dressed in the Gusher costume.

"How're you holding up?" Tim asked as he leaned against the doorframe, arms crossed over his chest. Tim had become more fatherly toward me since the team-building retreat. I liked him in that role.

Jay lifted the top of the costume into place, leaving his face visible through Gusher's open mouth. "You know what? I'm actually excited. I mean, it's not every day you get to be a professional sports mascot, right? That's cool to add to my resume."

I smiled, surprised by his positive attitude. "And you're not just a sports mascot, you're debuting this character."

Tim nodded. "True, true. You're setting the tone, creating a legend."

We chuckled, but Jay remained very serious.

"Any big plans for tonight?" I asked.

Jay's eyes twinkled. "Oh, you'll see. I've been watching a lot of mascot videos. I've got some tricks up my sleeve—or should I say, up my derrick?"

Tim groaned. "Don't say that to any woman. Ever. Under any circumstances."

I giggled. "I'm with Tim on this one, but I like the enthusiasm." I smiled. "Good luck out there tonight. We're rooting for you."

By the time Tim and I made it to our seats, the arena was buzzing with energy. Tim fidgeted in his chair. "I have this weird mix of anticipation and nervousness for Jay," he said. "And part of me wants him to fall flat because he's been a jerk."

I nodded. "Yeah, I feel that. I want this to go well for him, though. I mean, I know he planned for it to be me, but, mostly, I want him to succeed. That's what's best for the team."

Tim nodded, his gaze glued to the doorway where Jay would emerge.

As the lights dimmed, the announcer's voice roared through the speakers. "Ladies and gentlemen, please welcome your Texas Wildcatters!"

The team skated out onto the ice to thunderous applause. And then, with a burst of pyrotechnics, Gusher appeared at center ice.

Wow. That was cool. Jay had put a lot of effort into this introduction. I leaned forward, captivated.

"That shit." Tim whooped. "He's been holding out on us."

We cheered as Jay skated around the rink with surprising grace, high-fiving fans and doing tricks with his oversized hockey stick. The crowd ate it up. In fact, he was now receiving more applause than the players had. Always the sportsman, Cormac Bouchard met Jay-as-Gusher center ice and high-fived him.

"We're going to have some great content for the next couple of days," I said with a smile.

In a flash it was time for the puck drop, and the game was fast-paced, even more exciting than I'd anticipated. I cheered as Cruz got off a great block and Stolly flashed across the ice for an easy goal. The team really clicked when Jeff wasn't on the ice.

During breaks in play, Jay took his performance to another level. He challenged fans to dance-offs, led the crowd in cheers, and even attempted a backflip.

"Oh, I can't look…" I peeked through my fingers.

"He made it. That absolute shit!" Tim yelled, rising to his feet to cheer. "I knew he was a diva. I knew it."

By the third period, the Wildcatters were up a comfortable 3-0, and the second- and third-line players were gaining valuable minutes, including Jeff, who hogged the puck, created a turnover, and allowed the opposition to score.

The game ended to huge cheers for the team before the arena began chanting, "Gusher! Gusher!"

While the fans celebrated the Wildcatters' victory, Tim and I made our way down to the locker room. I found Jay still in the Gusher costume, but with the head off, surrounded by players and staff congratulating him on his performance. He was damp with sweat, but his grin was wide.

"Jay!" I called, pushing through the crowd. Tim came with me, beaming like a proud papa. "That was incredible! Where did you learn to do all that?"

He grinned, his face flushed with exertion and excitement. "YouTube, mostly. And a lot of practice in my living room. My neighbors probably think I'm crazy. Or really into martial arts or parkour or something."

Tim chuckled. "Well, it paid off. The fans loved you out there."

Jay turned to me and cleared his throat. " Zaila, I want to thank you. When I lost that bet, I thought it was the worst thing that could happen to me. But this...this was amazing. I've never felt anything like it."

Warmth rushed through me. This was yet another reason I loved my job—the unexpected moments of joy and growth. "Well, I'm glad you enjoyed it," I said. "Because you've got about twenty more games."

Jay's eyes widened. "Oh, right? I almost forgot about that part." He chuckled, and I hoped it was because he was excited about the next few months. "Well, if all the nights go like tonight, I'll be the best-loved mascot in any professional sport."

"You absolutely will," I said. "I have no doubt."

〜

Jay beat me to the office the next morning, much to my surprise. He seemed stiff, but he was beaming with happiness. "Ticket sales are up, and Gusher merchandise is flying off the shelves," he announced. "You know why? The fans can't get enough of little old me as Gusher. I'm a marketing goldmine."

I nodded, feeling just slightly uneasy. "That's so cool. Congratulations."

"You should go out with me tonight to celebrate."

I bit my lip as I shook my head. "I can't. I already have plans."

Jay's face fell. "With Gunnar?" he guessed.

I shook my head. "My mom. I told you, she's unwell, and I'm not sure how much more time I'll have with her." While true, I left off the detail that Gunnar would also be at my house tonight. Sometimes, maintaining professionalism felt like a balance beam that grew narrower and narrower the longer I walked it. But anyway, it was none of Jay's business.

Later that evening, we laughed so hard at Gunnar's story that my mother wiped her eyes with her napkin. "Oh, that poor man," she said. "Well, not really. He got what was coming to him, but you know…"

"I do," Gunnar said, his nod solemn.

Mom settled back in her chair as fatigue pulled at the corners of her mouth, causing her eyelids to droop. "You two should go out."

"What? Now?" I asked. I glanced at the clock, and it was after ten. "Um, no. I'm doing the dishes and going to bed." I elbowed Gunnar. "And my guess is you have to be up at…what? Five?"

He grimaced. "I probably should be, but I might just sleep in."

"Until?" I asked, eyebrows up.

"Six. Maybe even six thirty," he said.

"That's basically noon for the formidable CEO," I teased.

Gunnar's lips turned up, but his eyes darkened, as if he were thinking about something. "I can't remember the last time I woke without an alarm."

"Then it's been too long," Mom said, her tone pragmatic. "But you two really should go do things. You don't need to spend your time here with me."

"I love spending time with you," I said, reaching over to squeeze her hand, trying to keep Gunnar from noting the pulse pounding in my neck. He'd been the one to suggest we eat in, with my mom. It seemed that's what he felt comfortable with. If she pushed too hard, he might decide to stop seeing me.

I wanted there to be more between us, at least eventually. But I wasn't sure what Gunnar thought, though he certainly enjoyed Susan Monroe's company as much as I did.

"All right, then you two have fun. I'm tired." Mom withdrew her hand and rose. She grabbed the table and blinked a few times. Once she was stable, she hugged me, bid Gunnar goodnight, and headed to her bedroom. I kept my gaze on her retreating form, partially to make sure she made it to her destination, and also not wanting to face Gunnar.

"It's a good idea," he said after a moment. "I've wanted to have time alone with you but wasn't sure how to ask."

My heart pounded, and I kept my eyes averted as I collected the silverware and dessert plates, stacking them to carry to the sink.

"Zaila?" He trailed behind me, glasses in his hands. "What do you think?"

"I…" *I want you to be proud to be seen with me. Please tell the world we're together. I like what my parents had—an enduring love that was probably deeply passionate in the decades before I came along.* I pressed my lips together to keep the words from spilling out.

"Would you go out with me?" Gunnar placed his hands on my shoulders. He kissed my temple before nuzzling closer. "Let's do something fun—a movie. Is there anything good? I haven't been in ages."

"I'm sure we could find something," I said.

"Great." He spun me around and grinned. "Friday."

"Friday's the Wildcatters Gala."

Gunnar grimaced. "Right. That's important, and I have to go to it, though I'd much rather spend time with you." He ran his hand through his hair, mussing the smooth styling. "I have to give a speech, then schmooze with the mayor and governor."

I shuddered. That part of getting involved with Gunnar I wasn't prepared to handle. "At least I'm working the event," I said.

"We could go together, leave together," he said, his tone hopeful.

I placed my palms on his chest. "You'll be busy schmoozing."

He grunted. "But you'd add vibrancy—no, joy." He grinned. "You'd add joy to the schmoozefest. For me at least, and I'm selfish. You could tell them about the most recent book—"

I forced a laugh. "Stop. No one's interested in my reading list."

"You'd be surprised." His knuckles drifted down my cheek. "I'm fascinated by the depth and breadth of your knowledge."

When he talked like that, my defenses melted into nonexistence.

"Go with me." He leaned closer, his gaze intent. "Be my date. Come home with me. It'll be a late one. You won't have to disturb your mother."

I bit my lip. "I'll have to get ready here, and I already asked Jay if I could arrive about eight thirty, after Mom takes her pills."

A wrinkle formed in his brow. "But you could come home with me? We can bring breakfast or brunch here Saturday. Spend some time with your mother then."

My heart swelled. *He wants to spend time with me.* "Okay. I can pack a bag—"

"Do that now so you don't change your mind," he said. "I'll put it in my car, take it back to my place tonight."

I batted my eyelashes, mainly because I wanted to keep my own expectations at the appropriate level. "Eager?"

His breath fanned over my lips as he stared into my eyes. "You have no idea."

Gunnar didn't lean forward to kiss me, so I didn't push it. But I did make sure to slide my breasts across his chest as I sidled away from the sink.

By the time I returned with an overnight bag, Gunnar had loaded and started the dishwasher and wiped down the kitchen. He took the bag from me, hooking his free arm around my waist. He brushed his lips over mine again with gentle urgency before he stepped back, hunger clear in his eyes. "I can't wait to see you at the Gala, Z."

I saw him out and then touched my lips, dazed by the

potency of that brief kiss and the joy his nickname brought. It was a heady cocktail that allowed me to float up the stairs to my room. Friday couldn't arrive soon enough.

CHAPTER 20

Gunnar

I stood behind the bench, as I had all season thus far, my arms folded, jaw tight. At least this time it wasn't frustration. It was focus.

The scoreboard read 2–2, and we were in the third period, with less than two minutes until the end of regulation.

"Come on, boys," Cormac muttered as he tapped his stick.

The puck dropped. Fast. Fluid. The Wildcatters passed clean, working as a unit. No showboating. No solo acts.

Our other rookie, Brayden Blackwell—Jeff's replacement on the ice while I tried to offload him—skated hard to the crease and passed back to Cormac.

Slap shot.

Blue light. *Goal!*

The bench erupted with relieved cheers while the crowd roared.

My phone buzzed in my pocket. The social media team—probably Zaila, since she was the one with her laptop at the games—had posted a video of the goal. Caption: *Culture: earned.*

The arena announcer boomed, "Cormac Bouchard with the game winner!"

Cormac skated straight to Brayden and hugged him, whispering something in his ear. The rest of the team piled into a victorious huddle.

I let out a long breath, eyes lifting to the press box. Zaila stood against the glass, fist raised, eyes shining.

My phone buzzed again.

In the tunnel after the game, Zaila and the rest of the staff cheered. Cormac handed her the game puck with a big grin. "Keelie said you were smart and capable," he told her. "You've helped us reconnect as things were sinking. Man, oh man, I thought frisbee golf was gonna just be a time suck, but it was hilarious when Cruz got all competitive. It made us remember what it felt like to be a team. That's the stuff of legends right there, Z."

I smiled. That's where I'd picked up the name. The guys all called Zaila Z.

I came up beside her, beaming, wanting her to know I supported her. "Zaila's one of a kind," I said.

Cormac smiled as he and the rest of the team fist-bumped Zaila and me on the way past. "Yeah," he agreed. "She is."

Zaila arrived at the gala five minutes after I'd expected, though I'd been checking my watch for the past hour. She entered into the room in delicate silver sandals that showcased her cute toes, painted the same dark blue as her dress—the beautiful, rich blue of a midnight sky. Immediately I liked how it showed off her brown skin. It had thin straps and a corseted top that nipped tight at her waist, and a shiny, shimmering skirt draped down to just above her feet.

Her gaze swept the room, her red lips parted slightly, her smoky eye makeup highlighting her brown eyes. Half of her thick, dark waves were tamed into a twisted knot on the top of her head, while the rest cascaded down her back.

She was gorgeous, and I wanted to devour her. Glancing around, I realized others had noted my Cinderella's arrival and were checking her out. Possessiveness wasn't my style, but with Zaila, I wanted to stake my claim. Yet before I could move away from the droning conversation I'd stood through for the last ten minutes, Jay bounced over and spoke to Zaila. She responded with several nods before veering off to the left with him.

You built this team for Karl. For Cormac. For the culture, I reminded myself. *And here you are, staring at your social media strategist like a lovesick puppy. Get your shit together and focus on the task at hand…after you check out that perky little ass.*

I frowned as she beelined toward Jorge Salvados, a well-known sports journalist who wrote the most popular column in the city. He was about ten years older than Zaila, respected, established, and charming.

"You're not interested in the area's restructuring?" the mayor asked.

I refocused on the conversation. "My apologies. I was…considering something."

Chad Brennan, a local oilman who went through wives faster than most people worked through their cowboy boots, leaned in. "That pretty little thing in blue? I saw her too. That's a feast for the eyes."

We were about the same age, and Chad's date was younger than Zaila, wide-eyed and dewy, staring up at him with the adoration he seemed to require. Disgust rolled through me. I'd just read an article about a football owner who firmly believed his twenty-something girlfriend did not know he was a billionaire, that she was with him for his looks. I wasn't particularly interested in rating men's attractiveness, but I doubted that guy was considered a catch for his appearance.

I pursed my lips. There had been considerable chatter about Zaila and me after the staff retreat, even before there was a real reason for any chatter. Yet still, she remained interested. As did I, so we'd weather the storm, prove our relationship was nothing like that football team owner's or Chad's.

I turned toward the mayor, without responding to Chad. "Please excuse me. But know I'm committed to the rejuvenation of the locks surrounding the arena, and you're right; Frisco's an excellent model for how to brand the area and bring in more foot traffic."

I spent another hour and a half circulating the room before I made my way to Zaila. The ballroom had filled with the chatter of Houston's elite, but Zaila was engaged in what appeared to be an intense conversation with one of the team's sponsors.

"—but Hemingway's style, while groundbreaking, often lacks the emotional depth found in Fitzgerald's work," Zaila noted, her eyes alight with passion.

The sponsor nodded, looking a bit overwhelmed, so I interjected, "Ah, the eternal debate of the Lost Generation. Mind if I cut in?"

Zaila turned, a smile playing on her red lips. "Only if you're prepared to defend your position, Mr. Evaldson."

My cock twitched, as it always did when Zaila used my

last name. "I'm always prepared." I took a sip of my drink and enjoyed the faint flush that crept up her neck.

Despite what I *should* do, I would take Zaila home with me tonight. I would love her body as I already did her mind and soul. Fuck the critics—she and I deserved happiness. And we were going to get it.

The sponsor excused himself, leaving me alone with this amazing woman. We might be in a sea of bodies, but I couldn't care less. "So," I said, handing her a glass of Champagne from a passing tray, "you're Team Fitzgerald, I take it?"

Zaila accepted the glass, even as she protested. "I shouldn't. I'm working."

"I gave it to you. I want you to enjoy yourself. Plus, the next time you attend one of these, it'll be as my date, not just my employee." I stopped there, as I didn't want to spook her. I had plans for the evening after all. "So, it's best to take part in the niceties."

"Always prepared," Zaila murmured before she took a tiny sip.

"Fill me in on your thoughts about Fitzgerald," I encouraged.

Her smile widened. "The way he captures the disillusionment of the Jazz Age is a marvel. Top-notch lyricism. Let me guess, you're about to make a case for Hemingway's manly prose?"

I chuckled. "I've always been partial to Steinbeck. The humanity in his writing works for me."

"Steinbeck?" Zaila's eyebrows shot up. "How did I not know that? Gunnar, that's a plot twist I never expected. How fabulous! *The Grapes of Wrath* or *East of Eden*?"

"*Of Mice and Men*," I said. "There's something about the

friendship between George and Lennie that resonates with team dynamics."

Zaila nodded. "I never thought of it that way, but I can see where you're going. Still, I'd love you to elaborate."

As we delved into a discussion about literature's parallels to hockey, Zaila's quick wit and insightful observations drew me in—the moth to her flame. Our conversation flowed, touching on everything from classic novels to modern poetry. And soon schmoozing was the furthest thing from my mind. Why?

Because we fit.

"You know," I said, "I don't think I've had such an engaging literary discussion since my college days. And never at a hockey event."

Zaila grinned. "Well, we've already made our three-person book club."

"Your mother's the reason for your literary bent?" I asked.

She shook her head, that mass of dark hair moving tantalizingly over her shoulders. "My father. He was an expansive reader; it took a lot of work for Mom and me to keep up."

"Fascinating." The air between us charged, crackled.

Zaila must have felt it too, because after a shaky breath, she took a small step back, clearing her throat. "We should mingle a bit more. Can't have the team owner monopolizing all my brilliant conversation skills, though that sponsor didn't seem as keen to follow up on the topic once he realized I'd actually read both authors."

I laughed. "Sounds about right. Go sparkle. I'll find you when it's time to head out."

As I watched her walk away, I had to take a moment to breathe. Our intellectual connection was far more intoxicating than I'd anticipated. If I was this turned on by her mind, I wasn't sure how I'd handle the actual act of connection.

Though I couldn't wait to find out.

CHAPTER 21
Zaila

By the time the gala wound down, my feet and my cheeks hurt, but I felt effervescent after all the positive comments from colleagues, players, and even the mayor. Mainly though, I think I was high on Gunnar's heated glances, particularly in this public space.

He'd even winked at me from across the room. *Winked.* Excitement bubbled through me like the Champagne I'd had earlier. *Gunnar wants to take me home. Gunnar has plans for us.* I clenched my thighs together and willed my heart to slow its galloping pace.

"You need a ride home?" Jay asked.

"No, I'm good." I smiled.

"Want me to walk you to your car?" he said, hope in his eyes.

I had to shut that down. Right now. I swallowed hard, not sure what to say. I didn't want to give him any reason to turn back into the frustrated, angry version of himself he'd been after he lost the bet.

Then Gunnar waved me over toward the dignitaries he was sitting with. I dipped my head. "Thank you, Jay, but I'm still finishing up here. Mr. Evaldson asked me to discuss some options with him earlier this evening." *Kind of...*

Jay studied me a moment and then nodded. "Well, I guess I'll see you Monday."

"See you," I said. With a wave, I walked toward Gunnar, who rose from his seat and pulled out a chair for me. I looked back toward Jay to find him eyeing us, but I turned my attention to the man on my other side, smiling and offering my hand as Gunnar introduced me.

"This is Zaila Monroe, a very talented digital marketer, who helped create the Gusher the Goalie challenge. She and her team developed the new mascot, Gusher."

"Ah, yes, I saw those images," the rheumy-eyed gentleman said. "Fun stuff. I'm not much interested in the socials, myself, but my grandkids spend hours on their phones."

I smiled. "I've been told it's a different world."

"Very. Not bad, just moving at the speed of those microchips and semi-conductors instead of mail and telephone calls, as it used to in my heyday. So tell me, what got you interested in this digital marketing?"

"You sure you're ready for my answer?" I teased.

His eyes danced as he leaned closer. "I'm hoping it's juicy."

I chuckled. "Mary Shelley."

"What?" He blinked.

I grinned. "Ms. Shelley took the tools she had, a creepy vacation and her imagination, and created something no one had seen before. Social media's the same. It's not about duck faces or even tasty, beautiful meals; it's about what you bring to life with it."

"Fascinating," he murmured. He rapped his knuckles on the table. "I believe I'd better revisit Mary Shelley."

"And Jane Austen," I said. "She had such a witty, acerbic way of writing. Her books are so full of life. Those women wrote to be heard, to test ideas, to claim space in a world reluctant to listen."

"Mmmm... I see your point." He looked past me at Gunnar. "Keep this one close. She's got a great mind, seeing connections most miss."

"I plan on it." Gunnar's hand slid up my side to my ribs. My skin blossomed in goose bumps, and my heart kicked into high gear.

The older man chuckled. "I always knew you were a smart man, Gunnar. Well, I wish you both a happy evening."

We said our goodbyes as we rose.

"Ready?" Gunnar asked, staring down at me with his cool, assessing gaze.

I bit my lip as I nodded. "Yes." It came out breathy, needy. Because I was. I'd spent the last couple of days imagining Gunnar as a lover, and that made me more than ready for the full experience. Again, I had to press my thighs together. Needing to change the subject, I asked, "Who was that gentleman?"

Gunnar shot me a look. "Michael Dowd. He's the president of the most powerful business association in the state."

"Wh-what?" I asked.

Gunnar's palm warmed my lower back as he led me out to his car. He opened the door and settled me into the seat. Once he'd buckled in and started the car, he shot me a smile. "You charmed him," he noted with pride. "You really are an amazing woman, Rookie."

"I like that you call me that," I said.

He settled his free hand atop mine, where it rested on my thigh. "I like that, too."

I shifted in the seat to face him more directly before linking my fingers with his. "Thank you for inviting me back to your place."

I wanted to say more, but I chickened out. Perhaps it was Gunnar's age or status or…I wasn't sure. But I knew his rejection would hurt so much more than any of my previous boyfriends'.

Thanks to the late hour, the freeways were much less congested, and it wasn't long before Gunnar pulled up to an impressive set of wrought-iron gates. They slid open with quiet efficiency, and we then drove along a stretch of smooth herringbone bricks until we reached the house. Up lit by garden lights, the two-story home's red brick matched the impressive drive, and four white columns held up a second-story deck from which four more columns supported the pitched roof. A glossy black door with mullioned panes inset above the handle and on either side was centered between the farthest columns, while windows were spaced between the next two.

Large live oaks, maples, and a few other trees I didn't know the names of dotted the property, and between them was a carpet of emerald green grass. The place was tidy and impressive but didn't seem like a billionaire's residence. In fact, some of the players' homes I'd been to while filming them doing day-to-day activities were much showier.

Gunnar slid the gearshift into park and waited.

"It's beautiful," I said. "You know that."

He gave a faint nod. "But I want you to like it. To be comfortable here."

My brows tugged together, but he was already stepping out of the car and coming around to my door. He took my hand and

helped me out, then led me across the bricks, up a few steps to
the porch, and inside. A wooden staircase curved from the side of
the entryway up to the second floor, with wood-framed, French-
inspired windows making up the wall. The night was too dark,
but I could envision how the multitude of glass allowed plenty of
light during the day. Hardwood floors in a similar herringbone
pattern covered the entire lower level. They were warm and
polished to a high sheen.

"Want a drink?" Gunnar asked.

I shook my head, nerves slithering through my belly. Gunnar
moved closer and wrapped me in a hug. I hadn't realized how
much I needed the connection until I sighed out some of the
tension I'd been holding.

"You were the belle of the ball," he said. "I wanted nothing
more than to let everyone know you were there with me."

I smiled as I tightened my arms around his waist. "I doubt
that, considering how all those women were drooling over you."
I pulled back to smooth the lapels of his tuxedo. "You look
smashing in this."

His lips tipped up on the right side, and his glacial eyes
warmed as he looked down at me. "I'd like you to share my bed."

Oh my. I swallowed, because this was the moment. I could
demur, or I could jump into this thing with Gunnar wholeheart-
edly. I thought of my mother's illness, of my years of playing it
safe. I didn't want to be safe with Gunnar. I wanted to explore all
the messy, big feelings he brought out in me. *This is what I said I
wanted.* I took a deep breath. "Yes, please."

His smile dazzled me. Then his lips brushed mine, and I

closed my eyes, enjoying the sensations he evoked. The sensual slide of lips and tongue warmed my body and sent desire pulsing to my core. I wound my arms around his neck, arching into him, needing the friction against my pebbled nipples.

He kissed and licked and suckled my lips until they felt swollen, and I felt drugged. With a faint moan, he pulled back, took my hand, and led me up the stairs and down the hall to his bedroom.

It was large—as expected—with a sitting room that had more of those glorious windows, but my gaze settled on the king-sized sleigh bed done up in shades of pale and navy blue. Gunnar slipped his hand from mine and gripped my wrists. He kissed one palm, then the other.

"I hope you'll want to get naked so I can learn your delectable body, but if you'd prefer to sleep, I'll understand. There's no pressure, Zaila. Just…us."

I bit my over-sensitized lower lip as I stepped forward to undo his bow tie. I pulled it off slowly, then began to unbutton his dress shirt. "I'm fairly shy when it comes to nudity," I admitted. "But it's something I've wanted with you since…well, probably the beginning."

"The pull." Gunnar's eyes burned nearly white-hot with passion. "You feel it as much as I do."

I nodded. "You make me ache, Gunnar."

He cupped my cheeks and brought my lips up to his. "I'll make you sigh, moan, and scream, if you'll let me."

"Yes, please."

His lips slid over mine before I'd finished the word. Over the next hour, he stripped me, touching me with his fingertips first, then with his palms, tongue, and teeth, and he proved he was more than capable of making me do all three.

By the time we were both nude, in the center of that mattress with the softest sheets that had ever touched my skin, I writhed, covered in a fine sheen of sweat and panting with need.

His fingers dipped between my legs, finding me more than ready for him. He slid two inside me, groaning against my mouth as his thumb found my clit. He rubbed circles with a slow build that sent me tumbling into a prolonged climax that stole thought and breath.

He kissed me as I returned to myself and looked at me intently, seeming to memorize my features. "You are beautiful."

I blushed as I rolled toward him, hooking my leg over his hip.

His erection nudged at my center, and he narrowed his eyes as his nostrils flared. "I want you. Fuck, I need you."

I rubbed against him. "As much as I want you?"

"At least that much," he gritted out.

I rolled so that I was atop him, and his hands slid to my hips, molding my flesh in his palms and rocking my sensitive core against his groin. He released a string of words that were probably Swedish, his expression so full of passion that my breath stuttered.

"I want to be inside you now," he said.

I nodded. "Please."

He flipped me over with enough care that my head landed on the pillows. His biceps bulged and his glutes flexed as he reached into the nightstand and pulled out a condom.

"Watching you put that on is so sexy," I murmured, my gaze riveted as he rolled the latex over his girth.

"The things you say…" He rubbed his tip against my entrance, and I widened my thighs to encourage him. He slid inside me with intent, flexing that magnificent butt until he'd rooted as deeply as possible.

"You feel so good," I moaned as I arched up, desperate for friction. He braced his palms on either side of my head and gave me what I demanded…and more.

I reached my second peak before he did, and he continued to thrust into me with measured strokes until his jaw tightened and his pupils flared. A deep moan roared from his chest, and he dropped his head against my shoulder, panting. "Fuck. Fuck…"

I locked my legs behind his back and my arms around his shoulders as he recovered. Then we fell asleep entwined together, and I knew Gunnar Evaldson had found his way to my heart.

CHAPTER 22

Gunnar

I grinned as I woke many hours later to Zaila's soft breaths on my chest, her hair wild across my arm and neck. *Connection, intimacy...* Those were words I'd heard and thought I understood before. I hadn't, not until now.

Caring about and for another person, this woman, gave me a new purpose. For a long moment, I luxuriated in the pleasure of our physical connection. I tipped my head down to breathe in the faint hints of her shampoo before I disentangled myself from her embrace.

The next thing I wanted was her, sleep-rumpled and well-sated, moaning softly as she sipped her favorite coffee, a latte with lots of foam. I'd paid attention to her orders and ensured I had all the proper ingredients on hand. I padded out of my suite and down the hall to the guest room nearest the stairs, where I showered and brushed my teeth with the extra I kept stocked there, hoping the distance would allow Zaila to sleep longer. My plan faltered when I realized I didn't have a change of clothes or a robe to put on, so I went downstairs in a towel, hoping to find something to put on in the laundry room. My housekeeper proved too efficient, though, so with a sigh, I padded into the kitchen, shivering slightly as the cool air blew across my skin.

I started the coffee machine, making myself an espresso before pressing the series of buttons that would create Zaila's frothy drink. While I waited, I drank a large glass of water and noted that the bluejays in the backyard had pecked away all the birdseed once again. With a mental note to get more for the feeder, I picked up my coffee and sipped, enjoying the sunlight filtering through the leafy canopy that towered over my backyard.

Houston had taken some getting used to because it was large and not just American, but boldly Texan. That had created both a culture and climate shock when I'd first arrived. Now, while I still enjoyed other locations more—the city was built on a swamp and didn't have the gorgeous topography of my native Sweden—I'd learned to appreciate the city's arts and culture and its more modest topographical beauty.

I loved my hockey team and my house, and I was growing more certain I could love the woman in my bed, so Houston felt more and more like home.

The machine gurgled to a stop, and I picked up Zaila's mug. Carrying one coffee in each hand, I headed back up the stairs to my sleeping beauty.

I settled both our coffees on my nightstand and went to find a pair of sweatpants. I slid them on as I heard the bedsheets rustle, and I hurried back to the main room in time to see Zaila lift her head, squinting at the light. She was mussed adorably in a way that made my chest ache. Her gaze found me as I sat on the mattress, sliding in close to run my hand along her sleep-warmed cheek.

"Morning," I murmured, threading my fingers into her thick hair.

"Good morning." Her eyes smiled up at me even before her lips lifted. "I hope I'm not keeping you from something."

"Not a place I'd rather be," I assured her. "I made you a coffee."

Her eyes widened as I picked it up and handed it to her. She scooted upward to lean against the pillows and took a long sip. Her upper lip was soon coated in foam that she licked off before breathing out a contented sigh. "This is so good. Thank you, Gunnar."

I smiled as I joined her in leaning against the headboard and the pillows. "You're welcome." I took a much smaller sip of my espresso. "I loved waking up to you in my bed. I plan to do this often, just so you know."

Her smile widened. "It's my favorite wake-up, too."

We sipped our coffees in pleasurable silence before Zaila set down her empty mug. "I should probably get cleaned up."

"Sure." I waited a beat. "Mind if I join you?"

"Didn't you already shower?" She rose from the bed in all her nude glory, heading toward the bathroom door.

"Yeah, but I thought you might need some help with working the controls. Or with washing in some places. Or with any desire that built up overnight."

She giggled. "You know, I might. Give me a few to…" She trailed off as her cheeks bloomed pink. "I'll open the door when I'm ready for your company."

I settled back, running my hand down my abs. I enjoyed watching Zaila's gaze follow. "I'll be waiting."

Shower sex was better than anticipated, and I'd anticipated a lot. We got ready in a soft, post-orgasmic haze. Zaila was a no-nonsense woman, so she didn't bother with an hour-long hair and makeup routine. That said, I was waiting in the kitchen, having enjoyed a second espresso and more antics between the birds and the squirrels, when Zaila joined me. Her outfit today was a simple shorts-and-top set that showcased her long, tanned legs, narrow waist, and the tops of her shoulders.

"What's that called?" I asked, pointing to her outfit.

"A romper. I love them when it's hot out because they're so comfortable."

"You look great. Green's an excellent color for you."

She smiled as she stepped in closer and laid her hand on my chest. Then, she paused, almost as if she weren't sure she should proceed.

"I hope you're going to kiss me, and I hope it's going to last a while." I settled my hand over hers. "Because I'd really like that."

She rose on her toes in her gold sandals until her lips touched mine.

I held her close with my free hand, my palm settling on the top curve of her ass, and kissed her some more.

"Gunnar," Zaila said against my lips.

"Yeah?" I didn't want to pull back.

"I need to call my mother." She blinked up at me, worry clouding her eyes. "She's probably fine, but—"

"You need to be sure. I get that. Call her and let her know we're bringing over brunch."

Zaila bit her lip. "You don't mind?"

"That you're a responsible, caring daughter who worries about her parent's health?" I shook my head. "I do not. In fact, it makes me think even more of you."

Her expression softened, and I realized she'd been nervous. "Thank you for saying that."

"I mean it. The fact that you gave up your independence for your mom is not something I see from a lot of younger people."

Zaila shrugged. "That's probably because most of the younger people you deal with are professional athletes who are used to being catered to, not catering to others."

"That's valid," I said. "Insightful, too. Because I just thought most twenty-somethings were selfish."

Zaila shook her head. "I'm sure many are, just as many older adults are. But athletes are a special breed. They're used to being indulged and coddled. They aren't used to having to put in the emotional work for relationships. Well, in my limited experience."

"That's because our current rookies and first-year players are some of the most entitled little shits I've ever dealt with." I ran my hand through my hair, my good mood souring as I remembered my Jeff problem. The deal Silas and my GM had been working on had recently fallen through thanks to Jeff's comments about his lack of playing time. I was on the verge of sending him to the minor leagues. *So close.* "Make your call."

Zaila pulled out her phone but peeked up at me before she pressed dial. "You really don't like Jeff."

I shook my head. "I don't have to like the players, but I should be able to respect their work ethic and commitment to the game."

"Jeff doesn't meet that standard either," Zaila said.

Before I could ask if she was giving me her opinion or telling me what she thought I believed, she put her phone to her ear.

Once she was certain her mother was fine and more than happy to laze the morning away, she hung up. "We can take over brunch..."

I raised an eyebrow. "Or?"

"Or we could stay here for a while longer," Zaila offered, mischief in her eyes.

"And do what?" I asked, my hands falling to her hips.

She leaned in and bit my lip. "You could give me a tour of your house."

Nearly a week later, after the second win in a row for the Wildcatters—helped by Jeff riding the bench—I met Zaila in my office. The first game this week had been away, and I'd had dinner meetings the last two nights and then tonight's game. Dating me had to frustrate her; my schedule and lack of time with her certainly frustrated me. I struggled to find a chance to see her each day, and my calendar kept filling up more and more quickly, no matter how much I wanted to carve out time for her.

So, these stolen minutes in my office and at her mother's house were the highlights of my week. And I still missed holding her at night and waking up with her in the morning. That was part of how I knew this relationship differed from any other I'd had.

The moment Zaila walked into my office, I leaned down, my lips meeting hers in a tender kiss. The moment felt perfect and much-needed after the busyness of the last seven days.

"Well, well, what do we have here?"

I jerked back, my heart racing as I saw Jay Welks standing in the doorway, still half-dressed in the Gusher mascot costume.

I felt Zaila's muscles stiffen. I never wanted her to feel that way, tense and unsure, when she was with me. "Did you need something?" I asked Jay, my tone flinty.

"The big boss and his much-younger employee. Quite the scandal, don't you think?" Jay asked, his smirk growing.

I felt my jaw clench. "What do you want, Jay?"

He sauntered into my office, twirling Gusher's oversized hockey stick. "Oh, nothing much. Just better working conditions for the social media team. A raise wouldn't hurt either."

"You're *blackmailing* me?" I asked, incredulous. I felt Zaila huff as she turned to face her boss.

Jay shrugged. "I prefer to think of it as negotiating. Unless you'd rather the board hear about this indiscretion?"

I glanced at Zaila, who looked pale but determined. "Actually, the board is aware of my relationship with Zaila," I growled. She startled as she met my gaze. "Just as I informed Noelle." She was the head of the marketing department. "And HR."

"I didn't tell you, though, and that was my choice," Zaila told Jay. "Because I was concerned about how you'd react. Clearly I was right to worry. You thought you could sneak up on us and make our relationship dirty." Zaila lifted her chin, meeting Jay's gaze. "It's not."

"No, it isn't," I agreed. "And you skulking around, trying to get the goods on me doesn't match the level of ethics expected around here." I raised my eyebrows. "So, count this as your last warning. I won't give another one."

As Jay slunk from the room, a mutinous expression on his face, I slumped into my chair, the weight of this suddenly too much.

"Gunnar," Zaila said softly, "I don't think he took that well. What am I going to do?"

I looked at her, wishing I had a better answer. "Well, he can't touch me, but that calculating look makes me think I made a mistake in not firing him on the spot."

"That would have been bad, though, especially after Lydia—"

I nodded. "Which is why I didn't do it. But I'll keep a close eye on Jay."

"I'm glad you talked to the board, but…" She bit her lip.

"But?"

"Jay's my boss. I probably should have talked to him." She shrugged. "I wasn't sure what you wanted—"

"All of it," I said as I tugged Zaila into my lap. "I want everything with you. And now that Jay is aware, he won't bother you. I promise."

CHAPTER 23
Zaila

I worried for the next week, always expecting Jay to make a snide comment or undermine me, but he didn't. In fact, he continued as if nothing untoward had happened between us, though he was often out of the office for long lunches. One afternoon when Tim returned from lunch, he said he'd seen Jay with Jeff.

The next day, I went to lunch with Vivian and Paloma and saw Jay sitting in the same restaurant with our former boss, Lydia, of all people. "That's strange," I murmured.

"What?" Vivian asked. She'd been talking about her upcoming wedding, which sounded lovely.

"That guy back there—Jay Welks. He's my boss. He's talking to Lydia Breitbart, my former boss. Somehow it feels like they're bonding over the Gunnar-and-me situation."

"Oh, they are," Paloma said. She took off her sweater, putting her toned arms on display. "They have a Zaila hate club, I'm sorry to say."

"How do you know that?" I asked.

"Silas knows many, many things," she said with a wry smile.

"I was hoping you wouldn't notice them," Vivian said, her tone regretful. "We came here to keep an eye on them."

"Wait, why?"

"Because we don't trust them," Paloma said. "Jay wanted in

your pants. Just because you picked Gunnar doesn't mean he's cool with losing."

"We are married—or almost married—to athletes," Vivian added. "They take competitive to scary places."

"So…you're stalking them?" I asked, my stomach knotting.

"Pfft. No, though Naomi wanted to put a tracker on Jay. We wouldn't let her," Vivian hurried to assure me.

"Might not be a bad idea," Paloma muttered. "I don't like how intent they are." She pulled her gaze from Jay and Lydia to meet mine through the lenses of her glasses—cute, chunky turquoise frames.

"We can always let Keelie bring her golf clubs," Vivian said.

Paloma narrowed her eyes. "Not a bad idea."

"Can we just not? I'm kind of freaking out." I took a long drink of my water. "Tell me more about your wedding."

Vivian's grin grew, and her eyes gleamed. "Oh, you asked for it."

As the days passed, the lack of reprisal from Jay bothered me more than if he'd commented or gone back to being sullen, and his intense lunch with Lydia had waved all kinds of red flags. But those were feelings, not concrete actions, so I had nothing to tell Gunnar. There wasn't a problem, and I hoped the situation had righted itself.

Plus, Gunnar and I didn't get to see each other often, and we were finally spending this evening at his place. I wasn't about to waste it talking about Jay. My mother had gone to a bridge tournament with an old friend. Gunnar had booked them a suite at the hotel, and Mom had already sent me pictures, gushing about the amenities and the view of downtown.

Seeing her happy made me happy, and I'd just shown Gunnar *how* happy right here on his couch. He caressed my bare back with his fingertips as he nuzzled into my hair. The man loved my hair.

"I didn't think I'd be this constantly horny at forty-four. You've had me thinking about sex more in the last few months than I did in the previous decade. A shadow flitted across his expression, darkening it with something that looked suspiciously like guilt.

I sighed as I propped my chin on my hands and stared into his light blue eyes. "I'm twenty-four; you're forty-four. Yeah, it's a gap, but we're happy. I love spending time with you. I love how focused you are on me when we're together, both with our clothes on and off." His lip quirked up, and I grinned back, relieved to see him relax.

"I just... I worry about the future. What if—"

"What if what?" I interrupted, my voice gentle but firm. "What if you get hit by a Zamboni tomorrow? What if I trip over a hockey stick and break my neck? We can't control the future, Gunnar. You and I both know that." I leaned down and pressed my lips to his, offering comfort after the sting of my words. "You couldn't save your brother, just like I couldn't save my dad from that car accident, and I can't stop the progression of my mother's disease. I hate that so much, but life doesn't come with guarantees, no matter how much we plan."

His grip tightened on my hips, and pain flashed across his face.

I pressed on. "We're not promised tomorrow. All we have is right now, this moment. And right now, I love being with you."

Gunnar hugged me, his chin resting on top of my head.

"You're right," he murmured. "I just... I've never felt this way before. It scares me sometimes."

I leaned back with a smirk. "Well, old man, maybe it's time you learned to live a little. I hear it's all the rage with us youthful folk."

He chuckled, the tension finally breaking. "All right, Rookie. What does living in the moment look like to you?"

"Well," I said, pulling him towards the kitchen, "it starts with making some of those terrible dad jokes you love while you feed me dinner, and maybe planning our next adventure."

"Will you eat naked with me?" he asked.

"I think I can manage that...as long as I get a towel for the seat."

"But of course," he assured me with a laugh.

As Gunnar gathered ingredients, weight lifted off my shoulders. We might not have forever; no one did. But now was beautiful, and that was enough.

CHAPTER 24
Zaila

The next home game fell mid-week, which meant I'd spent the last three days pining for time with Gunnar. He was so busy, and while he texted often, face-to-face and body-to-body time remained elusive now that the season was in full swing. So when he pulled me through the empty parking lot behind the arena after the game, once everyone else had departed, I was ecstatic. The first raindrop hit my nose as thunder rumbled in the distance. With him close by, I barely noticed the noise.

The hockey game had ended over an hour ago, but these were the first moments we'd had together today, and the air between us crackled with tension—the kind that made my pulse stutter every time his fingers brushed mine.

"Gunnar, what are you—"

"Shh." He pressed a finger to my lips, stopping though we hadn't reached his car, his grin wicked under the flickering streetlamp. "Right now, I want to savor."

"Savor what?" I asked.

He smiled down at me, his expression tight with desire. "You." He leaned ever closer until his lips touched mine. Just like the first time—every time—we kissed, fireworks burst under my skin, heating my blood. He tipped me back and settled over me, his palm cradling my head as he deepened the kiss.

Thunder crashed and lightning rent the inky blackness, adding another layer to the electrical charge racing between us. His tongue slid past my lips and into my mouth, causing me to tighten my hold as I moaned. He made me so hot, so ready for more.

More lightning, more thunder. I didn't care about the weather, not as long as Gunnar kissed me, held me. Icy rain sluiced down my cheeks, soaking my blouse in seconds. I gasped, but Gunnar just spun me under his arm, his laughter rich and warm against the drumming storm. "Dance with me."

"You're insane!" I shouted over the downpour, but I was already moving, sliding against the slick asphalt.

Gunnar's hands found my waist, pulling me flush against him. "For you I am. Took you this long to figure that out?"

The man moved as if he'd been born for this moment, and the rain was just another partner as he guided me through a turn, his palm hot even through my soaked clothes. My heart hammered, equal parts exhilaration and terror, because this felt…real.

Like my parents' marriage.

Before I could catch my breath, ask to pause, to think, my heel hit a puddle. I squeaked as my feet shot out from under me. Gunnar saw me mid-fall, his arm hooking under my knees as he dipped me low, our faces inches apart. Rain dripped from his eyelashes onto my cheeks.

"Nice save, Mr. Evaldson," I breathed.

His smile softened. "I'll always be here for you, Zaila."

And then, because the universe has a sense of humor, my phone buzzed in my back pocket. Back on my feet, I pulled it out, the screen lit up with a text from Jay: Saw you two sneaking off. Cute. Just remember, he's not the settling type.

Gunnar's gaze moved over the screen. His jaw tightened.

I shoved the phone away, but the damage was done. The magic of the moment shredded like ice under a skate blade.

"Zaila." His voice was rough. "We need to talk."

My stomach dropped, and I braced myself, but Gunnar just cupped my face, his thumbs brushing away raindrops and some tears.

"I love you."

The words punched through me, leaving me breathless, weightless.

"I love you," he repeated, louder this time, like he was daring the world to argue. "And I don't give a damn who knows it. Not the team, not your coworkers, not the fucking press."

I stared at him, my lips parting... Up on my toes, I kissed him. Not gentle. Not sweet. A kiss that tasted like rain and recklessness, like every doubt I'd carried about our age difference, our professional disparities, melting away. Gunnar hauled me closer until there was no space left between us.

When we broke apart, gasping, he rested his forehead against mine. "I've wanted to tell you that—yell it from rooftops, really—ever since you schooled that stuffy old shirt at the gala with your literary knowledge. You were so unbelievably sexy."

"Why didn't you?" I asked.

He stared down at me. "You didn't seem ready."

I raised my eyebrows, ignoring the rain in my face. "I love you too, you ridiculous man."

His grin could've powered Houston for the month of August. "This is the best news." But then he frowned. "My love looks chilled," he announced, like the words *my love* weren't currently short-circuiting my brain.

I elbowed him. "I don't feel the cold."

He kissed my temple. "That's because all our love is warming you, Rookie. But you'll chill soon."

Perhaps he was right. And I did feel a bit of a chill as Jay's comments and smirks flitted through my mind. Deep down, I was unable to shake the feeling that I didn't fit into Gunnar's world, and perhaps I never would. But, then again, we could build a new one—where we fit so perfectly together.

CHAPTER 25
Zaila

A happy haze surrounded me for the better part of the next month. Gunnar Evaldson loved me.

The sexy hockey owner with the icy eyes that warmed just for me, that Gunnar. My Gunnar. The giddiness that came with our new connection allowed me to push aside my worry for my mother, and she was so happy for me that for a while, everything seemed perfect.

When I informed Tim, he just chuckled. He told me he'd decided we were perfect together after that first meeting.

"Lydia saw it, too," he said. "That's why she went off on you." His expression grew more serious. "What about Jay?"

"He knows," I said. "But…I'd prefer not to make a big deal about it, mainly because Jay's made it a little weird."

Tim's look told me he knew I'd understated the issue with Jay. But he didn't say anything more, so I didn't either.

At home, if I hovered, my anxiety over her condition setting in, Mom shooed me out of the house so I could spend time with Gunnar, something I was desperate to do. And while I appreciated the chance to get to know him better, he understood my need to be with my mom, so we settled into a routine of him bringing over dinner on Tuesdays and Thursdays, as long as there wasn't a game, and brunch on Sunday, where we lingered around the table, simply enjoying each other. Gunnar was too busy for much more than that, though he asked me up to his office for lunch as often as possible.

But then one afternoon the reality of her condition came roaring back to the forefront. Mom hadn't answered my texts all day—not even the cat meme I'd sent at lunch. She always responded to my texts. That was part of our deal; I'd continue to go to work as long as she assuaged my worry by letting me know she was okay. I didn't even care that she'd teased me about it. "*You're worse than a hockey mom with those check-ins,*" she'd told me. "*I'm fine, darling girl. I'll let you know when I'm not. Promise.*"

I left the office in a rush, as soon as I was able.

"Mom?" My voice echoed through the house after I'd fumbled with the locks, dropping my keys twice. My body shook in the silence, punctuated by the grandfather clock in the living room that ticked away like a bomb to my happiness.

I found my mother curled on the couch, her knitting needles abandoned in a tangle of yarn. Her skin matched the gray upholstery. I'd feared this moment for the past few months, and now it was here.

"Mom!" I skidded to my knees, my shoes digging into the carpet. Her hand felt like chilled paper when I grabbed it. "Please, please…"

"Z-Zaila?" Her eyes fluttered open, pupils dilated. "Can't… catch my breath."

The diagnosis we'd danced around flashed neon in my brain. I'd Googled every symptom, and I could repeat them like a terrible litany: chest pain lasting ten or more minutes at rest, shortness of breath, and the oh-so-obvious overwhelming fatigue.

"Where's your nitro spray?" I scrambled for her purse, sending Tic Tacs skating across the floor, as if that mattered now.

"Used it...twice." Her wheeze clawed at my ribs. "Didn't... help."

I whimpered before I bit my lip and firmed my chin. Angina should subside with nitroglycerin. Mom's symptoms had spiraled with incredible speed. This wasn't supposed to happen. We should have more time. I needed more time with her.

The 911 operator's voice crackled through my phone. "Ma'am, is she conscious?"

"Barely." I pressed my ear to Mom's chest. Her heartbeat stuttered like a rookie's skate on fresh ice. *Du-dum... Duh...........dum.* "Her pulse is irregular and seems to be slowing. Sh-she has c-c-coronary microvascular disease." Pushing the words past my stiff lips made them more real, made the situation too real.

"Paramedics are en route. Please stay on the line—" Mom's back arched off the couch, so I threw the phone aside, my hands on her cold cheeks.

"Mom, Mama..." I rolled her sideways, just as I'd learned from the online videos I watched obsessively. Her lips leached of color, then bloomed blue.

"Mama, you need to stay with me," I sobbed.

~

The ICU doors hissed shut behind Dr. Khatri as her lab coat flapped around her knees. Her expression was grim, matching my mood. "We've stabilized Susan with IV nitro and heparin, but..."

"But?" My nails bit into my palms. The past few hours had been sheer panic and the spiraling realization that every breath might be the first I took without a mother, as an orphan all over again.

"Her cardiac MRI showed diffuse subendocardial hypoperfusion." Dr. Khatri's tablet glowed with nightmare images of Mom's heart muscle streaked like storm clouds. "Severe coronary microvascular dysfunction. We're talking myocardial steatosis, possible progression to HFpEF…"

I stiffened, my mind both whirring and too sluggish to take in the medical jargon. "I don't understand all those terms. Will you break it down for me, please?"

Dr. Khatri opened her mouth, but then my mind clicked back into action.

"Oh…oh…Y-you're saying her heart's starving." I choked out the terms I'd memorized after way too many late nights looking up the disease. "The tiny vessels aren't delivering enough blood. It's…it's why the nitro didn't work."

Dr. Khatri nodded, her expression resigned. "We'll try enhanced external counterpulsation therapy tomorrow. But long term—and by that I mean later this week…" Her gaze dropped to Mom's DASI questionnaire in my lap, the one where she'd scored "Can't make bed without stopping to rest."

The walls in my periphery wavered as I tried to breathe through the reality. *Orphan.* The word slithered from childhood's shadows where I'd curled into the corner of the group home, before Mom and Dad had found me. I wasn't ready. I'd never be prepared to be alone again.

"Will those options prolong her suffering?" I asked, the words as heavy as my heart. "Or will they give her a fighting shot?"

Before Dr. Khatri could answer, her pager shrilled, and she glanced down at it, her eyes tired. She spun on her heel and tore back through the doors. She shoved them so hard, I could hear and see the chaos beyond.

"V-fib," a nurse barked.

I stood and followed, unable to stay in my chair, not while my mother struggled in that bed.

"Clear!"

Mom's body jolted under the paddles. My teeth rattled as I shivered.

"We got it! Got the pulse."

The doors swung shut in front of me then, and I dropped my head into my hands, my shoulders heaving. I wanted Gunnar here with me.

Oh, God. Gunnar.

He was supposed to come by the house. I'd forgotten entirely…

I looked around. I didn't have my phone or my house keys. Nothing. My mother was stable for the moment, but I…

I was alone.

CHAPTER 26
Gunnar

The conference room reeked of stale coffee and desperation. I jabbed my finger at the trade proposal sent over by my least-favorite team—the one who'd hired Leon, Karl's former head coach, as their offensive coordinator. This was probably because Lars, Karl's former teammate and the one I was certain had battered my brother, was now their GM. Once again, the leadership had proved to be rancid, self-indulgent, and irritating as fuck. Seemed perfect for Jeff, though that wasn't the outcome I wanted.

"You want me to gut my defense for a forward who can't stay out of penalty boxes?" I asked. "Are we playing hockey or Mortal Kombat?"

Lars leaned back, arms crossed. "He's got grit."

I scoffed. "Grit doesn't win Cups. Strategy does." My phone buzzed in my pocket—Zaila's dinner reminder. I silenced it. Again.

Fuck. This was taking too long.

"Or…you can give us your rookie," Lars said. "The one we wanted, but you took first to be an ass."

Ah, here we go. I set my elbows on the table. We'd arrived at the real reason for this meeting. Lars wanted Jeff, which was why we'd picked him up in the first place—why I'd insisted on drafting him despite the red flags. Anything to fuck with Lars Erickson and the coach who had cost my brother his life.

At least Jeff had tempered his public drinking now, and his numbers were improving when he played. But that wasn't often because he still wasn't gelling with the rest of the team.

Anyway, much as I wanted the asshat gone, I didn't want to give him to Lars.

Plus, Jeff had turned into a dark horse with the fans. He was flashy and social media savvy. He got the college kids to fork over money for merch and tickets, but that didn't mean I liked him or thought he was worth keeping around. I didn't. Despite his business acumen, he acted like an entitled brat.

Three hours into this meeting I hadn't wanted to take, the asshole wouldn't give up, though his deal remained like a bad pass. But at least I'd confirmed what I'd suspected: he wanted me to hand over the kid and one of my veterans so he could rebuild his team around Jeff.

At this point, I could be persuaded to release Jeff to Lars, but not my veterans. They'd been loyal, committed to the team and what we were building here. They were essential. "Neither Cruz nor Maxim Dolov are options," I told him. "And I don't make those decisions without my GM and coaching staff, seeing how such choices impact them, more than me." Granted, I'd made sure Silas and Pete, my general manager, were unavailable tonight because I preferred to weed out the bullshit first, only bringing in management when there was something worthwhile to discuss.

When I finally clicked off the video call, telling him not to reach out again unless he had an offer for Jeff and Jeff alone, I noted that the text I'd sent to Zaila earlier hadn't been read.

I frowned. That was odd. I glanced at the time. *After ten.* I scrubbed my hands down my face. I was hungry, angry, and, now, worried about Zaila and her mother. I lurched up from my desk, making sure I had my phone, keys, and wallet as I headed out the door to the parking garage. I called Zaila, a bit concerned I might wake her, but she didn't answer, which ratcheted up my concern.

When I arrived, her house was too quiet. No lights on. No answer at the door, which had my palms sweating. There was a spare key hidden under the garden gnome her mom had named Sir Squeaks-a-Lot, but I didn't need to use it because the side door was open. Zaila's keys were on the table when I entered the kitchen. The living room smelled of lavender and fear. Zaila's phone lay on the coffee table, her handbag on the floor next to the couch. A half-knitted scarf—Susan's latest project—was draped over the armrest. Tic Tacs dotted the floor, along with some plastic wrappings that appeared to be from medical interventions.

My stomach dropped as I rushed toward the front of the house.

"Zaila?" My voice cracked as I headed up the stairs to her room. I hurried back to the living room and picked up Zaila's phone, but it was password protected, and I didn't have that. I tucked it into my pocket and looked around. Grabbing Zaila's purse, I carried it to the kitchen. I found a couple of apples, crackers, and a block of cheese that I tossed inside. I switched off the light and locked the door before heading back to my car. It was getting close to midnight now.

"An ambulance came by about six fifteen," a voice to my right piped up. I turned and noted the slight form of a woman in a bright orange polyester housecoat. She had more wrinkles than anyone I'd ever seen, with wispy white hair and sharp brown eyes.

"Zaila or her mom?" I asked.

"Susan. We'd all been put on alert to check in on her. She didn't want to worry Zaila and have that sweet girl quit her big career. But Susan's been feeling right poorly."

"Are they at M.D. Anderson?" I asked. I'd told Zaila I'd make sure her mother got the best care there.

The old woman shrugged. "Dunno about that. Just that Zaila looked terrified when she climbed into the ambulance, and Susan wasn't doing too good. Just lying there."

"Thanks for the information," I said.

"She's going to need you," the woman added. "Zaila, I mean. That girl was close to her folks."

I nodded. Based on what Zaila had shared about her early life, it hadn't been easy. Her adoption had been a dream, so I hoped losing a second parent wouldn't ruin all the progress she'd made.

ICU waiting rooms were a linoleum-coated purgatory that reminded me of Karl's death, and the absolute last place I wanted to spend the night. I steeled myself as I hurried down the corridor toward the figure I recognized, huddled in a chair in the room's corner.

"Hey," I called softly as I entered.

Zaila jerked upright, shadows pooled under her eyes. "You came."

I crouched before her, knees protesting. "Always."

Her laugh sounded broken. "Your meeting…"

"Was ridiculous and means nothing." I cupped her face. *Cold. Too cold.* "You should've called."

"I…think I left my phone at the house." Her thumb brushed my wrist. "And…well, I was just processing."

"Processing what?" I asked. But the grief in her eyes told me. Her mother wasn't going to make it. Without thought, I rose and scooped her up. Once she was settled in my lap, with her head against my chest, I said, "Tell me."

"MVD crisis. She's…" Her voice splintered. "I can't lose her, Gunnar. I'm not ready. I haven't gotten over Dad."

I pressed my lips to her hair. Lavender and salt. "I'm here. However long it takes."

Her fingers dug into my forearm. "Don't you dare leave."

"Wild horses couldn't drag me away from you, Zaila. Wild fucking horses."

A little while later, she slept fitfully in an uncomfortable chair, her head on my shoulder. This. This fragile trust. This messy, beautiful collision of mismatched pieces. It was everything.

I'd built arenas. Won championships. None of it mattered compared to the weight of her in my arms.

"Love you," I whispered into her hair.

She stirred. "Hmm?"

"Rest."

"Glad you're here. I needed you."

"And I always need you, Zaila."

CHAPTER 27
Zaila

Later that evening, Gunnar's arm slipped around my waist, anchoring me as Dr. Khatri entered the waiting room to perch on the plastic chair opposite us.

"I'm sorry, Zaila. Your mother's heart... It's failing. We've done everything we can."

The words landed like a physical blow. "How long?" I choked out.

Dr. Khatri's eyes were kind. "We've already had a Code Blue, as you know."

I nodded, firming my chin so it wouldn't wobble.

"She's stable but skirting the edge of another episode. So...I'd say hours. Maybe a day. You're welcome to come back now, while she's awake. Please try to say your goodbyes."

My legs were as unstable as a newborn colt's as Gunnar guided me past the ICU double doors and to the chair by Mom's bed. "I'll give you some time," he murmured with a kiss to my temple.

I leaned over Mom, memorizing every line of her face. "Hey, Mom," I whispered.

Her eyelids fluttered open, and she smiled. "My darling girl."

I wanted to say something witty, make a joke to lighten the tension. Instead, the words tumbled out. "I'm not ready for this. I'm not ready to be alone again."

For a moment, I saw a spark of the vibrant woman who'd raised me. "Never...alone," she rasped. "My brave...girl."

Tears blurred my vision. "I love you, Mom. I love you so much. I'll always love you. Always be thankful you found me, saw me. Wanted me."

Her fingers twitched in mine. "Love...you...always."

We sat together, my hand over hers, but no more words came. She was peaceful, breathing more deeply than she had in days. I don't know how long I was there before the monitors wailed for the last time, but I remembered Gunnar holding me as orderlies wheeled my mother away. I sobbed against his shoulder.

The next few days passed in a haze of grief, soul-deep fatigue I couldn't sleep away, and logistics. So many decisions to be made now. Gunnar ensconced me in my house and set up his computer at the seldom-used dining room table, where he handled funeral arrangements and fielded calls from well-wishers along with his seemingly never-ending workload. I moved through it all like a ghost, barely registering the sympathetic touches and murmured condolences from him, let alone Vivian, who'd gotten in touch with me through Gunnar while we waited for news about my mother. She'd brought the rest of the CATS to sit with me, and some of the neighbors had stopped by as well to offer their condolences.

The morning of the funeral dawned surprisingly crisp and clear for a day in early November. I stood before the mirror, fumbling with the buttons of my black dress. My reflection stared back, hollow-eyed and pale.

Gunnar knocked. "Zaila? You decent?"

"Come in," I called, cringing. My voice was rough from crying.

Gunnar entered, looking somber in a dark suit. His eyes softened. "Here, let me help." He fastened the last few buttons. "There," he said, smoothing the fabric over my shoulders. "You look beautiful."

I let out a laugh as our eyes met in the mirror. "I look like hell."

"Hey." He turned me toward him and tilted my chin up. "You may be tired and grief-stricken, but you're exquisite to me." He brushed his lips against my cheek. "We'll get through this together."

I leaned into his touch, drawing strength from his unwavering presence. "Promise?"

"What did I tell you before? Wild horses couldn't drag me away."

Sometime later, the church was a sea of black, faces blurring as I made my way down the aisle. Mom's casket loomed ahead, draped in her favorite quilt—the one she'd used on the couch most evenings. Gunnar had remembered that little detail, and his thoughtfulness left me weak all over again, buckling my knees.

Gunnar's hand settled at the small of my back, steadying me. We took our seats in the front pew, and I gripped his fingers like a lifeline all through the service that passed in a fog of hymns and eulogies. When it was my turn to speak, I stood on shaky legs.

"My mom..." I began, voice cracking. I looked out at the crowd, panic rising. Then my eyes found Gunnar's. He kept his gaze on mine as he nodded, and suddenly, I could breathe again. "My mom was my hero," I continued. "She taught me strength, kindness, and how to make a the best spaetzle—a recipe she perfected because she knew I loved it." A ripple of laughter. "But most of all, she taught me love. How to give it freely, and how to accept it when it's offered."

My gaze locked again with Gunnar's. "She showed me that family isn't only blood. I mean, I was adopted—not hers biologically—but I always knew she and Dad loved me better than anyone else could have. She stood by me when I made decisions, listened when I didn't like the consequences that came from my choices, and held me up when I was knocked off my feet. I will miss her just like I miss my father, every single day."

I wobbled down the stairs and back to Gunnar's side, where he hugged me, pressing a kiss to my temple. "She'd be so proud of you," he whispered.

The reception was at a nearby restaurant—a fancy one because Gunnar was friendly with the executive chef. She had shut down for the day. Ida Jane, Keelie, and Millie dealt with the staff so I could sit at a table, not even pretending to pick at my food.

"Thank you," I said, catching Keelie on her way past.

She squeezed my hand and offered a smile. "No need to thank a friend for helping out."

Fresh tears blurred my eyes, but my smile was genuine. "I'm flattered."

"Pssh. I'm just telling the truth. Now, let your man take care of you." She leaned in closer. "It's a driving need with these guys. Give him that."

I hugged her and then Ida Jane as she bustled past, looking for one of the waiters. She was on a mission to get another pitcher of tea for the table where Mom's bridge friends sat with the Wildcatters huge D-man, Maxim Dolov, explaining the ins and outs of the game to him.

"He's gonna turn into a bridge-playin' terror," Ida Jane murmured. She shook her head. "That man can't do anything halfway."

I bit my lip to keep from laughing, shocked but also thrilled that I still could.

"Want some water?" Gunnar asked, appearing at my elbow with a glass.

I nodded, sipping the cool liquid. "I don't know how I'd do this without you."

His eyes crinkled at the corners. "You won't have to find out."

Hours later, when the last guests finally trickled out, exhaustion hit me harder than a freight train. Gunnar must have noticed, because he was suddenly there, arm around my waist.

"Come on. Let's get you home."

I let him guide me to his luxury sedan, sinking into the leather seat. The drive passed in comfortable silence, Gunnar's hand resting on my knee.

He turned toward my house, but with each mile, I stiffened more. Mom's death was real now. Before, I'd been able to pretend she was just....away, but now, going home to the emptiness overwhelmed me. "I can't," I gasped suddenly. "I don't want to go there."

Gunnar studied me for a long moment. "Okay," he said. "I have an idea. Do you trust me?"

"Yes."

He smiled, no doubt pleased with the speed of my response. A hint of mischief lit up his eyes. "All right. When we get there, go in. Pack a bag. Then we're getting out of here."

An hour later, we pulled up to a private airstrip where a sleek, midsize jet rumbled on the tarmac. I recognized it as Gunnar's private plane—the one he'd used when he came to the retreat.

"Gunnar, what—"

He cut me off with a gentle kiss on my lips, which tingled from the contact. It had been too long since we'd done more than snuggle. If Gunnar missed our connection as much as I had, we both needed some serious loving.

"You need to get away. Decompress. Let me take care of you for a while."

Warmth chased away some of the gnawing emptiness that kept threatening to swallow me. "But what about the Gunnar the Goalie challenge this weekend?"

This new idea—developed by Tim, Veronica, and me, would be my biggest event so far and had created tons of buzz on social media. After all the memes of Gunnar as the goalie, seeming to block shots from all of hockey's greatest players, we'd decided to put him to the test in real life. I was proud of the energy and fan connection we'd generated with the project, and I didn't want to miss it.

"You won't miss the challenge, and I have Noelle handling the last details since it's under her department," he assured me. "She heaped you with praise, by the way. Said there was very little for her to do."

"Oh, well, that was nice of her. But I don't really have the time off—"

"You do. I know you read the handbook, so you're aware that you get up to two weeks bereavement leave."

I blinked at him, realizing Gunnar had an answer for all of my half-hearted objections. "Where are we going?"

"That's a surprise." He grinned, looking years younger, clearly pleased with himself and that I'd quit trying to argue my way out of his gift. "But I promise, it's somewhere you can relax and heal."

As we boarded the jet, my shoulders eased for the first time in days. I took a full, deep breath as the plush leather seat enveloped me. Gunnar sat next to me, his arm around my shoulders.

"Thank you," I whispered, nestling into his side.

He kissed my temple. "Always, Rookie. Always."

I smiled, enjoying his cologne and warmth.

The jet roared to life, carrying us away from the pain of the past week. As we soared into the sky, I felt the first stirrings of hope. Whatever came next, I wouldn't face it alone.

Gunnar's heartbeat thrummed under my ear, a reminder that love endures. Mom's last words echoed in my mind: "*Never alone.*"

She was right. With Gunnar by my side, I wouldn't be.

CHAPTER 28

Gunnar

Hours passed, and then the North Sea stretched before us, a vast expanse of steel gray water that seemed to meld with the horizon. I watched Zaila's face as she absorbed the view through the floor-to-ceiling windows of my Swedish home. The tension in her shoulders, a constant companion since her mother's passing, eased further as she breathed in the fresh, salty tang.

"It's beautiful," she said, her hand against the glass.

I stepped closer, wrapping my arms around her from behind. "Welcome to Höga Kusten, the High Coast."

She leaned back into me, and I savored the feel of her body. "How high are we talking?"

"Nearly three hundred meters above sea level," I said, nuzzling her neck. "Highest coastline in the world."

Zaila turned in my arms, her eyes searching mine. "Gunnar Evaldson, are you secretly a geography nerd as well as a hockey nerd?"

I grinned, feeling lighter than I had in weeks. "Maybe. But it's a distant second to hockey. Want to explore?"

Her answering smile was like the sun breaking through clouds. "Lead the way."

We spent the afternoon wandering the rugged shore, the salty air whipping Zaila's hair into wild waves. The landscape was a study in contrasts, the jagged cliffs of red Nordingrå granite jutting out from the green forests and tapering down to the steely, volatile sea.

As we hiked along a trail, I shared stories I hadn't thought about in years. "My brother and I used to come up here every summer," I said, helping Zaila over a rocky stretch—she didn't need it, but I wanted to touch her again. "We'd spend hours exploring the islands, pretending we were Viking warriors. He was ten years older, but he indulged my imagination." I swallowed a lump of emotion. "That's why I bought this place. To remember the good times."

Zaila squeezed my hand. "That sounds amazing. I bet you were a fierce Viking."

I chuckled, and the sound surprised even me. "Oh, the fiercest. Until I tripped over my own feet and fell face first into a tidepool. Karl fished me out."

Her laughter rang clear and bright, and something in my chest loosened. It had been so long since I'd heard that sound. I wouldn't tell her so, but the depth of her grief had worried me. It was almost as if Zaila were slipping away...

As the sun dipped towards the horizon, painting the sky in muted oranges and brilliant pinks, we made our way back to the house. Zaila's eyes were clearer and her steps lighter. The change of scenery had seemed to work its magic.

"How about a sauna session before dinner?" I asked. We'd paused on the bench in the entryway to remove our hiking boots.

Zaila's eyebrows shot up. "A sauna? Why, boss man, are you trying to get me naked?"

Heat crept up my neck, as if I were blushing. *No, that couldn't be.* "I, uh... I mean, we don't have to—" Holy shit. I was blushing. Zaila's question had thrown me off kilter.

She cut me off with a kiss that was much too short but oh-so-sweet. As she pulled back, I anticipated the next one. *Soon,* I promised myself. This woman was my drug, more necessary than my next breath.

"Relax, Gunnar. I'm teasing. A sauna sounds perfect. But you'll have to explain the finer points to me, what with me being American and all that."

Getting to hold her made everything right in my world, so I once again ignored the voice deep in my mind that pointed out she was grieving, that she was on my payroll, that she was too young. None of that mattered when she made me feel whole.

Ten minutes later, we were ensconced in the cedar-lined sauna, the heat seeping into our muscles. I leaned back against the bench, closing my eyes and letting out a long breath. For the first time in what felt like decades, I allowed myself to fully relax.

"Oh my God," Zaila's voice broke through my haze of contentment. "Is that...is that a tattoo?"

My eyes snapped open to find her staring at my left biceps, where a small, intricate design was partially visible, peeking out from under the towel around my neck. I groaned, covering it with my hand. "Yes. A youthful mistake."

But Zaila was already prying my fingers away, her eyes dancing with mischief. "Oh no, you don't get to hide this. How did I miss it before?"

"I hid it," I said.

She narrowed her eyes. "Yes, you did. Always giving me your good side, huh? Well, let me see."

With a groan, I dropped my hand. The tattoo was supposed to be a tribute to my brother. I didn't remember going to the tattoo parlor, let alone describing what I wanted—I'd been wasted for days after I buried Karl. I knew I'd considered getting a tattoo with Karl's name and his hockey jersey number, but on my arm I had the words *amor vitae*, which translated to love of life, with what looked like a bent golf club instead of a hockey stick. The whole thing was embarrassing, which was why I'd kept it. Getting drunk, losing my sense of self hadn't brought Karl back, nor had it created positive outcomes. *Never again*, I reminded myself each time I looked at the stupid thing.

Zaila's lips twitched as she studied the ink. "Amor vitae," she read. Lifting an eyebrow, she met my gaze. "Love of...golf?"

I burst out laughing. The absurdity of it all, the years I'd spent hiding this ridiculous tattoo, proved hilarious. Zaila joined in, her giggles turning into full-blown guffaws as I explained the tattoo's ignominious origins.

"Oh, Gunnar," she gasped, wiping tears from her eyes. "That's...that's amazing."

I pulled her close. Sweat slicked our bodies, dampening our towels, and I wished she were naked. But now wasn't the time. Soon, I hoped. But not now. "You know what? It kind of is."

As our laughter subsided, I marveled at how good it felt to let go, to be silly and imperfect with Zaila. "Thank you," I murmured, kissing her temple.

She looked up at me. "For what?"

"For making me laugh. For being here. For...everything." Zaila's smile was tender as she traced the outline of my botched tattoo.

"No, no, I should thank you. This is just what I needed."

We stayed just like that for a while, the heat of the sauna and the comfort of each other's presence wrapping around us like a cocoon. This moment, sharing this place, reinforced my earlier revelation that I needed her. Not just wanted, but needed—like air, like the ice beneath my skates, like the beat of my heart. Zaila brought with her a sense of peace I hadn't known in years. Maybe ever.

When the timer went off, we stepped out of the sauna and into the cool evening air. The sky had deepened to a rich indigo, stars beginning to twinkle overhead. On impulse, I grabbed Zaila's hand. "Come on, I want to show you something."

I stopped long enough to grab us each a thick, fluffy robe and some clogs that I kept by the back door. Hers were too big, but she followed me as I led her down to the private dock jutting out into the sea. The water lapped against the wooden pilings, a soothing rhythm in the quiet night.

"Look," I said, pointing out over the water.

Zaila gasped as she saw what I was pointing toward: the faint, shimmering curtains of green light dancing across the northern sky.

"The aurora borealis, nature's best light show," I said.

"Incredible," she whispered.

I loved her like this—soft, awestruck, warm, and cuddly.

I loved who I was with her. Part of me wished we'd never return to Houston, to work and our lives—that we could stay here at the ends of the earth and soak in nature's wonders. I'd never deal with another irritation, just love Zaila until I quit breathing.

There was definitely merit in this thought. Though I wouldn't be able to follow through. Zaila would want to visit her mother's grave, return to work, and I was too enmeshed in my hockey team to let someone else take over the day-to-day details I handled. I'd been trying to find the right person since I'd started dating Zaila, but I hadn't yet, and I wasn't sure I could.

I wrapped my arms around her from behind, resting my chin on her shoulder. "Not as incredible as you."

She turned her head, a smirk playing at her lips. "Smooth talker."

"I try," I said. "I mean it, though. Zaila, you've brought light back into my life. Joy. Laughter. Things I thought I'd lost for good when Karl died."

Her eyes shimmered in the starlight. "Gunnar..."

"I'm serious. I know what you're going through, how much it hurts, how you want to run from it. And I know that you'll be stronger than I was, handle your grief better than I did because you're unstoppable, Zaila. It's one of the many things I adore about you."

She shook her head, overcome. With a quick movement, I scooped her up in my arms.

Zaila let out a squeal. "What are you doing?"

I grinned down at her. "Going for a swim!"

"Don't you dare—Gunnar!"

Her protests dissolved into shrieks of laughter as I jumped off the dock, plunging us both into the chilly North Sea. We surfaced, sputtering and laughing, the shock of the cold water exhilarating.

"You're insane!" Zaila gasped, splashing water at me.

I caught her hand, pulling her close. "Insanely in love with you."

Zaila's face broke into a radiant smile. "Well, that's good," she said, wrapping her arms around my neck. "Because I'm pretty insanely in love with you, too. And that was before you brought me to this magical place."

As we kissed with the aurora shimmering overhead and the cool sea lapping around us, the world seemed full of possibility, of joy, of love.

We swam back to the dock, climbing out and wrapping ourselves in the thick towels I'd left there earlier. As we made our way back to the house, hands intertwined, I couldn't stop smiling.

"What's got you so happy?" Zaila asked, bumping her shoulder against mine.

I squeezed her hand. "Just thinking about how lucky I am, how grateful I am for this second chance at happiness."

She leaned into me, her warmth a stark contrast to my chilly skin. "Me too, Gunnar. Me, too."

Inside, we changed into dry clothes and curled up on the oversized couch in front of the fireplace. As the flames crackled and danced, casting a warm glow over the room, we continued to talk.

"You know, I used to come here to escape," I said, running my fingers through Zaila's hair. "From the pressure of the team, the expectations, the...loneliness, I guess."

She tilted her head to look at me. "And now?"

I smiled. "Now it doesn't feel like an escape. It feels like coming home, all because you're here."

Zaila's answering smile was soft, her eyes shining with unshed tears. "I love you, Gunnar Evaldson. Botched tattoos, impulsive swims, and all."

I laughed, pulling her closer. "And I love you, Zaila Monroe. With all my heart."

CHAPTER 29
Gunnar

As we drifted off to sleep that night, Zaila's nude form pressed to my side, the sound of the sea a gentle lullaby in the background, I marveled at how much my life had changed. The stark beauty of the High Coast had always been a balm to my soul, but with Zaila here, it felt truly magical.

In the morning, we woke to the sun streaming through the windows, the sea a glittering expanse of blue. Over breakfast on the terrace, we planned our day. She wanted to do a kayaking trip through the archipelago, which I was in favor of as long as a picnic followed on one of the smaller islands.

As we paddled out into the clear waters, the red granite cliffs rising majestically around us, I felt a surge of joy so intense it almost took my breath away. Zaila's laughter echoed across the water as she raced ahead, her paddle cutting through the sea with surprising skill.

"Come on, old man!" she called, her eyes sparkling with challenge. "Can't keep up?"

I grinned, digging my paddle in deeper. "Oh, it's on, Rookie!"

I took Zaila to a hidden cove near another rocky beach, and she marveled at the ever-changing landscape. As we sat on a rocky outcropping, sharing sandwiches and stolen kisses, I realized that this moment, this woman, this life was everything

I never knew I needed.

"Thank you," I said, setting down my water bottle.

Zaila blinked at me. "For what?"

I gestured around us, at the breathtaking scenery, at the space between us. "For coming here with me. For helping me remember how to live, not just exist."

She reached out, intertwining her fingers with mine. "Thank you for bringing me here. For showing me there's still beauty in the world, even after...everything."

That night, as we sat on the dock watching a spectacular sunset, Zaila turned to me with a mischievous glint in her eye. "So, Gunnar Evaldson, oil and gas tycoon, ever thought about getting that tattoo fixed?"

I laughed, shaking my head. "No. It's a reminder of a different time in my life. Plus," I added with a wink, "it's a great conversation starter."

Zaila's grin widened. "Well, in that case, how about we get matching ones?"

I raised an eyebrow. "Matching tattoos? Isn't that a bit cliché?"

She shrugged, her eyes dancing. "Maybe. But who cares? We'll make it our own."

As I looked at her, silhouetted against the painted sky, I felt my heart swell with love and gratitude. "You know what? Let's do it."

"Promise?" she asked.

"I do," I said, enjoying the words, their permanence. I considered their implications but settled for this moment. For now.

Zaila's delighted laugh rang out across the water, a sound I'd never tire of hearing. We sealed our plan with a kiss, and I was once again speechless. This vibrant, beautiful woman had turned my world upside down in the best possible way.

"How would you feel about letting the team and staff know about our relationship?" I asked. My heart thumped against my chest as I waited for her answer.

"Are you sure you want to do that?" she asked, her brows pulling tight. "I mean, I'd love that, but I don't want to make things weird…"

"Why would they be weird?" I asked.

"Because, you know, I'm your employee. And younger." Her smile grew. "And so fun and interesting," she teased. "While you like to watch stock tickers and talk about ROI."

"Hey, don't knock stocks. My company shares helped build the Wildcatters." I stared deep into her eyes. "I love you. I want everyone to know that I plan to build a life with you. The fact that we met because you came to work for my organization just means we were meant to be together."

Her eyes went hazy, and she melted against me. "Okay. Let's let everyone know you're mine."

CHAPTER 30
Zaila

Four days later, the Houston skyline glittered like a mirage as our plane descended. I pressed my forehead against the cool window, watching the city grow larger, my stomach twisting with excitement and anxiety.

"You okay, Rookie?" Gunnar's warm hand covered mine on the armrest. "I know it's sooner than either of us wanted to come back, but there wasn't enough time to reschedule the Gunnar the Goalie challenge. This is the Wildcatters' only long weekend at home for the rest of the season."

I turned to him, drinking in the sight of his rugged features softened by concern. I offered a smile that I couldn't quite make real. "Yeah, I know. I guess I just have a lot on my mind."

His blue eyes crinkled at the corners. "Nervous about the charity event?"

I shrugged, not quite ready to voice the actual source of my unease. "It's a big deal, your return to goal."

He chuckled, the sound rumbling through me. "I'm going to be just fine."

"Oh, I know that. I've seen you play."

As we taxied to the gate, my worry increased, exacerbated by everything that waited for us, for me. I'd have to go back to my parents' house, figure out what to donate, what to keep, settle in with the memories, knowing I would never make more…

That task weighed on me even more than whether my colleagues would see me as sleeping my way to the top after Gunnar made his announcement about our relationship. I thought I'd moved past that worry, but now…the mere idea made me want to hide. Jay had already insinuated as much when he'd "caught" us together a couple of weeks ago.

The terminal's muted bustle was a stark contrast to the peaceful solitude we'd left behind in Sweden. Gunnar's hand rested on the small of my back as we navigated the thin throng of businesspeople wealthy enough to fly private, a gesture both protective and possessive. It sent a thrill through me, even as it deepened my uncertainty.

How public should we be? I knew there were pictures of us together; I'd seen a couple online when I'd checked my email. Still, as I glanced over at Gunnar's closed-off expression, the memory of our time at Höga Kusten felt like a dream. I wasn't sure those beautiful days would survive in the harsh light of reality.

Gunnar's brow furrowed when he glanced down at me. "You sure you're all right, Z?"

I nodded, forcing a smile. "Just jet lag, I think."

But as we entered his spacious living room a little while later, floor-to-ceiling windows offering a breathtaking view of the city, the weight of reality crashed over me. This was Gunnar's world—a world of wealth, power, and scrutiny. A world I wasn't sure I belonged in, where I wasn't sure I wanted to belong.

I was just an orphan.

Orphan.

That word. It was back, eating at me. I hated it. Hated myself for letting it burrow into my mind.

"Make yourself at home," Gunnar said, dropping our bags by the door. "I'll order some food. Any preferences?"

I shook my head, still looking out the window. The city sprawled before me, a maze of lights and shadows. Somewhere out there was the life I'd allowed Gunnar to whisk me away from. It felt a million miles away.

What must Jay think of me now? What about Tim? The rest of the team? I hadn't given a single thought to my coworkers until this moment, but they had to be irritated by my special treatment. I hadn't even told them I was going away.

Gunnar's arms slipped around my waist, his chin resting on my shoulder. "Penny for your thoughts?"

I leaned back against him, savoring his warmth. "Just... processing, I guess. It's different here." The pressure pinged at me from all angles.

He kissed my temple. "Different doesn't have to be bad, you know."

I turned in his arms, searching his face. "Gunnar, what are we doing? I mean, us. Here. How do we navigate this?"

His expression softened. "Well, you're my love, and I'm yours, so we'll figure out what we want that to be. One day at a time, Z."

His words were supposed to soothe me, but they didn't. One day at a time was fine for a vacation fling. Now I fixated on him calling me his *love*, not his partner or girlfriend. Just *love*. What did that mean? What did I mean to him? I tried to remember all the things we'd said to each other in Sweden, but now that hardly seemed real.

Still, instead of asking him, I tried to sort it out on my own. Who I was…what I was… But my mind grew more tangled, and I battled back tears. Maybe returning to Houston was a mistake.

It *was* a mistake. I didn't want to be here, not even for the Gunnar the Goalie event I'd been instrumental in setting up. None of this mattered, not really.

I wanted to be back in our bubble in Sweden, where none of this world could touch us.

Gunnar

Later that evening, Zaila curled into the corner of my couch. The loose sleeve of her oversized sweatshirt slipped off her shoulder as she brought her knees to her chest. In that moment, she appeared fragile. I hadn't pushed her to talk on the drive back from the airport, but I disliked the shadows forming under her eyes, the way she stared into the middle distance like she was next to her mother's grave again.

Returning to Houston had been a mistake. Zaila needed more time. Or maybe I'd just needed more time with her.

"You ate almost nothing at dinner," I said as I settled on the cushion next to her.

"I wasn't hungry," she murmured.

"I know. I've watched you pick at your meals for days, remember?" I slid closer to her, wrapping my arm around her shoulders and tucking her against my side, my cheek resting on the crown of her head. "You don't have to be okay, Zaila. Not with me."

Her throat worked. "Everyone keeps telling me to be strong, that I am strong. That life will even out and go back to normal."

"That's last part is bull." My voice was sharp, but I kept my touch gentle as I rubbed my thumb along the soft skin of her neck. "You don't have to be anything you're not ready to be. And It's okay if it takes you months to be ready to be anything but here."

For a moment, she didn't respond, and then the dam broke as sobs lifted her shoulders and tears wet my shirt.

"She was all I had," Zaila whispered. "And now she's gone, and I don't know what I'm doing anymore. Work feels pointless. I feel pointless. Just…flapping in the wind. I'm alone, Gunnar. It's so scary."

As I held her, I thought of Karl, of the days after the accident when I'd walked around like a ghost in my own skin. "I remember that feeling," I told her. "You probably always will, too. But, you, Zaila Monroe, are not pointless. You make people's lives brighter every day. Mine included. Even while you're grieving your parents, I'm happier than I've been in years. I don't think you understand how much you matter to me."

Her head jerked up, eyes wide and wet. "Oh. Oh, that's so… You don't have to try to make me feel better."

I sighed. "When Karl died, I shut down. I didn't let anyone in. It took years—meeting you even—to help me remember how to breathe. How to smile. To tell those dumb, horrible jokes that make me laugh even as my throat tightens because I'll always miss him. But it's okay now, because those corny one-liners make you smile."

I pulled her into my chest as her tears fell again. We sat for a long time, the only sound the hum of the fridge and her quiet sniffles. Lifting her head, her eyes red-rimmed but with fewer shadows, she finally whispered, "Do you ever think about what comes next? Not just work. I mean us."

I stilled. No one asked me questions like that. I'd been so careful not to jinx whatever this was, not to name it too soon. "Yes," I admitted. "I do. Every day. I thought I'd made that clear when I told you I was going to announce our relationship."

She tilted her head back to search my face. "And you're still going to do that?"

"Absolutely."

"This house," she whispered. "Does it ever feel like...*ours*?"

The question was so quiet I almost missed it. I cupped her face. "It could be. If you want it to be. Or I'll buy you another. Something you can enjoy decorating or renovating—make it your own."

Her breath hitched. "You'd do that for me?"

I skimmed my palm over her head, enjoying the silkiness of her tresses. "I'd do just about anything for you."

She straddled my lap. "Take me upstairs. To bed."

"Are you sure that's what you need?"

"Yes." She nodded. "And what I want. I need to feel alive, in this moment." She bit her lip, her dark brows tugging over her nose. "When you love me, it's like...like we're creating connections, these lines that hold us together. I...I love being tethered to you, Gunnar."

I swept her into my arms and hurried up the stairs as the hunger between us burned bright, then brighter. Being skin to skin with Zaila was a religious experience—a form of worship. The hunger between us grew with each coupling, as if we cemented the bond Zaila spoke of, and I exulted in it.

After, I held her close, trailing my lips along to her damp temple. "We'll figure this out, Zaila," I promised. "Together."

CHAPTER 31
Zaila

The next morning dawned bright and clear. I stood in front of the mirror, smoothing down my structured, boiled wool jacket. It was the last item my mother and I had bought together, and the lovely, bold green complemented my black midi dress and pumps. The woman staring back at me looked polished, professional...and overwhelmed.

Managing these events hadn't bothered me before, so I didn't understand where this anxiety had come from or why my mind refused to focus on the most basic of tasks. I bit my lip to keep it from quivering.

"You look beautiful," Gunnar said, appearing behind me. His hands settled on my shoulders, warm and reassuring.

I met his eyes in the reflection. "Gunnar, I... I'm not sure how to act today. Around the team, the donors and media... Should we, I don't know, keep things professional?"

Hurt flicked across his face before he schooled his features into a neutral expression. "Whatever you're comfortable with. I won't pressure you." He gave me a brief squeeze before he pulled back—much too quickly.

"I just...don't know when you plan to tell people about us, so..." I wished he'd wrap his arms around me, hold me tight, and refuse to let me go to this meeting.

"It's on my agenda," he said, his tone cooler than I wanted. "I plan to deal with it this week."

"Plan to deal"…like a business transaction. Dread settled, low and noxious, in my belly as we headed to Gunnar's car. The ride to the arena was quiet as the tension between us rose.

Gunnar squeezed my hand. "Ready?"

No. I wanted him to take me home. I longed to bury my face in his chest. I nodded because I didn't trust my voice, and after a moment we stepped out into the arena, and all eyes turned toward us.

"Gunnar!" A statuesque blonde in sky-high heels rushed up to air-kiss his cheeks. "We've missed you! And who's this little doll?"

I gritted my teeth even as I wilted under her scrutiny. Gunnar's hand found the small of my back again, steadying me. Yet he removed it too quickly, and the feeling of falling returned.

"This is Zaila Monroe," he said, his voice calm and professional—just like I'd asked for. So why did the distance make me feel *so bad*? "She's been instrumental in organizing today's event."

The collected group's smiles were polite, but I could see the questions in their eyes. Someone ushered us inside for the press conference before anyone could ask.

The next few hours passed in a blur of flashing cameras, microphones, and answers scripted by the PR department. Gunnar was in his element, charming the reporters with his trademark wit and self-deprecating humor. I stood to the side, clipboard clutched in my white, numb fingers, the perfect picture of an efficient assistant.

I hated every minute.

Sure, I was proud of Gunnar's calm command of the room, but I longed to be by his side, acknowledged as more than just staff. Yet I'd placed myself in this role. I felt an ever-growing sense of isolation as I realized how impossible it felt to fit into Gunnar's world.

As the press conference drew to a close, a reporter approached me. "So, Zaila, right? How long have you been working with Gunnar?"

I plastered on a smile. "Oh, just a few months. I'm still learning the ropes."

She nodded, her eyes sharp. "Must be exciting, working with him. He's quite the catch, you know."

Before I could formulate a response, Gunnar appeared at my side. "Ladies, if you'll excuse us. Zaila and I have some last-minute details to go over before the challenge."

He guided me away, and as soon as we were out of earshot, he leaned in close. "You okay? You looked like you needed rescuing."

I laughed, but it turned into a sigh. "My hero. Thanks for the save."

Gunnar's eyes searched my face. "Z, if this is too much—"

"No," I cut him off. "I'm fine. Really. Just adjusting. Everything…everything is harder." My voice broke.

"Yeah, I get that. If you need to step back—"

"Don't give me that out," I whispered. "I… I'll take it, and then I'll loathe myself for taking it."

He nodded, but I could see concern in his eyes.

"Time for you to suit up," I said, managing a smile.

Gunnar closed his eyes and sighed before turned toward the

locker room for final preparations. As he went, I felt adrift in a sea of uncertainty.

I headed for the ice and found the arena buzzing. Fans had turned out in droves. So many, in fact, that we'd sold out the event. I chuckled at the homemade Gunnar the Goalie signs I saw around the seats. I strapped on my headset, and as Gunnar waddled onto the ice in full goalie gear, the crowd erupted in cheers and laughter.

"All right, folks," I announced, my voice echoing through the arena, thanks to my mic. "It's time to see if our fearless leader can stop a puck as well as he can run a hockey team!"

The players lined up, each taking a turn firing shots at Gunnar. To everyone's surprise, Gunnar made nearly as many saves as the team's regular goalie, earning him heartfelt roars and high-pitched whistles of appreciation.

I couldn't stop smiling, and now on familiar turf, I felt more at ease. My hot man had the juice, and I was all over him showing off. I turned to the camera, offering a mischievous grin for the sake of social media. "And now, the moment you've all been waiting for. Thanks to your votes, the player taking the last shot on Gunnar the Goalie is—drum roll, please... Luka 'The Sniper' Stol!"

The crowd went wild as Luka, the team's star forward, skated to center ice. I braced myself, trying to look confident despite a flash of worry. *Please don't break any of his bones, Stolly. Or any teeth. Or anything...*

Luka wound up, his stick a blur as he unleashed a blistering slap shot. Time seemed to slow as the puck hurtled towards the net. Gunnar threw himself to the left, and by some miracle, his glove shot out at the last second, snagging the puck mid-air. The arena exploded in cheers as Gunnar lay sprawled on the ice, the puck clutched in his glove.

I rushed onto the ice, my device still broadcasting. "I can't believe it, folks! Gunnar the Goalie has done the impossible!"

As the players helped Gunnar to his feet, I felt a surge of pride. The way this event had brought the team and the fans together, this was what I'd wanted to achieve—okay, and maybe a bit of personal glory.

But even as I cheered, a part of me felt separate. Paloma and Vivian greeted me, bringing me into their group, just as they always did, but I remained detached. Nothing made sense, and if I stopped to think for even a moment, all I wanted was to leave.

That scared me more than anything else, because from the moment I'd learned about this position, I'd been so excited—not just to experience the sport live, but to live out a dream I'd shared with my father. Now it seemed lost, just as I was lost.

As the final buzzer sounded, marking the end of the challenge, the arena erupted in applause. Gunnar raised his stick in salute, his face flushed with exertion and joy. He lifted his head to where I stood near the ice, and our eyes met. He smiled, raising his hand to his lips, but his teammates mobbed him, and he was swept up in a sea of congratulations.

I was left wondering what he'd been about to do. A part of me didn't care.

"Come on," Vivian said, smiling. "Let's get down to the locker room so you can congratulate your man."

I smiled and nodded, though all I wanted was to disappear. I caught a brief glimpse of Paloma's frown and Ida Jane's concerned expression before Vivian whisked me away.

Gunnar pulled me into his arms the moment he walked out of the locker room, and I melted against him. He smelled fresh and clean, and his eyes danced with excitement. "That was even more fun than I'd hoped it would be," he said as he nuzzled his nose into my hair. "Thank you for setting it up, Zaila."

"Of course," I said, smiling.

He studied me for a long moment—long enough that I dropped my gaze. "Are you tired? Want to head home?"

I did, more than anything, but I didn't want to dim his joy. Gunnar rarely shared his emotions with the Wildcatters, and I wanted them to learn what a fantastic man he was.

"Of course not. We have a party to go to," I said, forcing a smile. I was pretty sure I failed, though, because Gunnar's expression dimmed.

"Let's go," I said, squeezing his hand.

"Hey, Z," Jeff called, waving as he and Jay walked by. I stiffened, not at all interested in talking to the self-centered man who'd gone out of his way to ruin his standing in the community and my pleasure in my job.

Gunnar wrapped his arm around my shoulders and led me away. "He seems friendly."

"I suppose." I said. "I know it's my job to work with him, but I just...I don't—"

"I'll talk to Jay tomorrow," Gunnar said. "I've been meaning to do that."

I stopped walking and faced him. "Don't. Please don't get involved, because that undermines my position with the team. While I don't care for Jeff personally, I can deal with him. And I need to. Myself."

Gunnar pressed his lips into a tight, unyielding line. "Fine."

I sighed. "Thanks. Now, about your party…"

"It's not my party."

I giggled. "Oh, you ridiculous man. Of course this is your party! Now, let's get you to it."

~

By the time we arrived at the upscale bistro Jay had rented for the occasion, the after-party was in full swing. Music pounded, and laughter filled the air as people sipped a wide range of beverages. The moment we strolled in, the players hailed Gunnar, and he disappeared towards the bar to hold court as the group hung on his every word. He waved me over, but I hesitated.

The reporter from earlier, a young woman named Melissa, sidled up to me. Tim had confided that he didn't like her, nor did Keelie, because she'd written a piece about how Cormac was past his prime. But Melissa and Jeff seemed to get along well, and Jay called her first when he wanted to increase visibility for a story.

While there was no accounting for preferences, I was pretty sure Melissa's camaraderie with the people who made me uncomfortable told me everything I needed to know.

"Quite a turnout, huh?" she said. "The Catters really know how to throw a party."

I nodded, grateful for the distraction. "Wildcatters. The complete name matters because it's an oil expression—"

"I don't really care about that." Melissa's manicured hand found my arm. "Listen, honey. A word of advice? Don't get too attached to the big boss man. Men like Gunnar... They're not the settling-down type. Trust me, I've seen it before, ad nauseum."

My stomach clenched because I was beginning to fear she was right. The moment we'd stepped out of our bubble in Sweden, Gunnar had seemed to cool to the idea of announcing our relationship. He hadn't pushed back at all when I'd asked earlier if I should keep it professional between us. I'd so hoped he'd tell me no, that he'd already sent out a press release. But he hadn't. And now I felt like a flag whipping in the wind, unsure where my emotions would flit next. The instability made me long for my mother, and a wave of grief gripped my chest.

Nothing felt right. I made my way to a quiet corner with a glass of wine I had no intention of drinking. Gunnar still held court, laughing and joking with Cormac and Stolly now. I leaned against the wall, feeling like an imposter. Was I just a little orphan girl playing dress-up in a world where I didn't belong?

As the night wore on, the doubts I'd been pushing aside since we left Sweden grew louder. What were Gunnar and I doing? How could this possibly work? He was a team owner and also an athlete who still had enough talent to compete against his own first line. And I was...an intern with a crush.

I startled, hating that line of thought. It wasn't true—I knew that. I tried to remember how I'd felt in Sweden. But I'd felt so alone since my parents died. After losing my mother, I was... adrift. I wanted to clutch tightly to Gunnar, and I believed he did love me, yet I worried I was too clingy. Too needy.

I set down my untouched wine and slipped out onto the balcony. The night air was warm, heavy with the scent of jasmine. In the distance, the Houston skyline glittered, beautiful and indifferent.

"There you are."

I turned to find Gunnar in the doorway, his tie loosened, hair slightly mussed. He looked so handsome, so out of my league.

"Splendid party," I noted.

He came to stand beside me, his arm brushing mine. "It would be if you were inside enjoying it."

I shrugged, not meeting his eyes. "I'm just taking a breather."

Gunnar's hand found mine, intertwining our fingers. "Z, talk to me. What's going on in that beautiful head of yours?"

I took a deep breath, the words I'd been holding back all day threatening to spill out. But looking at him—this man I'd fallen for so completely—I couldn't bring myself to voice my doubts.

I wasn't strong enough to stand without him. Not with my mother's death still so fresh. Anger and self-loathing twisted in my gut, and I struggled to breathe normally. I'd become the very thing my father had worked tirelessly to prevent. I was a woman who needed a man to help her through this world. I wasn't strong enough to stand alone.

Not yet…

Soon. I would take the next necessary step soon, but not yet.

I forced a smile. "Just overwhelmed, I guess. It's been a long day."

Gunnar studied me, his blue eyes searching. Finally, he nodded. "Okay. But remember, Zaila, you can talk to me. About anything."

As he pulled me into a hug, I buried my nose in his chest and breathed in his familiar cologne. I wanted to believe him, wanted to pour out all my fears and insecurities.

But standing here, surrounded by the glittering trappings of Gunnar's world, I'd never felt lonelier.

CHAPTER 32
Zaila

The Houston humidity caused my hair to poof and my eyes to burn before I'd even pushed through the Wildcatters office's glass doors on Monday morning. I adjusted my tote on my shoulder, my muscles tender from the tension that had ratcheted up with each day back in Houston. I missed Sweden, the sauna, and not worrying about what people thought of me. All of that had been easier to hold at bay while my mother was alive—while someone in this world loved me, knew me, and understood I'd never seek a rich, powerful man for his riches or his power.

My grief surged, still raw and jagged as a broken skate blade. I'd struggled to force it down so I could return to the rhythm of work. My mother would have wanted that. *"Live, Zaila. Don't let me hold you back."* Mom's words swirled through my head as I headed down the hallway.

"Morning, Z," Jay called from the cluster of desks that formed the social media bullpen in the center of the floor. He was too chipper, his smile a touch too wide. "Enjoy your vacation with the big boss man? Would have been nice if you'd told me, your actual boss, that you were taking vacation time you haven't yet earned."

I closed my eyes and swallowed. "I buried my mother last week, Jay." My voice was low, my throat raw as I fought the tears that pressed against my eyes. "I'm sorry about the short notice. I… It never crossed my mind."

"Your mom?" For a moment, Jay's expression softened, but then he lifted his chin. "Yeah, well, you should have. Since this is a workplace, and I'm your boss."

Tim came around the corner in time to hear those last words, and his expression turned murderous. He shoved himself between the two of us and wrapped me in a hug. "I'm so sorry about your mother, Z. Paloma stopped by and let us know what happened— well, those of us who were here. Jay's been taking long lunches." He shot Jay a glare as he placed his hands on my shoulder. "You okay? Ready to be back?"

No, I wasn't, and all I wanted to do was turn around and go back to Gunnar's house. Instead, I offered Tim a smile and nodded. "Can't wait."

He stayed at my side as I booted up my laptop and opened the dashboard. "What's all this?" I asked. "I didn't set up anything last week…"

I frowned as I skimmed the engagement numbers. After reading through the analytics, I froze.

The top-performing content wasn't A Day in the Life. It wasn't the nutritionist highlight I'd stayed up half the night editing. It wasn't the heartfelt clip about the team's anti-hate initiative.

It was Jeff.

"What's going on?" I asked.

Tim circled my desk and studied my screen. There were dozens of posts, an entire string of clips and carousels featuring the cocky rookie: Jeff laughing in the locker room, Jeff practicing extra drills, Jeff grinning with kids at a youth skate event. My Wildcatters header graphic—*mine*—now showed Jeff dead center, bigger than even Cormac, the captain.

My throat dried. I had made none of those edits. I hadn't been in the office. I hadn't had my laptop.

"Jay?" Tim called. "Did you queue all these Jeff posts?"

He ambled over, coffee in hand. "Hmm? Oh, yeah. Jeff's content has been fantastic lately. Fans love him."

"I never signed off on this," I said, meeting his eyes.

He shrugged. "It's all Wildcatters footage. It's fair game."

"But the balance—" My pulse kicked hard. "This looks like… like a personal rebrand. He's front and center on every channel. That's not how we—"

"Relax." Jay sipped his coffee. "You're making him look good. That's our job, right? Elevating players. And you happen to be the best at it."

I stared at him. *Making him look good?* This wasn't elevating— it was spotlighting one player at the expense of the team. Gunnar would hate it.

My phone buzzed on the desk. A text from Ida Jane lit the screen:

What's going on? Everyone's saying you're Jeff's PR girl now. Call me.

Before I could respond, a shadow cut across my desk.

"Ms. Monroe."

My stomach dropped. *Natalie.*

"Ms. Patel," I managed. My throat felt full of glass shards.

"Conference room. Now." Tim moved to follow, but she held

up her hand. "This is between Ms. Monroe and me."

"Oh, I'm coming along," Jay said, his expression gleeful.

The short walk felt like a perp march. The other staff on the floor pretended to be busy, but their sidelong glances burned. Inside the glass-walled conference room, Natalie didn't sit. She stood at the head of the table, shoulders squared, jaw tight. Jay closed the door with theatrical care.

"I'll be direct," Natalie said, her voice cold enough to frost the glass. "Why am I hearing that one of my interns is running a shadow campaign to rehabilitate Jeff Cross's reputation?"

My knees almost buckled. "What? No. That's not—"

Natalie cut me off with a raised hand. "The board flagged it this morning, and Mr. Evaldson is currently doing damage control. Engagement numbers spiked around Jeff. A suspicious concentration. Sponsors are asking why one untested rookie is suddenly the face of the franchise."

Was this why Gunnar hadn't told anyone about us? He must have known about these posts. Maybe he thought I'd done it to… I couldn't think of why. Spite him? No, he knew me better than that. I needed to talk to him. I reached for my phone, but at Natalie's sharp grunt, I pulled my hand back. "That's not—"

"Then explain this." Natalie slid a packet of printouts across the table. Hashtags. Clips. Graphics. My admin login had been used to credit every single one during the past week, while my laptop sat on my desk here and I was in Sweden.

My breath stuttered. I flipped through them with trembling fingers. The timestamps matched nights I'd been at my mother's bedside, then in Sweden with Gunnar. "Let me just contact

Gunnar," I said.

Natalie made an impatient noise, seeming surprised when I pulled out my cell phone. When Gunnar didn't answer, I sent him a message.

Natalie had said he was with the board. He'd get back to me, soon, and all of this would get cleared up. I sucked in a breath, calming myself so I could answer Natalie rationally.

"Yes, I gave Zaila Jeff's account, but it appears she's running a personal PR campaign for him on Wildcatters channels," Jay said with a smile. "That would be…a serious conflict of interest, wouldn't it?"

"That's not true!" my voice cracked. "I never made these. Someone's using my login. I haven't even been in the office for the past week."

That someone was obviously Jay. He'd said as much when Tim asked him a minute ago, hadn't he? God, how could I have considered him my friend? Given him the benefit of the doubt so many times?

Natalie's eyes narrowed. "So you're saying your credentials were compromised?"

"Yes. I was out of the country with Gunnar, on bereavement leave." I raised my gaze. "We left the day after my mother's funeral." Jay's expression was unreadable, but something hard flickered in his eyes. "I didn't have my computer because it all happened so suddenly."

"From where I'm standing? The evidence still points to you," Natalie said. "And evidently you have a close relationship with the team owner, so this is a very, very bad look, Ms. Monroe."

She leaned closer. "Gunnar's going to be censured over this, maybe fined. You will be, too. It will not be pretty, which means my entire team will work 'round the clock to fix your mistake."

Natalie turned to Jay. "And you—you were supposed to supervise this young woman, which obviously you didn't do. Not only that, but Mr. Evaldson came to me last week and reported that you were dumping all of your work on Ms. Monroe's schedule."

Jay's mouth dropped open. "That's not true! I do my work."

"Apparently, you don't. Because if you did, I wouldn't be in here explaining how bad this is for all of us, now would I?"

My chest heaved. *Don't cry. Don't let them see you break.* "Ms. Patel," I said, forcing each word past my raw throat. "I would never compromise the team. Never. My work, my loyalty is to the Wildcatters. To Gun—er, Mr. Evaldson."

Jay's eyes flared. "The integrity of this organization is not negotiable," he said. "You're right, Natalie. I'll suspend Zaila's admin access while IT reviews the logs. Until then, you're relieved of posting duties, Ms. Monroe. In fact, go home."

The floor tilted under me. Posting was my job. Without it, I was nothing here.

Gunnar, please respond. I need you…

My phone remained silent.

"You're relieved as well, Mr. Welks," Natalie said. "I'll be posting until we can sort this situation out."

"Me? But—"

"But *nothing*. As Ms. Monroe stated, she was out of town. All these posts came from her laptop, which was in this building."

Ms. Patel pointed to the IP address. "If she wasn't here, which is easy enough to confirm, then you'd better believe I'll be looking for the real culprit, and I will not be shy about letting the world know exactly what kind of creep would turn their jealousy against someone who's grieving." With that, Natalie turned on her high heels and disappeared.

I raised my gaze from the table to Jay. "I thought we were friends," I said as I pushed past the emotion choking me.

Jay shrugged as he looked away. "Lydia was right about you. And you were dead wrong about me."

Back at my desk, I collected the last of my belongings, my skin burning as the security guard stood behind me, watching my every move as if I'd actually do something nefarious. Still, a stubborn kernel kept expecting Gunnar to step in, to clear this up—to explain that we were together and I'd never betray him or the organization this way. *But what if he didn't know that?* I knew my emotions were spiraling, but I couldn't seem to bring them down.

Tim stepped into my office—my former office—his face white. "Jay took this too far. I'll get it sorted. Don't worry."

I sniffled and offered him a smile. "I haven't felt right since my mother died, Tim. Maybe this is fate's way of telling me I'm not meant to be here." I nodded to the security guard and headed toward the door.

"You know Gunnar's upstairs right now, fighting for you," Tim said.

For a moment that warmed my heart, but then it all crumbled. I used my shoulder to swipe away the tear on my cheek. "He shouldn't have to do that. All I wanted was for my work to stand on its own. Instead..." I'd made everything so much harder, so much worse. He was busy doing damage control because of me. Why had I ever thought we could make this work? My voice cracked. "I need to go." Tears streamed down my cheeks, which is why I didn't see Jay. I bumped into him as I stepped into the hallway and stumbled back. He gripped my elbows to steady me.

"Don't touch me," I snapped. "Don't ever, *ever* come near me again."

"Z—"

"Leave it, Jay," Tim snapped as we continued down the hall. "I told her to watch out for you, but clearly none of us knew what a true jerk you were. Now, the rest of the team and I will be marching your ass upstairs so you can tell Gunnar exactly what you did."

"I didn't do anything—"

"Then it won't be hard to explain your weekly lunches with Lydia Flores or Jeff Cross—"

"Are you spying on me?" Jay cut across Tim's tirade.

I frantically pressed the elevator button.

"I didn't have to," Tim replied. "Everyone knows you've had it out for Zaila since the mascot—"

I stepped in, and the elevator closed behind me, so I didn't hear the rest of that argument. Just as well. I was too busy falling apart.

CHAPTER 32
Gunnar

This meeting was a farce, one I didn't have time for. It seemed obvious that Jay had ambushed Zaila. According to Paloma and Vivian, Jay been at lunch multiple times with our former social media director, Lydia Flores. Still, I couldn't walk out of this meeting—not until I fully understood the board's issue with Zaila and the media backlash with Jeff. Protecting Zaila was my priority, even above the franchise.

That realization gave me a moment's pause, but then I decided I'd finally found my happiness, and I would not let anyone destroy it. *Dammit.* I'd *just* signed off on the press release about Zaila and me, and instead of celebrating that happy news with lunch in my office, I was neck-deep in this shitshow because I'd been overly confident in thinking I'd handled Jay.

Clearly I had not.

As if I'd conjured him, Jay stepped into the boardroom, fidgety and sweaty, with seemingly the entire third floor behind him. Tim led the group, his cheeks flushed. "Mr. Evaldson, Jay needs to speak to the board for a moment, please," Tim said. Even his clipped voice showed an anger I wouldn't have believed possible from the mild-mannered graphics director.

"We're in the middle of a meeting," snapped Don Rosenfeld, the president of a large regional bank and my oldest director.

"Which is why you need to hear this directly from the acting social media director," Tim said firmly. "It will be enlightening and should speed up the review process."

I would never have expected Tim, of all people, to interrupt a board meeting, but clearly, whatever Jay had done made it necessary in his mind. I studied Jay, wondering why I hadn't fired him. Well, I couldn't do all that work myself, and at first I'd needed to maintain distance from Zaila—and now I wanted time with her. Both those reasons had now come back to bite my ass.

"You really should hear what he has to say," Tim said, wiping his upper lip. "Especially since it has to do with the board's desire to censure Ms. Monroe for activities she never took part in."

With that, the board erupted.

"What?"

"How do you know that?"

"Why is everyone so captivated by this young lady?"

The questions flew around the room, fast and furious, but I kept my gaze firmly on Tim, and he met my eyes when he spoke again. "Some individuals inspire loyalty because of their actions. The team has made it clear that they will not let this go because Zaila is one of those people. I didn't just miss her this past week…"

I gritted my teeth, jealousy rearing its ugly head.

"…I found the quality of what we produce to be lacking while she was out on bereavement leave. Notably, that's the timeframe of the posts in question, while her laptop was on her desk." As Tim laid out the details, Jay flinched, his expression pinched.

"I've noted that our social engagement is down by half, outside of Jeff's posts," Silas Whittaker noted.

"That's because Zaila is the best at navigating our accounts," Tim explained. "And while she created most of the content that ended up on Jeff's pages—"

"So she was a cheat?" Don asked.

I wanted to punch him, but I remained in my chair…barely.

"Jay, why don't you explain exactly what happened last week while Zaila was on bereavement leave?" Tim said, nodding for the other man to step forward.

Jay shot Tim a poisonous look before he met my gaze. "I was the acting media lead, and I overrode HR so I could access Zaila Monroe's login information. I posted to Jeff's account, making it look like Zaila was favoring him. I adapted Zaila's pre-written content and hashtags and set up a schedule like she usually does for posting. That was wrong of me, and I take full responsibility for the breach. Ms. Monroe has acted with integrity throughout her time here. She led the charge in correcting our team culture and protecting our brand. We should thank her, not question her."

I leaned forward. "Lydia Flores, the former social media manager, was involved in this scheme?"

Jay swallowed. "Y-yes. It was her idea."

"Because?" Tim prompted.

Jay sighed. "She was jealous of Ms. Monroe's relationship with Mr. Evaldson. She was also seeking retribution for what she saw as Zaila getting her fired. And, well, Jeff is a distant relative, so she was angry about his treatment by the team as well."

"You're telling me that all this hassle—all these distractions— were because of petty jealousy?" Silas asked.

Jay gave a stiff nod.

Silas ran his hands down his face. "Christ. I just… That's awful. And you let Zaila be the scapegoat."

Jay gave another nod.

"That's slimy," Don muttered. "You're done here. I refuse to allow the destruction of someone's reputation because you were butthurt."

We all blinked at Don, who was close to eighty, for a long moment. He shrugged. "My grandkids taught me the slang. Seemed appropriate."

"Very," Tim muttered.

"Well, I think this meeting has been sorted," I said, rising from the table, buttoning my suit jacket. "Which is why I'm going to have my HR department work diligently through the staff to ensure such an issue doesn't resurface."

"You definitely need to get the staff's act together, unless you want it impacting the team's performance," Silas warned. "We have enough trouble there already."

I met each set of eyes around the table before I met Tim's, then Jay's. "You have my word that I'll handle everyone's issues with speed and efficiency. Jay, as Mr. Rosenfeld noted, your services are no longer required."

Jay swallowed as a strangled sound issued from his throat.

"We haven't decided if we're censoring you yet," Don informed me.

"Considering that has to be unanimous, and I'm voting no, it's already decided," Silas said.

I nodded his way in thanks. "Now, if you'll excuse me," I announced. "I have some details to iron out with the team."

"The Jeff issue is long overdue," Silas added.

"That's my first order. Tim, tell Zaila I'll be down to talk to her as soon as I can."

"Security led her out of the building ten minutes ago," Tim said.

"What?" I scrambled toward the door.

"Jay insisted she be removed," he explained.

I ground my teeth, frustration pumping through my veins. Now that Jay Welks was no longer employed, I had to get rid of Jeff Cross and his cancer on the team, but all I really wanted was to find Zaila.

Soon. As soon as I managed this clusterfuck, I'd find my way to her arms.

CHAPTER 33
Gunnar

The thud of sticks slapping pucks and the rumble of voices punctuated by whistles echoed through the arena. I paused inside the tunnel as I looked over the ice, homing in on my target.

Most of the CATS were now friends with Zaila, so they had to be aware of the issue Jay and Jeff had caused with my staff, and evidently Jeff's antics were once again dragging down the team—something Silas had told me just as Leon had popped his head through my door earlier, stating that the board had convened and requested me in the conference room.

Now that I knew what that had been about, I returned to the Jeff issue. As I rounded the corner into the arena, Jeff grinned at the offensive line, skating lazy circles as if he owned the ice. Stol, Naese, and the rest of the players avoided looking directly at them, like spectators at a fight they didn't want to stop but didn't dare join.

My jaw flexed. *This ends today.*

I descended the steps to the rink, boots echoing. Heads turned. The chatter died. Players nudged one another as I walked toward the boards.

"Cross." My voice carried, low and lethal. "Locker room. Now."

Jeff's grin faltered for a fraction of a second, then returned, cocky as ever. He flipped his stick up, resting it across his shoulders as though this were some game. "Sure thing, boss. We need to strategize about my brand, right?"

Murmurs rippled through the players.

My brand.

The words slashed across my conscience. I didn't wait. I turned on my heel and strode toward the tunnel. Jeff followed, sauntering like he was on the way to a photo op.

As we entered, the locker room smelled of sweat, soap, and old leather, which was the Wildcatters' cocktail. The other players trailed in behind Jeff, unwilling to miss what was about to go down.

Jeff flung himself onto the bench, sprawling like a teenager in detention. "What's the emergency? Didn't like the posts Zaila queued up for me?" His grin widened. "She's got a real eye for my best angles."

The words hit like a sucker punch. My vision narrowed. *Zaila.* He's dragging her name through this filth. I forced my hands to unclench. "You think this is a joke, Cross?"

Jeff shrugged. "Not my fault your golden girl figured out what sells. I mean, the engagement numbers don't lie. Fans love me. Sponsors love me. Maybe she does too—"

"Enough." The word cracked like a whip.

Jeff leaned back, smirk still in place, but there was a flicker of unease in his eyes now. "Hey, don't shoot the messenger. If she wants to build my rep while she's crying over her mom, that's—"

I moved before I thought. I slammed my fist into the locker behind Jeff's head, rattling the metal. Jeff flinched despite himself.

"Zaila's mother died last week, Cross, and you took advantage of that." I raised my eyes so that I met each of my players' stony gazes. "Her laptop was on her desk, not with her. I know because Zaila was with me last week."

Cormac and Maxim nodded, and Stolly and Naese crossed their arms over their chests, eyes narrowed, looking like club bouncers.

"This organization," I said, my tone sharp, "is built on respect. For the game. For the team. For the people who give their lives to it. You, Cross, have shown none."

Jeff scoffed. "I've shown plenty. You just can't handle that I've got charisma. You old guys—Cormac, Stolly—you're all jealous. I'm the future, and Zaila saw it. She—"

"Say her name again," I growled, "and you'll leave here in an ambulance."

A hush swept the room. Never had I threatened violence. I had never shown even a crack in my control. That's why I'd let the guys follow us in. I needed them to keep me from doing something rash, as well as act as witnesses as I tossed Jeff to the curb.

Cormac stepped forward, folding his arms over his massive chest. "We won't tell if you want to follow through on that."

Maxim cracked his knuckles. "Half-assed drills. Late to practice. Trash talk about wives. And now this crap with Zaila?" His accent thickened with anger. "I'd be more than happy to teach him a lesson."

Jeff barked a laugh. "You guys are pathetic. Hiding behind Daddy Evaldson because you can't handle a little competition. I've already got a brand. I'll be fine without you."

I stared at the pathetic little shit for a long, cold beat before I smiled. "Good. Because you're done here."

The words dropped like a guillotine.

Jeff blinked, the smirk sliding off his face. "What?"

"You're off the roster. Right. Now. Your contract buyout papers will be on your agent's desk within the hour. Security will escort you out. You are no longer a Wildcatter." I leaned closer. "If I have my way, you'll never play in the NHL again."

A stunned silence. Then, as if a pressure valve had released, mutters of approval rolled through the room.

Jeff surged to his feet, face mottled red. "You can't do that. I'll take this to the press. I'll tell them everything about your little intern sweetheart and how you let her run—"

Cormac moved in, fisting in Jeff's jersey, yanking him nose to nose. "Say one more word about her," he said, "and you won't have a face left to take to the press."

Jeff swallowed hard. For the first time, genuine fear flickered.

I inclined my head toward the door. "Out."

Two security guards appeared, no doubt brought by Silas, who now stood just inside the locker room door. Jeff tried to shrug them off, but they hauled him toward the exit, his protests echoing off tile and steel. He was still in his skates.

When the door slammed shut, silence fell like a weighted blanket.

I turned back to the room. "You give me your best. Every day. You respect each other." I thumped the large, handpainted Wildcatters logo on the wall. "That's the deal. If you can't do that, you don't belong here."

After a beat, Cormac stepped forward. "We've got your back, boss."

Nods passed from man to man. For the first time in weeks, the air felt breathable, almost relaxed—as close to *right* as it could be. The players would get back to an equilibrium quickly.

But my chest didn't lighten. I needed to find out what had happened to Zaila. I needed to fix it.

Shit. I'd known Jay was a problem. I'd known Jeff was, too. But I hadn't handled either situation correctly, and Zaila had paid the price.

The organization's halls were quiet, almost as if the staff held its breath. I passed through the social media bullpen, and the faint whispers between employees silenced. Tim had told me Zaila was gone, but my guts twisted when I noted her empty desk, her dark office, her laptop still sitting open, much like the wound I'm sure it caused her to be accused of disloyalty.

I'd now done what the team needed, protected my players and removed Jeff's cancerous presence. Cormac was happy, and the rest of the players were relieved. The organization would be stronger for it.

And yet…Zaila wasn't here because of my fuckup—my hubris that had told me I knew best how to deal with any situation. Just like with Karl. I'd been sure I should go to that party, sure it would be fun. Instead, because I'd mouthed off to the wrong people, angry with my brother for trying to keep me safe, I'd done much worse than simply hurt him. I'd gotten Karl killed. And I'd brought this situation to Zaila's feet because I'd decided

I could get Jeff to see reason. My overconfident foolishness had wrecked everything again.

My dead, beloved brother.

My grieving, beloved woman.

I kept fucking up with the *most* important people in my life.

I tried to call her again, but I was directed to voicemail; she must have turned off her phone. Dammit. I really wanted to talk to her, to make sure she was okay. She hadn't responded to my texts, but I still sent another.

I turned away from Zaila's empty desk and walked toward the exit. Each step was heavy, final, the weight of a man who had won the battle but failed to secure the only victory that mattered. I had to make this right with Zaila.

CHAPTER 34
Zaila

The comments from Natalie and Jay echoed through my mind for the rest of the day. I'd considered going home to my parents' house, but I couldn't stomach being there without them. With nowhere else to go, I'd ended up at Gunnar's, just as I had for weeks. Their words circled through my head as I circled the living room yet again.

"PR spin... Gunnar's gold digger... Unprofessional..."

I didn't fit in Gunnar's world, and people immediately assumed the worst of me. They immediately began talking about me. Natalie had made it clear that when most people looked at me, they didn't see Gunnar's partner. They saw someone temporary.

I couldn't do temporary—I wouldn't. I made another loop around the living room as doubts slipped under my skin. Hadn't I wondered if he really meant it before? Just last night, when he'd rolled close and whispered "*love you*" against my hair. I'd wanted to believe those words—him. God, I wanted to. But everything else seemed to work against that.

I smoothed my palms over my skirt, staring at my reflection in the darkened window. The woman who looked back seemed small, uncertain. Not the Zaila who walked into boardrooms without flinching. I was no longer the woman Daddy would be proud of. I was flailing...failing.

If I stayed here with Gunnar, I'd lose myself piece by piece. I already was. This uncertainty about my place, and about whether I even had an internship at this point, only increased my anxiety as I waited for Gunnar to make our relationship real, as he'd promised to do. Instead, I floundered, unsure and unaware of what was happening—between us but also within my team at work, let alone the larger organization.

I watched the press conference, my stomach rolling and dropping before it hardened as Gunnar ended it, stepping away from the mic without ever mentioning that he and I were dating. He'd barely mentioned me at all—instead focusing on Jeff, Jay, and Lydia, making sure to name them and detail their part in the plot to distract and hurt the Wildcatters organization.

Perhaps I was just a footnote.

That thought caused more hurt and confusion to grow, so perhaps it was better to leave before Gunnar pushed me out. *Yes.* That was smart. I'd walk away while I could still stand on my own two feet. Here I just seemed to sink deeper and deeper into quicksand.

It was past time for me to get on with my life. To find something where I wouldn't be temporary.

Gunnar

This whole day had been anticlimactic, though it should have felt like a victory. Jeff Cross could no longer cause chaos or pain, and the Wildcatters could breathe again. Instead of relief, though, for the entire drive home, Zaila's empty office weighed on my mind.

When I entered, the house was quiet. Zaila sat at the kitchen island, her long, elegant fingers wrapped around a mug of tea. The lamplight caught the purplish smudges under her eyes. She lifted her head and gave me a polite smile, the kind you'd give a stranger holding open a door.

"An eventful day," she murmured.

"Yes, and I was frustrated because I missed you," I said. "I'm so sorry that happened."

"I'm okay."

Zaila wasn't okay. It was like I could see her slipping away, and now I wasn't sure if it was the grief or the hell Jay had put her through. "I'm sorry the meetings took forever, but I had to hash out details with Silas and talk to the press. We had to sort through Jeff's contract, the lawyers—long day."

Her gaze dropped to the tea. "I heard he's gone."

"Yeah." I dragged a hand over my face. "It really should have happened sooner. That's on me. I didn't because…" I trailed off, not wanting to delve into the mistakes that had caused Zaila so much pain.

She nodded. "I'm glad. For the team."

"I want your time with the Wildcatters to be happier," I said with a long sigh. She stiffened, her head still bent. "It'll be better when you return. I'll make sure you have the support you need." I crossed to her and brushed my fingers over her shoulder. She didn't pull away, but she didn't lean in either. She was just…still. Too still.

"Zaila. Please, tell me. Are you okay?" I asked, my heart thumping against my ribs.

"Fine." The word was flat.

I wanted to press, but I was bone-tired and afraid that if I pushed, I'd break whatever fragile thread still tethered her here. After a long moment of debate, I let it go. We'd talk soon, when we were rested, when I had the ring I'd commissioned.

Everything would be perfect.

She rose from the stool, setting the mug in the sink. "I'm tired, and I need to make sure I have everything together for Lennon and Vivian's wedding."

"Zaila—"

She glanced back, her expression unreadable, before she offered a small smile. "Like you said, it's all fixed now." She headed upstairs. "Both Jeff and Jay are gone."

Later, when I slid into bed after wolfing down a sandwich over the sink, she was already on her side with her back to me. I curled close and rested my hand on her waist. She didn't move, didn't give any indication she was awake, though I was pretty sure she was.

"Love you," I whispered into her hair.

Her breathing was steady, even. Maybe she was asleep. Well, I wouldn't wake her. We'd talk after the wedding.

CHAPTER 35

Gunnar

My day started much too early—at 4:00—with an issue at one of my oil fields and spiraled from there. By the time I returned from the crisis, which my staff had worked diligently to mostly contain by later afternoon, I had just enough time to prepare and get to Lennon and Vivian's wedding with Zaila. I was dragging from lack of sleep and worry about her subdued demeanor the night before.

Zaila remained quiet on the way to the wedding. I wasn't sure if she was grieving her mother or unhappy about the way things had gone at work yesterday. Probably both.

"You'll be able to return to the office Monday," I told her. "The Jay/ Jeff situation is all sorted."

"Great."

Her clipped response surprised me. Something was deeply wrong, but my phone rang, and I had to walk my executive team through the crisis-response protocol, not finishing the call until we pulled up at Cormac's house.

She waited near the car, and I took her hand in mind, surprised to find hers shaking. "I'm glad you're here with me," I told her as I we entered and looked for a spot among the seats that had been set up on my team captain's huge back lawn. This had become the location of choice for most team social events. I pointed toward two in the back, as I did not want to deal with pleasantries while I was still exhausted from the recent multi-time-zone travel and too little sleep. "Though if I could have made up a good-enough excuse to skip this wedding, I would have," I muttered.

Zaila dropped her gaze and smoothed the silky fabric of her dress over her knees. "Marriage is a big step."

Something in her tone niggled. "You'll tell me what's bothering you later, won't you?" I asked. As much as I wanted her to talk to me, this wasn't the time or place.

She shook her head, looking away. "I'm not sure it's fixable."

Or maybe it was. "Zaila…"

The music started, and Zaila turned her attention forward. I'd thought she was tired last night, but she continued to pull away from me even now, and I didn't like it. While Lennon and Vivian exchanged their vows, I reflected on the past few days. Nothing had been right since Sweden. I'd take her back there—clear my schedule and spend a week…no, a month focused solely on her.

I startled from my planning and clapped as Lennon kissed Vivian. I turned to Zaila. "Are you upset about work? I'm certain that's all going to be fine. The board knows the truth, and I'll make sure everyone else does too."

She looked past my shoulder. "No. Surprisingly, I'm not concerned about my position. Oh! Ida Jane is waving at me. She checked in with me yesterday, and I think it would be nice for me to reassure her in person." She turned and headed toward the CATS. I followed her, but then Silas called my name.

I sighed, wishing I could ignore him, but I couldn't, especially since we now had a gaping hole in our offense that would require careful planning to keep our players healthy for the season.

"Leon in Boston snapped up Jeff," he said without preamble as I approached.

I nodded. "Yes, I'm not surprised. That may be the best place for him. Those two will butt heads until the team implodes."

Silas narrowed his eyes as if considering a problem. "Yeah, probably. Leon's a pain in the ass, too. Can't stand the guy."

I hated him because he'd done nothing to protect my brother all those years ago when he was the head coach for Karl's team in Oslo—in fact, he'd riled up the players, pushing buttons and leaning into old, tired clichés about the gay community. But spilling those secrets wouldn't bring Karl back, so I kept my mouth shut.

Silas shook his head. "The kid doesn't take any coaching. I don't know how he got through college with that attitude. I'm still furious his coach noted none of this. When I called him, I told him so. He said everyone expected Lars in Boston to draft him, and no one liked the guy. It was supposed to be a brilliant plan."

My need for retribution had gummed up Jeff's almost-certain transition to Boston. I rubbed the back of my neck. I needed to let Karl go—not the memories, but the pain surrounding his death. That was holding me back with Zaila, as well as with my hockey team. I wasn't as clear-eyed as I needed to be because of my hatred for Lars and Leon.

"Jeff's good, but so is everyone in this league," I said. "Now he has to work, and he doesn't know how."

Silas and I continued to talk while I tracked Zaila in the

crowd. She had a glass of Champagne and smiled at the CATS, who'd dragged her into their circle. I scowled as Zaila finished her glass and picked up a second from a passing waiter.

She didn't drink; we'd discussed this before. Clearly, the situation from yesterday still bothered her. Of course it did. And that was on top of grieving both her parents' deaths.

Fuck. Zaila was spiraling, and I'd let her. That ended now.

I excused myself and headed toward her, determined to pull her to the side and finally get her to open up, but I was waylaid for the next hour with my general manager, Pete Riggs, who pulled me into the house to discuss possible trade options that would fit our team's mentality and needs.

I speared my fingers through my hair as I glared at him, my jaw tight. "I'm not offloading Cruz or Maxim. They're the backbone of this team for as long as they want to play. Figure it out, but do not promise one of the guys who's keep the team in playoff contention."

Frustrated and starving, I headed outside just in time to hear Naomi Kramer say, "Let's dance."

I'd missed the food, and I'd been an inattentive date to Zaila right when she needed my full focus.

"Adam, I need those delicious hips of yours pressed against mine." Naomi grinned at her husband.

Adam leered as he handed Luka Stol his beer. "Whatever my beautiful bride wants."

The deejay picked an upbeat, fun song, and soon everyone was breathless and a little damp from exertion. I looked around for Zaila and saw her heading toward Vivian and Lennon.

I beelined that way as well.

"I wanted to wish you two all the best," Zaila said as I came up next to her. She smiled at the newlyweds, but her eyes stayed haunted. "And to thank you for the invitation." She clasped Vivian's hand in both of hers. "It's been a pleasure getting to know you."

I frowned as I hovered at the edge of the group. That sounded like a formal goodbye, not just an exit from the wedding.

"Thank you," Vivian said. "We hope you had fun."

"Oh, I did. It's so nice to see a couple in love, so willing to broadcast it to the world."

I stiffened, and my gaze lingered on Zaila's face. *What the hell is she talking about?*

Vivian smiled at Zaila. "Lennon's my person."

Zaila laughed. "Ah, *Grey's Anatomy*. I watched all the seasons during the pandemic." She leaned in closer, her brown eyes sparkling. "McDreamy filled my dreams." She cast a sly glance toward me. "But then, I have a thing for older men. He's mature. Knows what he wants."

As the music shifted, Naomi and Adam joined us, as did Maxim and Ida Jane, and I fought the urge to scoop Zaila up and carry her out of here. I wasn't in the mood for taunts and mind games. I wanted her to tell me what troubled her so I could fix it, and we could go back to being happy.

"You mean as opposed to the college students your age?" Vivian asked, blinking innocently, before she sent me a sly glance.

Everyone knew about Zaila and me. Right? Well…no. I hadn't formally announced that we were dating, though I'd made no secret of it either. But some people might still wonder… *Ah, shit.* I needed to issue a press release so that the world would know Zaila Monroe was mine.

"So those young men don't do it for you?" Ida Jane asked. Her gaze slipped toward mine, and I saw the calculation in her eyes. I took another step closer.

"Hmm… No. I like a man," Zaila said. "One who's confident, knows what he wants and isn't afraid to go after it."

I scowled down at Zaila, who stared back. "This is neither the time nor the place, Zaila."

"I'm sure you're right," she said, looking away. "What do I know about relationships, anyway?"

"What. The. Fuck?" Naomi murmured. She shoved her glass at Adam and went to Zaila, placing a hand on her shoulder. She clasped her other hand around Zaila's and tugged her away from me.

"She doesn't need to talk to you," I said.

Adam stepped forward, likely reacting to his wife's growing anxiety. "Zaila gets to decide that."

Vivian and Zaila nodded as my eyes widened and my jaw dropped. "You think I'd hurt her?"

"You just did," Lennon said, his hands fisting. "By telling her what to think or do."

"Oh, he won't hurt me," Zaila said with breezy confidence.

"For fuck's sake, I'd never hurt her," I said, somewhere between flabbergasted and offended.

"It's true," Zaila said. "He won't hurt me. At least not physically."

That had Adam, Maxim, and Cormac growling. They'd protect this woman they barely knew against a man who could disrupt their lives.

Zaila looked at the guys, eyes wide. She offered them an impish smile and a faint shake of her head. "I didn't mean it like that. I just meant he's broken my heart because he doesn't want you to know we've been dating and sleeping together for the past six weeks. Though I saw it in the paper this morning, so I guess everyone knows I'm Gunnar's floozy." With that, Zaila turned back to me.

I stepped forward, opened my mouth to negate that ridiculous comment, when Naomi said, "You earned this job when you long before you ever started a relationship with Gunnar. Don't let one headline take that away."

Vivian and Ida Jane stepped toward Zaila, offering her their silent support. "So, now that I've spilled the tea and am no longer Gunnar's dirty little secret, I'm going to go—before I totally ruin the vibe." Zaila met my gaze and offered me a sad smile. "Goodbye."

She turned to Vivian and squeezed her fingers. "Sorry, but not that sorry." With a last smile at Naomi and Ida Jane, Zaila hurried off.

I remained rooted to the spot, staring after her. When Lennon stepped forward, I held up a hand. "It's none of your fucking business."

By the time I got around to the front of the house, Zaila was gone.

CHAPTER 36

Gunnar

I was so tired of the endless questions and needs from everyone around me. The only time I'd felt whole in years—decades, really—was with Zaila, but I'd been so busy second-guessing myself that I made her doubt what was between us.

I went to the parking area, only to find my car blocked in by the happy couple's limo, so I found a corner near the catering tent, braced my hands on the table, and bowed my head. My chest ached like I'd taken a puck straight to the ribs.

I did this. I'd broken the best thing to ever happen to me because…what? My feelings were hurt when she said she wanted to keep things professional when we returned from Sweden? I hadn't been forthcoming, hadn't admitted that her uncertainty fed mine, so I'd hesitated to send out that press release about our relationship.

"There you are, Gunnar," Ida Jane said as she marched across the tent like she owned the place, flanked by Keelie, Paloma, Vivian, and Millie. The squadron of hockey wives carried…holy crap. Were those cucumbers and face masks? Where did they get those? This was Lennon's wedding.

Naomi and even tiny Hana narrowed their eyes at me, giving off a serious and terrifying we're-not-asking energy.

"What?" I asked, raising my hands, palms out. "I can't take

another round with you right now. I'm strategizing how to get Zaila to forgive me."

"Good." Hana nodded.

"That's an excellent first step in any intervention," Naomi said.

Keelie placed her hands on her hips. "And he finally traded the slimy little suck up."

"That's nicer than what I would have called him," Ida Jane said, her eyes flashing.

"Really?" Millie shoved her glasses up her nose. "What would you have called him?"

"A shit bag," Ida Jane noted.

"Well, he was a snot-nosed whiner when security escorted him out," Paloma said. "I cheered when he left the building."

"Me, too," Hana said. "He called Paxton old and slow."

"Jerk," Keelie snapped.

All the eyes returned to rest on me.

"What?" I scrubbed my hands down my face as the women continued to eye me with pity. "Who died?"

"Your common sense." Paloma sighed. "And hopefully you're willing to relinquish your dignity."

Keelie dumped a spa kit on the smooth, formerly clean surface of the table. "You need soothing, and then you need to listen to everything we tell you so you can get your woman back before she does something exceedingly stupid."

I glared, but Ida Jane sat me down and slapped a cucumber slice over each of my eyes. "Hold still. You have bags for days. You don't want to go to Zaila looking every one of your twenty years age difference."

"Of course I'm going to Zaila. Has Lennon's limo moved? I'll go right now." I tried to sit up, but multiple sets of hands held me to the chair while the pressure on my cucumber slices increased.

"Look, Gunnar, I know you're the team owner, so don't let this blow back on Luka, but I need to tell you that you're acting like a damn fool." That was Millie.

"Zaila's terrified, Gunnar," Ida Jane said. I could tell because of her thick, sweet accent. "Not of you—of being left. Again. Just like always."

"And you've reinforced that she isn't a priority by not keeping your word about going public," Naomi said.

"Yesterday you did the presser, but didn't mention your relationship to Zaila at all," Hana said.

At least I thought it was Hana because her voice tended to be the softest.

"Not cool, my dude," Naomi added.

"Definitely not helping your cause with a woman who was adopted," Paloma said. "I talked to her, you know. Her parents tried therapy, in case Zaila had abandonment issues, but she was fine as long as she felt secure in her relationship with them."

"Dying parents really screw things up," Hana said on a sigh.

That smacked me like a cheap shot. I yanked off a cucumber. "She's my top priority."

Millie shook her head. "No. If she were your top priority, you would have insisted that security return her work badge and told the press corps that she's your partner."

"You didn't do that," Naomi pointed out, rather unhelpfully.

"She's protecting herself. Her mom just died, and you…"

Millie's voice dropped. "You didn't even take her out on actual dates."

"Which made it easy for her to think she wasn't important to you," Keelie added. "Though that clearly isn't the case."

I blinked at the women surrounding me as I gradually processed their words, my blood running cold. By swallowing my feelings instead of airing them, I'd created the space between Zaila and me. At the time, I'd thought it best to focus on the team, but I'd failed Zaila—failed to show my grieving woman that she was the center of my existence. She needed that reassurance right now, after losing her parents. She'd been reeling before we left for Sweden and all those fears rushed back when we returned to Houston—with good reason. I hadn't made Zaila feel like she belonged with me—to me—as I'd said I would. She'd been able to doubt that I loved her because I hadn't told people I did.

I didn't just love her, though. I needed her. But I hadn't shown her how much—not in the ways she needed to see and feel it.

Swallowing the lump of frustration and self-directed anger proved difficult, but I managed—barely. I'd made a point to talk to Ida Jane about how Zaila's early years of abandonment had affected her, and yet, I'd let my concern for a business, for public appearances, take precedence. At least that's how Zaila took it, from what she'd said earlier.

My priorities were skewed, and I hadn't pushed firmly enough for what I knew was right. I'd let fear when she questioned us, even a little, take hold. When Zaila asked for us to remain professional in public, I'd failed to realize that she was as afraid of us, of our future, of me leaving her, as it seemed I was of her leaving and hurting me.

I pursed my lips as I flipped back through all our interactions. I'd never told her that I considered her my equal, that I wanted her by my side during meetings, downtime, and kayak rides, as well as complex negotiations, not just in my bed. I'd never once told her that every time she smiled at me, her eyes bright, I felt whole. Like I deserved a family—like she was my family.

While I'd waffled, other people had planted doubt in her head. I'd let her worry she was temporary, dispensable, when she was the one person I couldn't imagine losing.

Now, I worried I had.

The thought scraped my insides raw. The minute I could get out of here, I was heading to Zaila's house, and I wouldn't hold back. I'd fight for her—with every word, every gesture, every damn thing I had.

Because the truth was simple: the Wildcatters, the franchise, the wins—they were pieces of my life. But Zaila? She was what made *me* feel whole. And I wanted to do—be—the same for her.

Ida Jane sank into a crouch beside my chair, her manicure of team-colored polish noticeable as she wrapped her fingers around the armrest. "We've all been there. You think you're prepared, you think you have it all together, but then you get hit with the biggest board slam of them all: a love that means you have to go all in or lose everything."

Paloma shuddered. "That's terrifying—giving someone else control over your happiness. After my boys grew up, I was afraid to love again. Even once I met Trix—that's Silas's, and now my, daughter—I struggled with letting myself love her." Her smile warmed. "Thankfully, that girl is simply too lovable to hold back. By the end of the first day with them, I was a goner."

"You're doing a version of what Pax did," Hana said. "You decided the solution for her without actually talking it out." She seemed to be the most emotionally lethal of the group, which wasn't fair.

Why was it always the quiet ones?

"I wouldn't have ever walked away from her," I exclaimed.

"You did yesterday," Naomi said.

"And you've been really aloof at the wedding," Keelie added.

I opened my mouth, then shut it.

"I'm going to make an educated guess here, since I'm the licensed therapist," Ida Jane began.

"You work with kids," I mumbled.

"And since you're acting like one, you're within my wheelhouse," she shot back.

No wonder Maxim was so enamored with his wife; she had a backbone of steel.

"Now, as I was saying, my hypothesis is that you believe you deserve to be alone just as much as Zaila's afraid of being left all alone."

I stared at her for a long minute. No one moved, no one seemed to breathe.

"I was sure I deserved to suffer when I was hurt in that car accident," Hana offered. "That I was being punished for not being the woman Pax needed or deserved."

"Not unlike you losing your parents, who were on the

way to your hockey game," Paloma said. She patted my clenched fist.

"And I have to assume losing your brother, Karl, a few years later made it easy to ice people out," Millie said. "I thought that's what you were doing with me until I realized that's just how you move through life."

I remained silent, digesting what they'd said, how I'd let my coping mechanisms lead me to loneliness, regret, and heartbreak. This emotional place sucked, and I'd figured most of that out myself, but having these wise women shove it in my face as they empathized with me and Zaila made it all click: I had to tell Zaila the whole ugly truth.

She had to understand why I ran from such an involved, loving relationship to one that was so careful and controlled, meticulously managed. It wasn't her; it had never been her—I was protecting myself, though he would hate that. *Hate it*. And yet…I continued to do so. Either I'd have to suck it up and deal with my past, or I'd have to let Zaila go.

The second option wasn't happening.

"Are you all always this good at the emotions?" I asked them.

"Yes." They all nodded.

"That's why we have such a cohesive team," Paloma said with a smile. "We keep the guys emotionally healthy."

"Sorry, Gunnar, but you're messing up the juju we've worked so hard to establish," Millie said.

"Now that Jeff, the real problem, is gone, we need you out of your funk and all-in with Zaila so we can redirect to keeping our men happy and focused on the game," Keelie said.

"I…"

Hana gave my shoulder a soft pat. "You don't have to thank us."

I stared at her, mystified.

"But you need to show Zaila that you want her in your life and that she can trust you to be there for her in all situations," Naomi said.

They all smiled before Keelie added, "And we have just the plan."

CHAPTER 37
Zaila

"I hate Gunnar Evaldson." I moaned into the toilet bowl, tears streaming down my cheeks. With a weak hand, I flushed the sick before flopping onto my back on the too-small bathmat. Despite the heat, the tiles were cold, and my skin was clammy.

Shivering, I stared up at the ceiling in my parents' house. Tomorrow was Monday, and I'd need to find another job.

I also needed to stop drinking wine, because hangovers were the pits.

I'd half expected him to show up last night, but he didn't. That's when I knew our relationship was over. Tears sprang to my eyes all over again, and I let them slide along my damp temples. *One more minute of wallow before I push myself up and get on with the day.*

The only good thing was that my parents weren't here to see this mess.

Once I finally picked myself up off the floor, I turned on the water in the shower. After a few minutes, the warm spray revived me, and I dressed in a flowing skirt with an elastic waistline, as I could handle nothing restrictive around my sensitive midsection. My stomach was really out of whack.

By the time I walked into the kitchen, my queasiness had returned, along with some abdominal discomfort. I frowned, and with a sigh, I headed toward the stove. But then I stopped.

Gunnar stood at the enormous windows that looked out over the backyard, hands shoved in his pockets. He was backlit, so I couldn't see his eyes, but his head tipped like it always did when he had a problem to solve.

That problem was me. Except I didn't want to be a problem.

"Zaila."

I cleared my throat. "Why are you here?"

"Because I wanted to see you," he said.

I clenched my hands into fists. "Well, I've been seen." I swallowed, but my mouth was parched.

He stepped forward, his gaze narrowed. Part of me felt as if he could actually see what was happening in my body.

"Zaila."

My gaze shot up to his. I watched his pupils dilate. He liked that I listened to him. Lightheadedness caused me to sway.

"Are you okay?" he asked, his tone softer than I'd ever heard it.

So unGunnarlike. I blinked up at him, annoyed that fatigue continued to cling to me when he looked so utterly perfect.

"Zaila, you're so pale. You look unwell. What's wrong?"

"I…" The words stuck in my throat because I remembered his response when I'd asked him point-blank about us: *"You're so young. You have your whole life in front of you. In twenty-five years, I'll be almost seventy, in thirty, I'll be elderly, and you…You'll still be in your prime. Why would you even consider tying yourself to me, knowing you'd have to be a caregiver? I don't want that for you."*

Instead of hearing him tell me no, as I had before, now I saw and listened to the concern in his words—for me. He thought he was too old, and maybe he was, but that didn't stop my feelings for him. "Ah, I understand." I smiled a little, though my eyes welled. "I'm so sorry I didn't grasp what you were trying to tell me."

He stepped closer, concern pinching the skin between his eyes. "Something is wrong. Tell me. Whatever you need, I'll help you."

Just as he had been when my mother died, Gunnar Evaldson was a good man. A wonderful man. I wished he could see himself as I did.

A terrible cramp seized my abdomen. I gritted my teeth against the shriek that built in my throat as I doubled over, panting. "Oh, this hurts…" I gasped, panic ripping through my chest, followed by pain.

"You're bleeding. Good God, Zaila…." Gunnar lunged forward, his arms outstretched, fear flaring in his eyes as another terrible pain ripped through my midsection, stronger than before.

I focused on my breathing as my insides tore apart. Then… nothing.

Gunnar's concerned face was inches from mine when I blinked my eyes open. Lord, he had beautiful eyes, like diamonds reflecting the bluest sky. I beamed at him, enjoying the floating sensation. While I didn't remember being intimate with him, I must have, because this was how I always felt post-orgasm. "Hi."

"You terrified me."

"Blunt, as usual."

He shifted on the mattress, and I felt his hip with my knee. Strange. Gunnar kissed like a god and touched me as if I were the finest porcelain. Yet sitting next to me, wanting to be close, seemed out of character.

"Dammit, Zaila."

"What?" I asked, noting the strain around his mouth and the echoes of terror in his eyes. "What is it?" Then I slumped back against the too-hard pillow, my memory rushing back. "I started bleeding...the cramps."

He shook his head, his gaze never leaving mine. He made a rough sound as if the words cost him. "It was an ectopic pregnancy. You arrived at the hospital before your fallopian tube burst."

I shook my head. "That's...that can't be right."

His lips kicked up for a millisecond. "I would never lie to you, Z. Especially about something that important. But not about anything. I need you to know that."

I tried to push into a sitting position, but my abdomen to ached too much. "Ectopic...did I lose my ovary?" I whispered.

His expression was solemn. "No, but it's damaged."

This time, panic rose, circling with desolation. "Did I lose my ability to have kids? Gunnar, can...can I have a child?" Hysteria gripped my guts and rose in my throat.

His eyes slid closed for a moment. He smoothed away the wetness under my eyes before he cupped my cheek. "Well, you have two ovaries, so I don't think so, but I don't really know. But I need you to know something: I would have adored our child nearly as much as I adore you," Gunnar said, his voice thick.

I pressed my cheek into his palm as we locked eyes. "I can't believe I was pregnant. What happens now?"

"Ah, well, the doctor said she'd talk to you."

Admitting he was less than on top of the scenario told me just how rattled Gunnar was. The reality of his words sank in: I had been pregnant. And now…had I damaged my ability to have a child? Anger, hurt, and confusion pinged through me, and I realized how much I wanted to have children—Gunnar's children—one day. I tried to swallow and ended up coughing. He grabbed the cup from the rolling tray and positioned the straw at my mouth. I took a small sip before I turned away.

"When can I talk to the doctor?" I asked. I needed to not get carried away. This didn't change anything about my situation with Gunnar. Of course he wasn't going to leave me bleeding on the floor. But why had he come to my house? What had he wanted? I shoved my hand through my hair, wincing when something caused a sharp pull on my scalp.

"Easy," Gunnar murmured. He extricated my hand from my hair, and I stared, open-mouthed, at a gorgeous, thick platinum band set with tiny diamonds spiraling in two rows toward a bluish-purple stone. He plucked a couple of long, dark hairs from the prongs holding the larger row of baguette diamonds closest to the stone.

"What…" My gaze shot to his before dropping to the ring, then back up. "What…"

For the first time since I'd known him, Gunnar seemed unsure. His cheeks flushed, and he fidgeted with the ring, spinning it to sit in the middle of my finger.

"What…" My brain and mouth were no longer connected. I couldn't get another word to form in my muddled, fascinated state. The ring was so pretty. Gorgeous. My breathing escalated.

"It's musgravite. The moment I saw the stones, I thought of you."

"What's it doing on my finger?" I asked. *Yay! A complete thought and an important question.*

He cleared his throat, his thumb rubbing my knuckles before returning to caress the ring, then back to my knuckles. "I put it there."

Duh. I sure as heck hadn't. "Why?"

"So the doctor would tell me—"

"You wanted access to my medical chart." Anger and revulsion pushed up. "Of all the manipulative—"

"I've been waiting for it to be ready for the last month. I picked it up this morning, and I wanted to ask you to marry me when I came over today. I wanted you to know how much you mean to me. How much I love you."

Gunnar's soft words caused my jaw to snap shut. I stared at him, my gaze darting right, left, trying to read something in his expression, his eyes.

"What...what..." *Dammit!* He'd reduced me to an incoherent pile of mush again.

For the second time, Gunnar looked unsure. I'd never seen him as anything other than completely in charge, composed, all-knowing.

"I wanted to give it to you after that night we danced in the rain, but it wasn't ready. And I worried you weren't ready either. But that was more about my failings and my fear than about you, Zaila."

I blinked at him. Apparently, he'd rendered me mute—the

sweet, gorgeous, romantic asshat.

"I knew then, as rain danced over your luscious skin, that you were the only woman for me," he said with a quiet assurance I adored. "I knew I wanted to spend every waking minute with you. Every laugh, every breath, every day. You were, are, and will always be my love, Zaila. I'm sorry I didn't make that clear, spell out what you meant to me sooner. And I'm sorry I haven't done a better job of letting the whole world know."

Some machine beeped faster, almost like a squirrel's chitter. I shook my head. "But you've implied for weeks that I was too young, too naïve, that I'd messed up your carefully laid plans—"

Gunnar's gaze was steady but dark, and he seemed to gnaw on his cheek. "I hesitated because I'm used to control, to compartmentalizing, to not caring so much. But none of those things is possible with you. And none of them is what I want."

The beeping slowed a bit as I processed his words.

"Now, how are you feeling?" he asked.

The diagnosis terrified me, not going to lie, even to myself. "Um…okay, I think." I looked up at him, managing a smile. "But Gunnar, I deserve more than a pity engagement."

His lips quirked up. "What if it's you taking pity on me?"

I rolled my eyes. "As if. You're Gunnar Evaldson. Billionaire. Corporate genius. The most eligible bachelor in the world."

"I hate that insipid title," he grouched. "Look, I want you, Zaila. I always have—from the moment you doused me in Coke. Or I suppose I could say baptized me in cola." His eyes twinkled, and I giggled.

Damn him, he still made me laugh at the dumbest things.

"I gave you that ring because I wanted to, Zaila. I need you in my life. Take some time to think about that. Take all the time you need. I'll make sure you get –are being given—the very best treatment. Hell, the moment even a whiff of a word gets out, I bet Vivian Cruz will be at my door with her stethoscope, proclaiming herself your personal nurse. And that's because I adore you, Zaila."

Warmth flooded me as I thought about my friend…and how I'd dropped a bomb at her wedding. I winced as I considered Vivian's potential reaction. I hadn't thought about it at the time, too hurt by Gunnar's dismissal of me.

"My guess is that Vivian can't stand me," I murmured.

"That's where you're wrong. She and Keelie have been hounding me every hour since you walked away. 'Get off your fat ego and get Zaila before someone with an actual brain in their head beats you to her', Vivian told me."

I blinked. "She didn't."

Gunnar chuckled. "She did."

I shook my head. "Wish I'd seen that."

"In fairness, she was pretty worked up, and she apologized later. Profusely, while begging me not to take her outburst out on Lennon."

"You won't."

He nodded. "I didn't. I won't. Those CATS gave me the kick in the pants I needed to see things clearly. They are terrifyingly efficient and empathetic." He clasped my hand, and I luxuriated in the warmth of his palms. "I don't want to pressure you, but I do hope you'll consider being my wife. Actually, I'd much prefer you become my wife. And I'd be happy to issue a press release and shout it to the rafters. I want you with me everywhere. Be my partner. You made me a better person."

"I…" My brain couldn't withstand this level of emotion. He was destroying me in the most romantic of ways, and I loved him all the more for it. "I just don't understand. What changed? Why this now when you've been so careful and cautious for pretty much our entire relationship?" I thought for a moment. "Except in Sweden. Something was different there."

CHAPTER 38
Gunnar

"I was different there because that's a special place for me," I explained. "Because of Karl."

I didn't want to do this now, but Zaila needed to understand. "As I told you, Karl was murdered. *And* it was my fault." The words ached as they came out of my throat, and they landed like tiny knives, driving into my skin, chest, heart. "My parents' deaths... Those were because of me, too. So, you see, I...well, I believed I couldn't keep you, not if I wanted you to actually live."

I met her gaze, and her eyes were soft. "How could Karl's death possibly be your fault?"

Guilt and shame roiled in my gut. "I mentioned Karl's partner, a man, to his coach, Leon Johanson."

Zaila's lips formed a perfect O as understanding hit.

"This was nearly thirty years ago—beliefs were different. It was totally cool for Karl to be raising his younger brother and living with a male friend, who helped with the responsibilities, but it was not okay for Karl to be in a relationship with that male friend."

"And they weren't understanding. Not in the locker room," she said.

I bowed my head. "They weren't. They didn't want a...a..."

"I get the idea," Zaila said, her tone dry.

"Leon didn't want a gay man on their team, so he told Lars, his enforcer, about Karl's lover. It didn't matter that he was the lead scorer, that he could bench-press more than most of them. Once they knew, all they could see was his sexual orientation. He was no longer a person." The horror of that still grabbed me by the throat. I clenched my hands into fists.

"The last thing Karl told me was a stupid joke about a bluebird. I snorted—didn't even laugh—because I was pissed at him and Johan for not letting me go to a party. I went anyway… Well, I got there, hung out for a bit and ran my mouth to Leon and Lars about how Karl wasn't fair, considering he was at a party as well. Their faces changed as I spoke, and I just got this bad feeling… So a little while later, I left."

"Lars showed up at the bar that night—the one I'd told Leon Karl liked to go to." I swallowed. "I saw the end of it, when Karl was so beaten and bloody. He…he'd protected Johan, made sure Johan got out of the club. Lars didn't like that." I met her troubled gaze. "If I'd just said nothing to Leon—"

Zaila scoffed. "That's like me saying if I'd been a better baby, cried less, my birth mother wouldn't have given me up, and I wouldn't have a hole in my heart that believes, even now, no matter what I tell myself, that the people I love, who I need, leave."

I offered a flat smile. "Well, you were an infant. I was an eighteen year old."

"Who trusted the wrong person. Your brother's teammate, and, I dare say, a supposed friend."

I nodded. "He and the other four players who took turns holding and beating Karl spent fifteen years in prison, but it didn't feel like enough. I mean, Karl's gone forever. They get to move on with their lives." My voice cracked as I sought to control the emotions blasting through me. This was why I never spoke of Karl; the grief still felt fresh.

Zaila leaned forward with a faint wince, telling me her abdomen ached. Before I could react, her arms were around me. Her head rested on my shoulder, her nose in the crook of my neck. "That's a terrible burden, and I'm so sorry you carry the weight of Karl's death."

She didn't tell me I was wrong again, didn't say my dear brother was in a better place. She just held me as I shook, the emotions seeping from my muscles.

"I'm better," I said after a while, rubbing her back. "Thank you."

"This is what you did for me," she said, her voice filled with wonder. She shifted back on the bed as she stared, her expression awestruck. "You comforted me through the worst of my grief, and I didn't see that." She whispered the last words. "Because I was so focused on my fears." Her eyes widened, and she swallowed. "Gunnar…"

I took her hand. "Do you remember what I told you back when we started being us? I told you wild horses couldn't drag me away. I meant it, Zaila Monroe."

"My middle name is Alice," she said. "It's my mother's middle name—something we share."

"I love that," I said, smiling. "Zaila Alice Monroe, I adore you. Completely. Still, I lost my way somewhere. When you pulled away, when the demands of reality intruded and we were no longer safe in our bubble, I let doubt take hold of me." I kissed her knuckles. "That's on me. I failed you—failed myself. I let other people's comments, their opinions, my desire to keep things neat and orderly, matter more than they should." I smoothed her hair back before I cupped her soft cheek. "I'll always love you, Rookie."

"I love you, too, Gunnar. I…I'm sorry I ran away."

I kissed her, enjoying the connection, needing to feel the livewire attraction that simmered between us. Once we were both breathless, I pulled back. "It's okay. I mean, you're young and reckless. You had to do something—"

"If you compare me to Jeff, I'm going to take this ring off and get you tossed out," Zaila said, her eyes narrowed.

I chuckled. "I'd never. But if the rookie shoe fits…"

Zaila shook her head, but I saw that sparkle in her eyes. "I acted like a dumbass. I should have told you how I was feeling instead of pulling away. I'm sorry."

"So did I, and so am I." I closed my eyes for a moment, letting the insecurity and hurt of the last week wash away. "I never want to go through something like that again, which is why I promise to talk to you—to be honest with you when you ask me a question. Like why I didn't take you out on dates. I see how you could have gotten something twisted in your head, thinking I was hiding you or embarrassed to be seen with you." I cupped her cheeks again, needing her to see my vulnerability. "Then, when you said you wanted us to remain professional, I just…I just thought…"

"That I'd changed my mind about being with you, and you'd be alone again, hurting more than before." She wrapped her hand around my wrist, drawing us closer together. "I was so afraid about not fitting into your world. I worried you were right, and I was too young, too gauche." She rolled her eyes, and I smirked and shook my head. "We're a pair. So much anxiety and grief because we don't know how to say what needs to be said."

"I have to tell you, even at my age, baring my soul is terrifying."

"Right there with you." She blew out a breath, then smiled. "But now, I feel good—great. Like I share your burden and you share mine, and somehow everything is lighter."

"Good way to put it."

We say quietly for a while. A nurse came in to check Zaila's incision and vitals. Twenty minutes later, the doctor spoke to us about Zaila's condition. While both ovaries were intact, one fallopian tube had been removed after being damaged by the ectopic pregnancy. Zaila still had one fully functional ovary and fallopian tube, though, so she remained able to bear children. Now that Zaila was awake and her vitals looked good, she could be discharged tomorrow, as long as she continued to rest. I promised I'd make sure she did so.

Once we were alone again, I clasped her hand in mine. "So…I break you out of here tomorrow. Got any plans?"

She nodded, her eyes shining.

"I do. I have to answer the question you haven't asked me." She lifted her left hand and flashed the ring.

"I don't want to ask you here, so if you want to take it off—"

"Not a chance, Gunnar." Zaila closed her hand into a fist and settled it on the far side of the bed. "You put a ring on it, and its staying."

A flutter of serenity blossomed in my chest as I grinned. "All right. I'll keep that in mind for when I get to propose."

"I want to go back to Sweden."

I smoothed her hair back and kissed her temple, contentment a warm blanket around me. "You got it."

EPILOGUE
ONE MONTH LATER
Zaila

"Only you would do something like this," Gunnar grumbled.

But I could tell his opposition was all bark, kind of like the small, shaggy dog curled up in my lap. I shrugged, biting my cheek to keep from smiling. "Well, it wasn't like I could organize the pet adoption day and not adopt a pet, Gunnar. That reflects poorly on the organization."

His shoulders slumped. "Dammit. I've never had a dog. They're messy. And needy. And—"

"It's high time you learned how to be a pet dad," I cut in. "It'll be good practice for…"

I frowned, my lips pressing together. We weren't actively trying for a child, though Gunnar felt his age and a stronger need than I did. I knew this because he'd told me so. But I wasn't positive I was ready for that much change yet. Still, I loved the idea of family, just not *quite* yet.

"My daddy was fifty when I came into his life," I said. "He was a calming, soothing influence on me. I want that for our kids."

"We'll talk about kids and adding to our family later," Gunnar said, rubbing a palm up and down my back. "After I get used to the fact you brought home a dog."

"He'd been in the shelter for weeks, and the staff said he'd be put down." I might have added to the wobble of my chin to sell my point.

"They knew you were a sucker for a dog," Gunnar muttered, his eyes burning with glacial ice.

"Well, I was. I am. Have you actually looked at him?" I pulled from Gunnar's embrace and bent down. My incisions weren't tender anymore, and I felt better each day. The CATS had set up a calendar for the past month to ensure I wasn't left alone for long, organized by Paloma, who was truly the most amazing woman. I aspired to be her when I grew up. Thanks to her, Vivian, Keelie, Ida Jane, Hana, Naomi, and Millie, I was part of a family again. Losing my mother had left me rudderless for a while, but I'd found my determination now, my spark.

A significant reason for that was the man in front of me. He'd confronted his fears to make sure he was the best possible version of himself for us. That didn't mean we were always able to communicate easily, or that there was never any tension. But I'd come to accept that part of what made us work was that we had to remain on our toes. Most of our tension came from outside forces. Gunnar and I had, quite accidentally, forged something strong and time-tested. We were better together. The Wildcatters were better when we worked together, too, which the CATS and the rest of the staff frequently remarked on. In the past few weeks, I'd really bonded with Vivian and Hana, who, like me, were quieter than the more vivacious Ida Jane and Naomi. I liked their introspection and willingness to let me work through my issues at my pace.

I hadn't realized how rare that was until I'd lost that full-throated acceptance from my parents.

The dog shifted, scooting closer, his ears tilting forward as if listening to us, his light brown eyes gleaming as they pleaded for the love he'd already engendered in each of us—though Gunnar was reluctant to admit it. I reached down and petted his head, enjoying the soothing softness of his ears.

"I can't believe you named him Hat Trick," Gunnar muttered, but I caught the hint of a smile ticking up the corners of his lips. I was now well-versed in Gunnar's tells.

"Well, he got out of prison, made me fall in love with him, and scored billionaire-doggy status all in one day." I shrugged. "Those are some impressive stats."

"It had nothing to do with the fact that Luka Stol and Cormac Bouchard each managed a hat trick against Jeff Cross's new team the night before?"

I widened my eyes before blinking up at him as I bit my cheek to stifle the smile threatening to burst forth. "I never thought of that."

"Liar." Gunnar chuckled even as he pulled me close, his lips at my temple, warming me as I snuggled closer.

~

I started back at work a month after my surgery as the associate social media director, a position that offered higher pay and a better title, but most of the same tasks as I'd had before. I had a job I loved, and Tim was my boss now. It was great collaborating with him. We were all happy with the arrangement.

Being engaged to the big boss man had perks, too, because even Natalie had apologized to me, and then asked for my help with a tricky issue that Gunnar had assured her I'd be willing to solve. I did, and now Natalie and I planned to have regular strategy meetings.

The CATS had invited me to their away-game-watching parties, and I adored being included in their group. We were at our house, the one I shared with Gunnar, for tonight's playoff game, and the Wildcatters would battle Montreal. Of course we'd all wanted to attend the game, but it was the first of the series. We'd decided to hold off until the next rotation back to Montreal, if needed, so we could celebrate or commiserate with our guys when the series ended.

However, it soon appeared that celebration was already in order after the guys decimated Montreal's defense and scored three times in the first quarter. Under Cormac, the guys were playing smart and loose—and they looked like the champions I knew they were.

Ida Jane leaned around Vivian and tapped my knee. "Did Gunnar tell you Jeff's 'fresh start' lasted all of thirteen games, including the one where Cormac and Luka scored six goals to Jeff's nil before he was sent back down to the minor leagues?"

I nodded and buried my face in my margarita so they would miss my satisfied smile.

"He pitched such a fit about the demotion he's now serving a month-long suspension, the longest in the league," Paloma added.

I shook my head. We weren't sharing anything new. We just liked this story.

Vivian grinned, her eyes dancing. "Jeffy boy is going to be force-fed humility, even if he fights it kicking and screaming."

Ida Jane clanked margarita glasses with her before slamming

back her drink. She opened her eyes and gave a satisfied sigh. After watching the massive screen for a few seconds, she said, "We need to discuss the second line. See that? I'm not happy with the guys' interactions there. What's going on, and how do we fix it?"

The second line had just scored a goal, but there had been a stutter between the younger players, which had almost led to a missed pass.

"Well, we can find the younger guys partners," Hana suggested. "Pax has been telling them how much happier they'll be in loving, long-term relationships."

I leaned forward, elbows on my knees, as I soaked in lessons on how to improve the team dynamic.

"I'm going to tell Gunnar to hire you all," I said later that evening, deep into my second margarita and late in the third period. We'd turned down the game because the guys were up four-one. "You're really smart."

"And you're really toasted," Keelie said with a tipsy giggle of her own.

"We don't want to be on the payroll," Paloma said. "We like what we do."

Naomi gave a sharp nod. "But that doesn't mean we won't do our damnedest to make sure our team performs at peak."

"Oooh, did you hear about Lydia and Jay?" Millie asked as she set down her phone.

I shook my head.

Millie grinned. "Their gossip empire collapsed."

Naomi made a blow-up sound as she opened her hand.

"People realized they didn't actually like listening to them,"

Ida Jane said. "I bet that stung."

"Jay's hanging around like a bad smell. He's dating a woman from the ticket sales department named Eileen, and I think it's to get the scoop on the organization," Keelie said. "I hope Eileen knows what she's getting into."

"Considering how often they undress each other with their eyes, I'd say she's quite happy in the relationship," Naomi said. "It's more than you and Gunnar, Z." She smirked.

"Oh, please, they aren't any worse than you and Cormac," Naomi said.

"Or Lennon and me," Vivian added.

There were murmurs of agreement among the ladies.

"Admittedly, we do that often," I said. "Gunnar's quite a catch, a man in his prime."

"Love looks good on him," Paloma said with a smile.

Naese scored a goal, and Hana jumped up, doing a hip-thrust-shimmy dance.

That brought another round of giggles.

"At least Eileen can't tell Jay anything he can use against the team," Keelie said.

"And we'll keep it that way," Paloma agreed.

When the game ended, Gunnar stepped out of his office, where he'd been watching the game, and rolled his eyes at us even as he organized rides home for each of my friends.

~

Later that night, as I got into bed, I stared up at the ceiling.

"What's wrong?" He settled his rump next to my hip.

I shook my head. "Nothing."

"Rookie, you promised."

I bit my lip as I swallowed the latest knot of emotion. "I'm just feeling sorry for myself, sad about the pregnancy." I sighed as I closed my eyes. "I got invited to a baby shower."

Gunnar gathered me into his arms, and I rested my head against the thick slab of his shoulder. "Ah, my love, that brought all the grief forward."

I wrapped my arms around him because I'd learned that leaning on Gunnar didn't make me weak; it made me human. I appreciated his ability to hold me—and hold me up sometimes— just as I did for him when his demons came in the night.

"It's been just over a month since the surgery, and my mom was gone just a couple of months before that. It's all been…a lot." I huffed out a breath.

"You overloaded."

I nodded, my eyes squeezed shut. "But I want to go. I love that the CATS invited me."

Gunnar smoothed my hair. "You can be pleased and sad together. Hell, you can be happy and grief-stricken at the same time. I spent months that way, when I was courting you."

I giggled, remembering his bad dad jokes as we waited out the thunderstorm. "Why did the bicycle fall over?"

"What?" he asked, sounding confused. I pulled back to meet his gaze.

"It was two-tired!"

Light bloomed in the icy depths of his eyes as he grinned. I'd never tire of that smile, which he still graced me with too infrequently. "Ah, I see. You've been holding out on me."

I shook my head. "I looked that one up today, in case I needed it." I hesitated. "I might have bookmarked a site. You know, so I had some options."

He swiped at the damp skin under my eye. "Ah, well. Karl would be proud. Did it help?"

I nodded. "A couple of months ago, I would have hated to admit that there's magic in those puns. But Karl was really on to something. Your brother was a smart man."

"He certainly was."

Gunnar kissed me with such sweetness that I melted deeper into his embrace, wanting to stay there forever.

When we finally parted a few moments later, I blinked away the funk that hit me whenever I thought about my surgery, the loss, and my prognosis. There had been some tough weeks, which was part of why we'd waited on our wedding. Plus, Gunnar still had to officially propose. Though we both knew he'd ask me and I'd say yes.

For now, instead of making our commitment front-page news, we enjoyed our deepening relationship. Plus, I wanted nothing to detract from the team's momentum. They were three games from the Cup. While Gunnar had told me I was more important—and I could see the truth shining in his eyes—I'd gotten caught up in the excitement of my first championship run. Gunnar, being the sweet man he didn't want others to know he was, had indulged me, but I could tell he was impatient to cement our relationship.

Truth be told, I was impatient, too. Much as I enjoyed my work and the organization, I wanted more of the emotional security Gunnar offered. That had once felt self-indulgent, but now, thanks to talks with the CATS, I understood that it was a normal response to my upbringing and my place in life. Plus, as Naomi had said, *"Putting a ring on that gorgeous man's finger is a coup de grace I don't think any of those 'perpetual-bachelor' people see coming."*

During the past month, the CATS had stepped in and stepped up. While my parents had loved me and told me often, this group of ladies showed me their love daily through their actions. Vivian and I were especially close, and I'd talked to her almost daily since coming home after the ectopic pregnancy. Being a nurse, Vivian had lots of thoughts...most of which turned out to be positive and helpful. I swallowed as a lump formed in my throat, feeling so thankful to have such amazing women in my life.

"I want to get married soon," Gunnar said. He ran his fingers through my hair with slow, steady strokes, and I sighed, soothed, by his ministrations.

"You still haven't asked," I pointed out, even as flutters bloomed in my belly. *Is he going to ask me? Now?* I bit my lip, shoving down the giddiness pressing against my breastbone.

"Hmm..." He rose from the couch and held out his hand. "Come with me." I slid my hand into his warm, large palm, a shiver of delight skating over my nerves. This man made me so happy.

"Where are we going?" I asked as I trotted a half-step behind him.

"You'll see."

He opened the back door and led me outside—and into a magic fairyland of twinkle lights, flowers, and soft, sensual music.

"What...how?" I gawked.

"You've been busy—a bit distracted, even." Gunnar *tsk*ed, but his cool eyes danced with growing amusement. "A rookie mistake."

"And you took advantage?" I asked, tipping my head back as the smile I'd held in stretched across my lips. I loved bantering with this man.

"Of you? Never." He nipped at my earlobe. "You mean the world to me, Zaila. And I know it'd probably be smarter to wait so the news cycle doesn't mix our personal life and the team's, but, honestly, I don't care. You're what matters. I hate that you don't wear your ring when you go to work. I hate that I can't tell every man I belong to you."

My heart melted more at those sweet words. Gunnar empowered me—showed me how to advocate for myself—every day. And here he was, doing so again *while he proposed.*

"So, I don't want to wait." His pale gaze held mine as he pulled out my ring—the one he'd given me last month. He must have gone up to our room, into our closet, and taken the ring out of its box. "I want this on your finger, my promise to you that you can look at every day. I want you to remember that you're the most important person in my world, and that I'm happiest with you at my side. So...will you wear my ring to work and the game tomorrow? Will you show the world how much I love you?"

I cupped his lean cheeks as I rose on my toes, our lips just touching when I murmured, "Yes."

His mouth curved upward into a grin before he tugged me closer and kissed me breathless. He slid the ring onto my finger and pulled away just long enough to spin me closer.

Hat Trick, visible through the large windows, barked and wagged his tail.

I laughed and kissed him again. "What do you think about Hat Trick being ring bearer?"

Gunnar grimaced. "I think it's fifty-fifty that your mutt eats or loses the rings."

I bit my lip to hold in a giggle. "So…you love the idea?"

His eyes crinkled. "I do."

I snuggled into his chest as I admired my ring. Gunnar held me, swaying to the music. I loved him like this—relaxed, unguarded, *mine*. "Can we get married at the end of the month?"

He rested his cheek atop my head. "If that's what you want, we can make it happen."

"At home," I said. "I know we could go somewhere fancy, but I want to be in our home, with our friends who have become our family when *we* become a family." I clasped his large, callused hand in mine, imagining a wedding ring on his finger.

"Then that's what we'll do."

"Then we should go to Sweden," I said, tipping my head back so I could gauge his reaction. "Hat Trick will love the ocean."

Gunnar cursed under his breath, but there was a happy gleam in his eye that he didn't bother to hide.

"You know what I love most about you, Gunnar?"

He shook his head, his expression open and yearning. We craved this connection with each other, and we'd worked past our own damn selves to get here.

"I love how you put me first, make me feel valued." I kissed him. "Loved." Kiss. "Wanted." Kiss.

"You are all those things, Rookie. And more." He leaned in closer, his cheekbone brushing mine as we danced under the lights and stars, twinkling into the darkened sky. "You, Zaila Alice Monroe almost Evaldson, are the single most precious thing in this world."

ACKNOWLEDGMENTS

Thank you, Jessica Royer Ocken, for your editing skills. My book always turns out soooo much better after you've worked your magic.

Thanks to my beta readers: Antje Worledge, Kate Newman, and Rachel Childers. My goodness, you ladies are amazing! You make me think, you make me work harder, and you make me so, so thankful to share this love for romance and a good story. I'm forever in your debt. Thank you.

Thanks Charity Chimni for your expertise, listening skills, and amazing proofreading skills. I'm so thankful to have you on my team! I seriously cannot thank you enough.

Chris, this may well be my favorite cover you've ever made me. Thank you so, so much! You are incredibly talented. Just saying…

My lovely readers: well, clearly, without *you*, none of this would be possible. The fact that you trust me with your time is the greatest compliment. Thank you so, so much.

ALSO BY ALEXA PADGETT

Wildcatters Hockey Series:

Another Powerplay, Book 6

Another Face-Off, Book 5

Another Goal, Book 4

Another Hit, Book 3

Another Shot, Book 2

Another Charge, Book 1

Oblivion Series:

Sweet Oblivion

Craving Oblivion

Sultry Oblivion

Forever Oblivion

An Austin After Dark Book:

Deep in the Heart

Broken Rose of Texas

Austin By Morning

Standalone Steamy Romance:

Trail of Secrets

The Seattle Sound Series:

Sweet Solace

Between Breaths

Many Sounds of Silence

Striker's Waltz

Hold You Close

A Moonlit Serenade

From the First

Midnight Dance

Moonshine Eyes

When We Fell Down

Seattle Sound, The Collection: Books 1-3

Seattle Sound, The Collection: Books 1-5

ABOUT THE AUTHOR

USA Today bestseller Alexa Padgett's books have garnered accolades from prestigious organizations, including *Kirkus Reviews*, National Indie Excellence Awards, and *Publishers Weekly*.

Alexa spent a good part of her youth traveling. From Budapest to Belize, Calgary to Coober Pedy, she soaked in the myriad smells, sounds, and feels of these gorgeous places, wishing she could live in them all–at least for a while. And she does in her books.

She lives in New Mexico with her husband, children, and Great Pyrenees pup, Ash. When not writing, schlepping, or volunteering, she can be found in her tiny kitchen, channeling her inner Barefoot Contessa.